RUNNING Out Of Rain

Eventually, all storms break for a little sunshine...

♥PRIME
OF LOVE
The Series

Book One

By

LORI LEGER

CAJUNFLAIR
PUBLISHING

ISBN-10: 1940305209
ISBN-13: 978-1-940305-20-2

Copy Editor: Karen Sue Burns

ACKNOWLEDGMENTS

A shout out to my friends/book clubbers, critique partners, Karen Sue, Joan, Melissa, and Trish for reading this through, editing, and telling me what works and what doesn't. It takes a village, and you are mine. And to DonnaMarie Tamucci-Denson, whose OCD, when it comes to finding errors, borders on phenomenal. Her one flaw being she's a Dallas fan, amongst a bevy of Saints fans, but I love her anyway!

Once again, thanks to my husband, Mike, for keeping things afloat as I strive to meet deadlines, fight with formatting, book covers, and other various publishing woes. You're still the best, and the *only* man I want in my life. Love you, babe.

To Amanda Miller Lapoint, for the awesome, awesome, AWESOME hand crocheted afghan and matching pillows with my name and logo crocheted into them. I am still stunned every time I see it. Thank you!

Locale Acknowledgments: D.I.'s (Basile, LA), The Town and Country Club, aka Chicky Town (Riceville, LA.), LuLu's Lounge and The Circle Top (Both were located in Gueydan, LA back in the day), The Lake Shore Club, The Red Rose, The Regatta Seafood and Steakhouse, The Wave Café, (All are or were located in Lake Arthur, LA)

A shout out to the good people of Louisiana, especially those of Cajun lineage who know the difference between a good gumbo and a bad one, store bought roux and home-made, and why you should never eat boiled crawfish if the tails are straight. We are kind and generous, we are intelligent, strong, and resourceful, we are proud Americans—we are Cajuns.

And *Cajuns* . . . like country boys . . . will survive.

Note from author: I've changed the names, but use the same locations of several cities and towns, such as Lake Charles (Lake Coburn), Kinder (Kenton), Lake Arthur (Lake Erin), and Gueydan (Gardiner) in all of my series set in Louisiana, as shown in the map I've included. I know and love this part of my state therefore I've chosen to include it in my stories.

DEDICATION

To all women out there over the age of fifty, whether you've found love, are still looking for it, or are comfortable enough in your own skin not to need anyone else around. If your purse "essentials" have altered from lip gloss, mascara, and eye-liner to panty-liners, tooth floss, and bi-focals—this book is for you. It's a reminder that just because there's a little silver in the hair, doesn't mean the pump isn't primed for passion.

Also to anyone who's had to deal with the heartbreak that is called Alzheimer's disease, whether it's yourself or a loved one . . . bless you all.

Musical Soundtrack:

Gary Allan – Every Storm (Runs Out of Rain)
Lee Benoit – *Johnny Can't Dance*
Lee Benoit – *Lover's Waltz*
Wayne Toups – *The Back Door*
Paul Young – *What Becomes of the Broken Hearted*
James Otto – *Somewhere Tonight*
Chuck Wicks – *Hold That Thought*
Billy Currington – *Must Be Doin' Somethin' Right*
George Strait – *Troubadour*
George Strait – *I Believe*
Blake Shelton – *Home*
Loretta Lynn – *You Ain't Woman Enough (To Take My Man)*
Clifton Chenier – *Louisiana Two Step, Oh My My*
Wayne Toups – *Take My Hand*
Wayne Toups – *Two Step Mamou*
Jo-El Sonnier – *No More One Time*
Jo-El Sonnier – *Step it Fast*

GLOSSARY of Cajun Terminology

Putain – Bitch, Prostitute (Poo-tan)
Envie – urge, need, to want something (Awn-vee)
C'est bon – It's good (Say-bawn)
Ca c'est bon – Used as a stated fact: It is good! (Sah say-bawn!) OR in question
form: Was it good? (Sah say-bawn?)
C'est toute la meme chose – It's all the same thing (Say to la mam shawz)
Ma petite femme – My little girl (Ma p'teet fahm)
Mon coeur – My heart (Mawn kur)
Mon vieux – My old friend (Mawn vyuh)
Chienne – A female dog (Shee-yan) said quickly (Sh-yan)

Map of South Louisiana
Real and *Fictional* towns in book

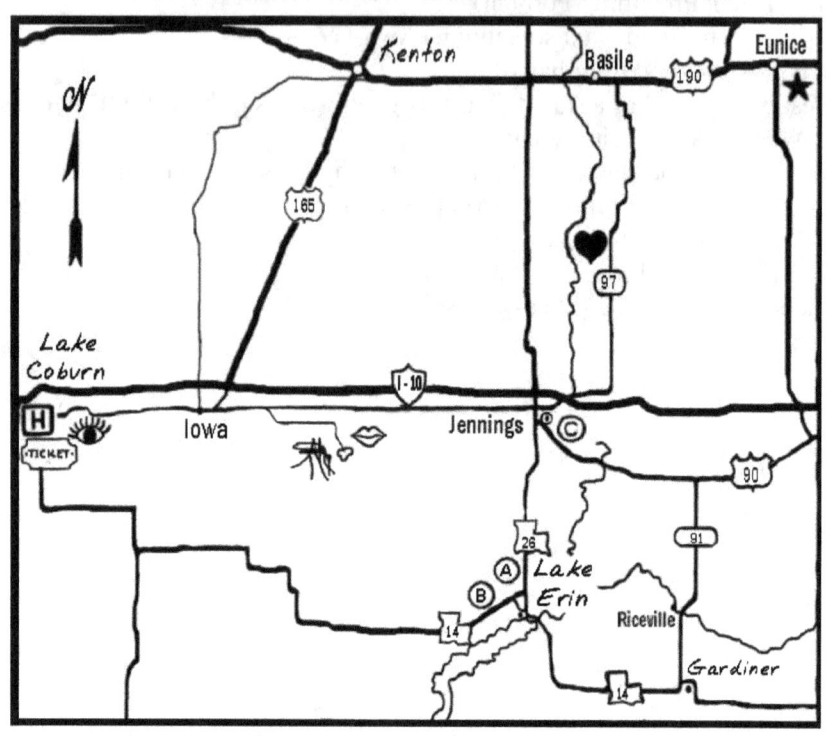

LEGEND:
- Ⓐ *John Michael's home*
- Ⓑ *John David's (J.D.) home*
- Ⓒ *Cyn and Bessie's home*
- Ⓗ *Lake Coburn Memorial (Cyn's Workplace)*
- 👁 *1st Sighting (John Michael & Cynthia)*
- ♥ *1st Date* (D.I.'s)
- ᴛɪᴄᴋᴇᴛ *2nd Date (Mall Theater)*
- 👄 *1st Kiss*
- *Mosquito Swarm at Pond*
- ★ *3rd Date* (Queen Cinema 3)

Prologue

November 15th
Tonka City, Oklahoma

Everyone expected Cynthia to be strong. To deal out comfort to her three grown children like face cards in a stacked deck. Yes, they'd lost their father, but she'd lost so much more. So, how the hell could she comfort others when she was dying inside?

This was the ultimate deal breaker. She and Gene were supposed to grow old and senile together, happy and in love. Yet, here she was, barely fifty-two years old, widowed, and about to say one last goodbye to the man she'd married over three decades ago. Whether or not she'd be an angry, bitter widow was still up for debate.

Members of the "brotherhood" of firefighters from departments throughout the state of Oklahoma were in attendance—all co-workers, connections, or acquaintances from her husband's thirty years as a firefighter. They'd come to pay homage to the "chief", given testimonials as to what a good man, co-worker, brother he was.

An impressive display of uniformed men and women lined the perimeter of the room. The fire engine waited outside, polished to a shine, ready to take Chief Ellender to his final resting place.

After a few last words from the minister, everyone filed slowly from the room. Dr. Cynthia Ellender approached the open coffin with her two sons, her daughter, and son-in-law—all still in shock from the recent revelation. The scandal her husband had bequeathed to his family, one that would likely rock this town for years to come, still raw and fresh in their minds.

Poor Trini, shamelessly spoiled by her father, broke down in dramatic fashion, as always, relishing the chance to be the center of attention. One look from Cynthia had her daughter's husband and brothers leading the twenty-five year old from the room to wait outside.

Finally, she alone remained. The funeral director stood at the door, along with six uniformed pall bearers chosen to transport their chief to the engine—none of whom dared to meet her gaze.

She released a long, slow breath and faced her husband one last time. She stared at the man whose bed, whose very life she'd shared—the man she *thought* she'd known everything about. They'd kept their secrets, but never from each other—or so she'd believed.

She reached inside the coffin, ran her hand over the broad chest, smoothed down the single row of brass buttons over his class "A" jacket uniform. Her fingers made a feather light pass over his badge, the various cords and patches. One last time she touched the five bugle pin adorning his collar, the five corresponding stripes on his sleeve, the white gloved hand arranged so carefully over his cap.

Cynthia leaned close to the handsome face, the sexy mouth she'd kissed thousands of times. In a voice wracked with a mixture of bitterness, shame, and fury, she whispered the very last words she would ever speak to her husband.

"You son of a bitch . . . how *dare* you?"

Chapter One

May 31st
18 months later
Lake Coburn, Louisiana

John Michael Ferguson stepped out of his F-250 pickup onto the hospital parking lot, his heart pounding with excitement. He'd had to wait too damn long before becoming a grandfather but dang if Cat and Zachary weren't popping them out two at a time. After a complicated pregnancy, they'd come a month early and Cat had nearly paid the price. She'd severely hemorrhaged during the emergency C-section, but had fought her way back. And now he was the proud grandpa of fraternal twins, a girl and a boy.

He took several steps toward the hospital entrance and stopped to stare back at his truck. "Come on, Pop. What the hell you doing back there? We've got some babies to hold."

His seventy-seven year old father stepped gingerly from the truck and growled his reply. "Look, we didn't all spring from the valley of the jolly green giants, you know. If I fall out of this too-tall-truck of yours onto the pavement, you'll be the one changing my damn diapers after I break something." He slammed the door, continuing his grumble fest. "It's bad enough you almost killed me coming over here, driving too fast. Now you want me to make a mad dash across the parking lot to get to something that ain't going anywhere. They're newborns—it's not like they can walk out by themselves." He shook his head. "Kids today got no damn patience."

John couldn't help but grin over his dad, John David "J.D." Ferguson, calling him a kid, at fifty-three years old. "Watch your step, Pop. There's a curb." He pointed to the sidewalk in front of his father.

"I see it. I'm not blind."

John removed his good straw Stetson and passed a hand through his thick hair. "That's not what the people at the DMV say." His low-spoken reply somehow carried to a man who had to have the TV blaring in order to hear.

"I can see plenty good enough to drive. Those assholes at the DMV don't know what the hell they're talking about. Communists—the whole damn bunch of them."

"I know. It's a conspiracy to keep everyone with common sense from driving their own vehicle. It couldn't possibly have anything to do with those cataracts clouding your vision."

"I don't have cataracts."

John sighed. "I know, and you don't have an enlarged prostate, either. It's perfectly natural to go to the head every ten minutes. May as well put the damn diaper on you now, and then you can fall out of my truck anytime you want to."

"Eh, go on with you." The older man waved him off before heading for the entrance, stopping long enough to pull a handkerchief from his pocket. He wiped his face with the square of cloth decorated on one corner with the initials JDF hand-embroidered in bold blue lettering. "Feels like summertime."

John Michael had to agree. Even at 9:00 a.m., the day showed all the signs of the heat and humidity common to southwest Louisiana in mid-Spring. Never mind the miserably long, hot summer in the forecast. "Tomorrow's June 1st— the beginning of hurricane season. I wonder if we'll have any worth naming this year."

"That's a kind of wait-and-see thing. The National Weather Center's predictions haven't exactly been spot on lately, have they?"

"Nope, they've fallen far short for several years, thank God." It occurred to him Zachary would need extra help battening down the Lake Erin Feed & Supply store's hatches if they *were* hit with any storms from now through November. He'd likely be worrying about more important things, like keeping his wife and new babies safe.

They stepped through the automatic doors of the entrance and headed for the elevators. John pushed the button for the third floor. He looked down at the man he'd passed up in height somewhere around the age of fifteen.

"You know, we're at a hospital. I'm sure there are some fine urologists here—and I know they have an optical clinic on the north side of the building. We could get you some appointments." All he got for a reply was an ominous growl. "It's called maintenance, Pop. To keep in top running shape—like changing the oil, refilling the washer fluid, and rotating the tires on a vehicle."

"It's called minding your own business."

"You *are* my business when you think I should be at your beck and call to haul you around town." The doors whooshed open at the second floor and an older woman boarded. Judging by the look on his dad's face, her presence saved him from a verbal tongue lashing.

By the time the doors opened onto the third floor, his dad had obviously decided to let it go—for the time being anyway. He knocked lightly on the door to room 324, pushed it open at his daughter-in-law's call to enter. He grinned at Cathryn, propped up in her bed and holding a baby. He whispered a silent prayer, thankful she'd made it through the process of bringing life into this world. Pale, but beautiful, she sat there beaming at him.

John could barely remember a time when Zachary hadn't been crazy about Cat McDaniel. It had started somewhere around sixth grade—had taken nearly twenty years for his son to do something about it and get her to marry him. Since then, she'd infused some much needed joy into their family.

"Hey there, Poppa John—or should I say Paw Paw John? Wash your hands first and then come on over here and introduce yourself to one of your grandchildren."

He did as she told him and approached the bed to give her a gentle hug. "How's my favorite daughter-in-law doing?"

She kissed his cheek. "Does it still count if I'm your only daughter-in-law?"

"It absolutely counts. I could have twenty of 'em and you'd always be my favorite. Which one do we have here? Scratch that, he's swaddled in blue so this must be my new grandson." He took the infant carefully and sat in the chair nearest her bed. "Hey, young man. I'm your grandfather. But you can call me Paw Paw John." A gruff throat-clearing from the door had him looking up at his dad.

"Excuse me, but that tagline's been taken already, boy."

Cathryn chuckled. "Hey Paw Paw John."

"Exactly!" He nodded and pointed a thumb at his own chest. "*I'm* the only Paw Paw John in this family." He puffed out his chest to his son. "You gotta be oldest and ugliest to get dibs."

Cat waved off his comment. "Pfft, there you go fishing for compliments again, Paw Paw. You know darn well there's not an ounce of ugly on you."

"Ugly is as ugly does," John growled. "And it's not my fault five consecutive generations of Fergusons displayed a complete lack of imagination in naming their sons. That's why Beth and I steered clear of it when we had one. Zachary is a nice, strong, perfectly acceptable name. And more importantly?" He leaned forward to make his point. "It's *not* John."

The older John chuckled as he greeted Cathryn at the bed and kissed her forehead fondly. "Forget him. How's my girl? You had a pretty rough time of it, I hear."

She gave him a one shouldered shrug. "I'm good, still a little weak, and they limit my nursing sessions, but I'm getting stronger all the time."

J.D.'s arthritic hand lingered on her head for a moment. He blinked several times and finally gave her a satisfied nod. "Good to know. Where's the other one? I didn't come here prepared to wait my turn. Hell, I thought I'd have my own bundle of joy to hold."

Cathryn chuckled. "She's in the nursery. Her pediatrician is doing some blood work and running tests to ensure everything is as good on the inside as it is on the outside. She should be back soon."

Zach pushed open the door, carrying a large cup of coffee in one hand and a bottle of orange juice in the other. "Hey, we got us a party going on in here, or what?"

"Now we do. Hey Zachary, that's a handsome little man you've got there."

"Yes sir, I have to agree with you." He shook his grandfather's hand and pulled him close for a one-armed hug. "Wait until you see our daughter, Paw Paw. She's going to be every bit as pretty as her mama."

"A looker already, huh?"

"You bet." Zach approached John, stood bent at the waist, resting his hands on his thighs to watch his sleeping son. "What do you think, Pop?"

"Well, Son—" Suddenly overcome with emotion, John had to blink to clear his eyes. "I think I can get used to this real quick. Congratulations."

Zach beamed at his father and accepted the hand shake he offered. "Thanks."

All eyes pivoted toward the doorway as the pediatric nurse entered, pushing the portable bassinet into the room. "Here's the other half of the dazzling duo. We'll leave them in here to visit for another thirty minutes or so."

Cat waved at the woman. "Thank you, Ms. Jackie."

John stood to get a better look at his granddaughter. He grunted before casting a glance in his son's direction. "Oh man. Are you ever gonna be in trouble in about fourteen years."

Zach snorted. "I hear you." He reached out for his son and turned to his grandfather who was finishing up with his hand-washing, obviously anticipating his turn. "Paw Paw, you want to hold your great-grandson?"

J.D. deposited the paper towel into the trash receptacle and turned, wearing a gleeful expression. "Well, hell yeah. Why else would I have suffered through your dad's death defying driving skills?" He took over the chair John had previously occupied and clapped his hands together. "Hand him over."

Zach settled the baby into its great-grandfather's arms, and the infant's eyes opened wide. He stared into the older man's face, as though studying him, or committing to memory, every laugh line, every wrinkle, and every work worn surface.

J.D. checked out the baby boy. "Hello, young man. What's your name?"

"Caleb . . ." Cathryn spoke, barely over a whisper. "Caleb Paul Ferguson."

Without looking up, J.D. nodded and smiled. "Paul, after your father. I'm glad to hear that. He adjusted his hold on the child. "Caleb Paul Ferguson," he repeated. "A fine name for my first great-grandson."

John cleared his throat loudly. He lifted the baby girl from the bed, gently cradling her in his arms. His gaze ricocheted from his granddaughter, to his daughter-in-law several times. He nodded, smiling at Cat. "Yep, she's got her beautiful mother's features written all over her." He walked over to the chair next to where his father sat, holding Caleb, and seated himself. "What's this little beauty's name?"

Zach approached, spoke reverently, as though he were about to reveal some great truth. "Her name is Cassandra, Pop—Cassandra Beth Ferguson."

John's heart skipped a beat when he heard the name. He turned to Cat, who sat sniffing, tears running down her pretty cheeks—obviously emotional at the scene. "Beth..." His voice broke as he cleared it and continued. "Bethie would approve." He met his daughter-in-law's gaze. "Thank you, Cat."

Cathryn nodded, accepted the tissue Zach handed her, and then latched onto his hand as he sat beside her on the bed.

John scanned the room—his father, himself, his son, and two grandchildren—four generations of Fergusons here in this room. As much of a thrill as it gave him to be a part of it, he was keenly aware of the missing presence. He knew if his wife could speak to him from the grave she'd say it was her biggest regret—not being a part of her grandchildren's lives. He gave Cat an encouraging smile. He suspected she was thinking the same thing about her father not being around to see his daughter's babies.

Beth and Paul would have both loved this.

John checked the time, realized their visit was nearly over. "Before we go, Paw Paw *Johnny* would like to hold them both at the same time. May I?" He grunted in satisfaction as Zach placed Caleb in the crook of his free arm. He gazed from one to the other, noticing the various differences and similarities of facial features between his two grandchildren. "Look at 'em, would you?"

His dad walked up and chuckled. "Yep, that's an armload of pooters, right there."

John laughed in agreement. He heard a soft knock at the door, but didn't bother to look up. Another in the continual flow of nurses or techs, he supposed, who'd attended Cat's every need. He blocked out all conversation as he concentrated all his attention on his two beautiful grandchildren.

"Don't you look good holding those two?"

The pleasant female voice broke into his silent reverence of the two infants. "Probably not as good as I feel, but thanks anyway." He looked up, grinning, and did a double-take at the woman standing before him. "Cynthia?" He squinted, to make sure he was seeing correctly.

Hands resting on her trim hips, the woman smiled and nodded. "I would have known you anywhere, John Michael. I swear, other than that distinguished looking salt and pepper hair of yours, you look exactly the same." She crossed her arms. "You suck for that, you know."

"Cynthia Anne Robicheaux . . ."

The pretty redhead's green eyes sparkled with laughter. "Nobody's called me Robicheaux in a long time." She touched the name tag clipped to her lab coat's lapel. "It's Ellender now. I married a man from Oklahoma."

He frowned, trying to recall having seen her in the past thirty-five years since graduating high school. "You've been an Okie all this time?"

She nodded. "Two weeks after graduation, I took a bus to Oklahoma to spend a month with my grandparents. I met Gene my fourth week there and never returned."

"Until . . ."

"Six months ago. I lost my husband a year earlier and our three kids have scattered to different areas. I decided it was time to come on back to Louisiana. I want to spend time with mom while she's still here."

"I'm sorry about your husband." He smiled as he remembered a particular incident. "Your mom baked the best red velvet cakes. Oh man, the pudding-like filling and cream cheese icing. Damn, that was good eating."

Cynthia nodded exuberantly. "She still does."

The elder John cleared his throat and spoke up. "Robicheaux? Are you Ham and Bess's daughter?"

"Yes sir, do you remember me?"

He slapped his thigh and laughed. "Now I do. I remember you tagging along with your dad everywhere he went."

"I bugged you mercilessly to see those new chicks every time you got in a new batch." She went over to give him a hug. "How are you, Mr. John?"

He nodded. "I'm good. And Johnny's right about your mother's red velvet cakes. That's when people baked 'em from scratch. Not these crappy mixes with no taste." He shook his head. "It broke my heart not to make your dad's funeral a few years back. I was with my wife at Lourdes Hospital in Lafayette. She was fighting her own battle with the big 'C' at the time."

Cynthia's face fell. "Oh. Did she . . ."

"No, she beat the cancer. Sometimes I wonder if . . ." He stopped, wiped his mouth with his hand.

John Michael met Cynthia's curious gaze. "Mom has Alzheimer's Disease. She's in a continuous care facility now."

"I'm so sorry." She reached out to his father, touched his arm gently. "Have you looked into the support groups here for the families of those afflicted with the disease? Sometimes it helps to talk about it with others in the same situation."

He cleared his throat with a loud harrumph. "Thanks, maybe I'll look into those."

John Michael and Zach exchanged looks equal in their levels of skepticism. Both implying, *Yeah, old man, sure you will.*

"So—" Cynthia swiveled and pointed to Zachary. "You're the father, obviously. You look too much like John Michael not to be his son."

"I am and extremely proud of it."

"Well, I need to speak to both you and your wife about a particular procedure for," she checked at her paperwork, "Caleb."

"What procedure? Is something wrong?" Zach's voice registered panic.

John Michael groaned. "I think she's asking about a circumcision, Son."

Cynthia gave him a quick nod. "You are correct. I'm the pediatrician and I'm here to answer any questions the two of you may have on the procedure, or to help you decide, one way or another."

John David stood quickly, adjusting his belt buckle. "Holy crap. I don't need to be here for this conversation. Are you about ready to go, Johnny?"

"Sure am, Pop. Doesn't sound like anything I want to hear about, either." John stood carefully, handed his granddaughter to Zach, and placed his grandson carefully in his designated bassinet.

He leaned over him. "Poor little booger." He gently tucked his grandson's blanket around the tiny figure. "I hope she does a good job, for your sake. Sometimes, they botch those things, you know." He looked up to find a host of eyes upon him. "Well, not me—and I'm sure you'll do a good job, Cynthia. I'm just sayin'."

His dad snorted. "Well, looks to me like your sayin' ain't helpin' much. Let's go, boy. It might be best to make our exit before they start tossing stuff at us."

John grabbed his hat and nodded at everyone. "I'll be back tomorrow, probably without the old guy, since he finds my driving so appalling and all." He found Cynthia's eyes pinned to him. "Cyn," he said, slipping in the nickname he'd called her in high school. "It was good to see you."

"You too, John Michael." She smiled again. "Maybe I'll see you again before they leave the hospital."

"I hope so." He nodded at her and ducked out of the room, grateful his old man had exited the room without witnessing the wink she'd sent his direction. The old fart would jump to foregone conclusions in a heartbeat. He pulled the door quietly closed, and turned, only to have his father in his face, wearing a smug expression.

"I gotta hit the can again, Johnny."

"Of course you do." He shook his head as his dad disappeared into the men's restroom. He stood there in the corridor, twirling his truck keys in his hands for several seconds, thinking about Cynthia's wink. What exactly, if anything, had she meant?

"You're still here."

He spun on his heel to see her approach, wearing the same captivating smile she'd possessed all through high school. "Waiting on Pop, as usual." He used his thumb to point at the restroom door. "His second home, lately."

"Enlarged prostate, huh?"

"Yeah, but don't let him hear you say that. He's in denial." He smoothed the rim of his hat trying to come up with a better topic of conversation.

"Those are two beautiful grandchildren you have in there. Are they your first?"

He nodded. "If Zach has anything to say about, they'll be my last. He almost lost that sweet girl in there."

"I heard about it when I came back from my day off. It got serious during delivery but she's fine now. It's remarkable how well the twins have adjusted to the environment outside the womb, though. Not a single sign of respiratory distress, none of the usual complications to babies of premature birth. Mother and babies are perfectly fine. There's no reason to believe her next pregnancy will be troublesome. Each one is different."

He waved his finger between the two of them. "You and I know that, but who's going to convince my son?" He shrugged. "Of course, if Cat wants more children, I have a feeling they'll have another go round at it. So, what did they decide about the procedure?"

She grinned. "Helmet head."

John winced. "Poor little guy. When?"

"Since they were a month early, I've advised them to wait a couple of weeks. They'll decide whether to bring him back here, or use their own pediatrician, or even use a specialist."

He cocked his head at her answer. "I didn't realize the medical profession had circumcision specialists."

Her laughter rang out between them. "Not specifically for circumcision but a pediatric urologist. Whomever they choose, your grandson will be fine." She grabbed her buzzing phone and read the text. "I need to be somewhere." She slipped it back into her pocket and grinned at him. "You know, some of my best memories from home involve your dad's feed store."

He nodded. "The shipments of chicks, I know."

She lifted one shoulder. "Yes—and those hay bales." Lifting her hand, she wiggled her fingers in a wave. "See you around, John Michael."

Cynthia spun on her heel and walked away from him at a brisk pace. She'd been a pretty little thing in high school, and she still was. No denying he'd always had feelings for this particular redhead.

John turned, paced an impatient trail in front of the restroom door, waiting for his father.

He froze in his tracks. *Hay bales.* Suddenly, a memory flooded his mind, as vividly as if it had happened yesterday, instead of forty years ago.

He'd spent all afternoon unloading a trailer full of hay bales. Cynthia had shown up with her dad and offered to help, nothing less than an insult for a young man of thirteen. She'd hung around to watch him nearly bust a gut trying to impress her with his speed and strength. He couldn't remember the details, but he'd ended up kissing Cyn that day.

Somehow he'd forgotten all about the late summer event responsible for providing him with enough fantasizing to last all through junior high and most of high school.

John swiveled in the direction she'd headed, in time to see her turn back for a second look at him. Still within earshot, he caught her light-hearted laughter as she sent him a final wave and turned a corridor to disappear from view.

How in the hell had he forgotten Cynthia Anne Robicheaux?

Cynthia rounded the corner and headed to the nurses station. Bee Tate stopped what she was doing, rested her pudgy fists on ample hips and raised one curious brow.

"What's got you grinning like the Cheshire Cat? You see the Mad Hatter down there or something?"

Cynthia froze in her tracks. "Les Miles is here? Really? Where?"

Bee's chocolate brown face twisted in confusion. She cocked her head, causing her silver wig to skew the slightest bit. "Who the hell is Les Miles? Is he a character in Alice in Wonderland, too?"

"Les Miles. You know, head coach for LSU? Tiger football?"

Bee gave her head a violent shake, further skewing the mound of unnatural silver curls atop her head. "Girl, you're giving me a headache with all this nonsense. I don't watch college football. And what the hell does that have to do with a story about a trip down a rabbit hole?"

Cynthia thought about trying to explain how the press had come to label Coach Miles the Mad Hatter after particularly entertaining interviews and because he always wears a white hat. It required far too much effort for someone who wasn't a fan. "Forget I said anything."

Bee pointed one stubby brown finger at Cynthia's face. "A diversionary tactic if ever I saw one. What did you see down there?" She waddled to the end of the corridor.

"Bee—what are you doing?" Cynthia's comment came out in a low hiss.

Bee stuck her silver topped head around the corner. She turned back to Cynthia, wearing an ear to ear grin. "Lawd! I know why you were grinning, now. That's a mighty fine looking man over there. Do you know him?"

"He's the grandfather of the Ferguson twins."

Bee's mouth twisted in a grin. "My, my, my—I had four of my grandfather's alive at the same time. Not a one of 'em looked as good as he does. Nuh-uh. Nope. I'd have remembered that, fa sho."

"He's an old friend from my home town."

"Ah—now we're getting to the crux of the situation. You *know* Mr. TDSH." She explained the acronym when Cynthia directed a clueless stare in her direction. "Talk, Dark, and Sexy as Hell."

Cynthia shrugged one shoulder and walked around the desk. "I knew him a long, long time ago. This is the first I've seen of him since our high school graduation." She pulled up a file on her tablet, entered some information on Caleb Ferguson. "They opted for the circumcision, in case you were interested."

"Poor little baby boy."

"I know."

"Are you doing the procedure?"

"I suggested they wait a couple of weeks but I will if they ask me to. They may decide to bring him to their own pediatrician though."

"Maybe they can get the good looking Paw Paw to bring him in so you can strike up a conversation with him."

Cynthia rolled her eyes. "I doubt it."

"Maybe he'll come along for the ride."

Cynthia cringed, remembering having to sit through the procedure for her own sons. "It's not exactly the kind of thing men want to witness."

Kevin, the vertically challenged, highly obnoxious X-ray technician who seemed to thrive on her rejection of him, approached from her right. "*What don't we want to witness?*"

"Circumcisions."

She didn't have to see his face to know he cringed.

"Oh, hell no. I'd rather be beaten bloody and thrown into a pool of sharks. A barbaric religious practice."

Cynthia shrugged one shoulder. "These days it's done for hygienic reasons and to prevent complications."

He shivered. "I don't care, and if you gals can't find a more pleasant topic of conversation, I'm leaving."

Bee turned on him. "Don't let the door hit you where the good Lord split you, Kevin. Buh-bye."

He sent a glare Bee's direction before pivoting slowly toward Cynthia. "I have tickets—"

"No."

"But they're—"

"Kevin! You've asked me out no less than a hundred times. My answer has been no. It's always going to be no."

"They're great seats."

She turned on him, her hands splayed. "How many times do I have to tell you I don't date in the work place? I've seen too many people end up in more drama than it's worth."

Kevin cocked his head sideways in what his co-workers called his giant cockatiel move. "Ridiculous!"

Bee approached, and gave him a light shove on the shoulder. "She's right, Kev. Heck, even dogs know not to poop where they eat. It surely seems like you'd have realized that by now. Besides . . ." She stopped to send Cynthia an exaggerated wink. "There's a new bull in the pasture."

"Good grief." Cynthia gathered her things and headed for her office. "It's suddenly come to my attention that you people know too damn much about my life."

Bee's laughter followed her out of the room. "And you're just now realizing this? Welcome to the fishbowl, honey."

Cynthia pushed open the door, her arms loaded down with groceries. She kicked it shut, staggering to the snack bar to dump the bags.

"You know you can make two trips, don't you?"

She scrunched her face, annoyed her mother caught her at this again. "I know. I don't want to."

Bess Robicheaux gave her daughter a one armed hug then focused her blue-eyed gaze on her. "Stop being hard-headed like your father. I don't want you to hurt yourself."

"Can I quote you next time I hear you've been climbing a ladder to pick figs out of that old tree out back?"

Her mother placed her fists on ample hips and cocked her head, before giving her short, snowy-white waves a gentle shake. "Well, I wasn't raised to see good fruit rot on the ground, by dang it! Besides, a lot of people get too much enjoyment out of my baked goods to let those delicious figs go to waste."

Cynthia brought a bag of canned goods to the pantry, glanced up at the shelves full of fig preserves, along with pears, blackberry and muscadine jellies, and multiples of others of which she couldn't quite read the labels. Her mother spent lots of time picking and canning fruits and berries. She spent even more time baking it up into delicious pies, fold over tarts, and other delicacies. Most of which she brought to the local nursing homes or food banks for distribution to the destitute. Sometimes, she put together baskets for people she'd heard were having difficulty making ends meet. Sometimes, she brought them to people just to see them smile.

For a woman who'd never had a career, she sure stayed busy. "You're a good egg, mom, but promise me you'll let me pick the figs from now on. If I'm too busy I'll hire someone to do it for you."

Bess pursed her lips. "I'll think about it. How was your day?"

Cynthia put two cans of stewed tomatoes on the shelf. "I had a good day. Lots of road construction going on in the city around Lake Coburn Memorial. It feels like I'm driving in a maze. I could have done without the lane I-10 lane closure. It took forty-five minutes to drive the thirty miles from Lake Coburn to here." Here, being Jennings, a city of 10,000, located sixty-five miles east of the Texas and Louisiana border on I-10.

She emptied the bag and closed the pantry door. "You will not believe who I saw today at the hospital."

"From your tone, I suspect it's someone I know."

"A set of twins were born on my day off. Preemies, and from what I hear, it got pretty hairy in the delivery room. The mother hemorrhaged and coded at one point. She's fine though."

"Who are the parents?"

"The father is Zach Ferguson from Lake Erin."

"Zach Ferguson . . . there was only one family of Ferguson's left in Lake Erin, so he must be Marilee and J.D.'s . . ."

"Grandson. He married a Cathryn McDaniel, also from Lake Erin."

"Cat—she's Ellen and Paul's daughter, right?"

Cynthia shrugged. "I'm not sure. Gone over thirty years, remember? I vaguely remember Paul McDaniel, but I have no clue who he married."

Bess frowned. "Well you couldn't have seen Paul, he passed away around the same time your father did."

"I saw John Michael and Mr. J.D. Did you know Ms. Marilee has Alzheimer's? She's in the latter stages, from the sound of it." Her mother's face fell.

"I didn't know. Poor Marilee—after fighting so hard to come back from cancer, too."

"Mr. J.D. said she was in a bad way in Lafayette when Dad passed."

Bess nodded. "I remember. We'd cross each other during chemo sessions sometimes. The treatment nearly did Marilee in, but she was so determined not to leave J.D."

"She made it through, but she's leaving him in another way, I'm afraid. I told him about the meetings we have in the area for the families."

Bess made a face. "Those old men don't go to therapy. They think it's their duty to take on the whole world." She clucked her tongue. "So this is John Michael's first grandchildren?"

"Sure is. Who did he marry, Mom? I know he's a widower, but I can't recall if she's anyone I knew."

Her mother tapped her forehead as though trying to remember. "I think she was from Lafayette. She'd spend the summers with relatives in Lake Erin, but the family's name escapes me right now. So, Johnny's a widower. Seems like I remember a particular summer you had it pretty bad for him. If I remember correctly, he's the one that started your father on the path to worrying."

Cynthia chuckled. "Whew, you remember correctly, Mama. I was thirteen when I developed a bad case of the 'I wants' for John Michael."

Bess slapped her thigh at a particular memory. "Ham had a fit when he caught you writing Mr. and Mrs. John Michael Ferguson all over something in your room one day."

"Yeah—it was my wall, so a *fit* would have been appropriate."

"Hadn't we recently painted it for you?"

Cynthia nodded. "Yes, you did. And I can totally understand how furious Dad was with me now, but at the time I thought he was being terribly unfair. After all, it was *my* room and *my* wall. Why shouldn't I be able to plaster it with the love of my life's name in permanent black marker?" She shook her head. "Thirteen year old girls are so ridiculous." She smiled at a particular memory. "Mmm, that was right after he kissed me."

"What? At thirteen? Where did he kiss you?"

"I'm almost sure it was on the mouth."

"Oh poo! You know what I'm talking about."

A low chuckle issued from Cynthia as she shook her head. "It was once, and forty years ago, mom. What are you going to do? Give me a retroactive grounding?"

Bess burst into laughter. "I suppose you're right. But I'm still curious about where it happened."

"I got my first kiss behind the feed store building—he'd been unloading bales of hay from a trailer, stacking them in the shed out back. I think he was showing off a little for me." She laughed. "I think I wounded his ego by offering to help. He said no, of course, but I remember watching him and even at thirteen years old his arms were muscular. I'm pretty sure none of the other guys our age were nearly as well developed. It was my first time at really becoming *aware* of a boy as . . ." Her voice trailed off.

"Are you trying to tell me he awakened my thirteen year old daughter's sexual desires?"

Cynthia grinned at her mom. "Yeah. I guess he did. He took my hand, pulled me between two tall stacks of hay, and he kissed me." She placed one hand over her heart. "It was so romantic."

Her mother gave her a bland look. "You and I clearly have different perceptions of romance."

Cynthia burst into laughter. "Whatever, Mom. It was perfectly acceptable for my very first kiss."

Bess frowned. "I'm not sure it was your first. I remember having to go to school to justify the black eye you gave a little boy in third grade for kissing you."

"Well, John's was the first kiss I actually *wanted* from a boy." She fanned her face. "He was good looking then, and all through high school, but you should see him now. He's the perfect combination of Jim Caviezel and Pierce Brosnan, with a little bit of Sam Elliot thrown in for good measure."

Her mother nodded. "He's got good genes. J.D. and Marilee are both good-looking people. Johnny gets his height from Marilee's side of the family, though. J.D. never reached six feet tall and from what I can remember Johnny was quite a bit taller than his dad."

"Mr. J.D. looks good for a man his age though. It's so sad about Ms. Marilee."

"It doesn't seem fair. That family has had its share of heartache already—the daughter they lost back in the '70s."

Cynthia's eyes widened at total recall of the horrendous event. "I've been gone so long I'd forgotten."

"I think the entire town of Lake Erin tried to forget it." Bess sniffed and wiped the corner of one eye with her pinky. "The Ferguson's have weathered some terrible storms. Of everything Alzheimer's has taken from my old friend, Marilee, I pray it took the memory of Jenna's death from her first." She picked up the bagful of bathroom items and headed toward the hall. "It's too much rain for one family, I tell you. Too darn much rain."

Her mother's comment brought back a flood of memories for Cynthia. In an instant she was transported back to a fall morning at Lake Erin high school—her and John Michael's sophomore year. One week after his sister, Jenna, had been crowned the football team's homecoming queen.

Cynthia was sick, running a fever and she'd been heading to Ms. Jane's office to call her mom. Her hand was on the door knob when it wrenched open, and John Michael rushed out, wild eyed and shaking his head furiously, nearly knocking her over.

"No! There's no way in hell my sister's dead. I don't want to hear it!" He'd paused in front of her, his frantic gaze locked onto her for a second before he rushed to the heavy glass lobby door and shoved it open. He hit the street, running like a scared rabbit in a full-out sprint. In seconds, he'd disappeared from view.

She'd turned at the sound of soft sobbing, saw his parents standing there, Ms. Marilee in tears, Mr. J.D.s mouth set in a grim line. Both of them visibly devastated—their son in a state of absolute denial.

She'd walked over to where the couple stood and gave Marilee a gentle hug. The poor woman had latched on to her, collapsing into heartbroken sobs.

Cynthia's biggest regret had been missing the wake and funeral because of the flu. By the time she saw her classmate again, some cataclysmic shift had occurred between them—altering what had always been an easy, relaxed friendship, bordering a little on the flirtatious. After that day, he barely spoke to her, and when he did, his demeanor was stiff, uncomfortable. For the remainder of high school he couldn't seem to look her in the eye.

Thank goodness that phase had passed, because seeing him today made her realize how much she'd missed seeing John Michael's eyes. Eyes such a beautiful shade of blue she still referred to the color as "Ferguson blue".

Chapter Two

John hesitated for a moment at the door, stopping long enough to send up a brief prayer. *Please let it be a good day for dad's sake.* He followed his father into the room, stopped inside and waited.

Marilee Ferguson turned her head to face them, her eyes blank.

And there it was. The cue telling them both she had absolutely no idea who they were. God, he hated this. Visits on days like this sapped him of energy, made him want to turn tail and run out of there before one word was spoken. But his dad forged ahead, as usual, determined to make her remember.

"There's my girl. How are you today, Marilee?"

John Michael held his breath, hoping her next words wouldn't be accompanied by a terrified scream or a look of suspicion and panic as they sometimes were. Instead, she cocked her head to the side, narrowed her eyes in concentration. "Do I know you gentlemen?"

He released his breath slowly as his dad chuckled and nodded.

"I believe we've met a time or two." J.D. held out a fresh bouquet of Forget-Me-Not flowers to his wife. "John David Ferguson, ma'am, but you can call me J.D. to make it easier. This is my son, John Michael."

Obviously relying heavily on her friendly Cajun roots, Marilee accepted the flowers graciously. The corners of her light brown eyes crinkled as she beamed up at her husband, the crow's feet and laugh lines a testimony to the years of a happy life, despite the previous rough patches. "Oh thank you, they're so pretty. These must be my favorite, I think, because I always seem to have them in my room. It's so nice to meet you, Mr. Ferguson. I'm sorry I'm not who you think I am. I don't know any Marilee. I'm—I'm—ah, I seem to be having a senior moment." She closed her eyes, frowned, opened them again. "Jenna. I think my name is Jenna."

John had to take a step back, watched in amazement, as his dad took less than a split second to compose himself.

J.D. smiled, leaned over to place a chivalrous kiss on his wife's hand. "It's very nice to meet you, too. Jenna is a beautiful name for such a beautiful lady."

He shot a glance in his son's direction—still smiling, but the sparkle in his eyes somewhat dimmed.

John took a deep breath and released it slowly. He stepped forward to place a comforting hand on his father's shoulder before kneeling in front of "Jenna's" chair. It broke his heart every time he had to do this but he did it anyway. He'd do anything to keep some kind of link between himself and the woman who'd given birth to him, loved him, and nurtured him throughout the first fifty-three years of his life. The least he could do was to return the favor in her last years, whether she recognized him or not.

He extended his hand, met her curious gaze. "I'm John Michael, Ms. Jenna. It's a pleasure to meet you."

The drive from the nursing home to the hospital was a quiet one for the two men. John waited until he parked his Ford truck in an available spot in the parking lot before turning to his dad.

"You all right, Pop?"

The old man wiped his face with one hand, shook his head. "It wasn't supposed to be this way, Johnny. We were supposed to be together." He stopped suddenly, faced his son. "But then again, I'm preaching to the choir, here, aren't I? At least your mother's alive."

John nodded. "Yeah, she is. That doesn't change facts. You're every bit as alone as I am."

J.D. nodded. "I am, but you don't have to be, you know. I can't see Bethie wanting you to live out the rest of your life without someone to go home to. Maybe it's time to move on, Son."

John stared ahead at the hospital, couldn't help but think of his beautiful, sweet Beth and wonder if his dad was right. The thought had him wondering if he'd see Cynthia today. Immediately, he felt a wave of guilt wash over him. "God almighty, I miss my wife. I know she's gone, but I'll always love her." He looked over at his dad. "But I guess I'm preaching to the choir too, aren't I?"

J.D. nodded—his expression a combination of sadness and acceptance. "If you find someone else, it doesn't mean you have to stop loving your wife, Johnny. Marilee and I had almost sixty wonderful years together before this disease started affecting our lives. You deserve the same chance to grow old with someone."

John nodded. "Maybe you're right." He grabbed the door handle. "We'll see, anyway."

Cynthia approached the third floor nurses station. "Bee, here's the form you called about. I can show you how to access the electronic file though. You have a printer right there."

"Uh huh, yeah I know." Bee whisked the paper from her hands and dropped it carelessly onto the desk. "But if I had, look what you would have missed. That fine hunk o' man is here again, and I did not imagine him craning his neck to look for you." She pushed her toward corridor A. "I sent Patrice in there to change his daughter-in-law's sheets so "Mr. Tall, Dark, and Sexy as Hell is waiting outside the room for the all clear to go back inside. You can thank me later."

Cynthia balked, but the smooth foam soles of her shoes acted as useless, grip-less glides as Bee pushed her out into the center of the corridor's intersection. She turned to gape at her, and then heard her name being called. She spun around to see John Michael standing outside the room, as Bee said. He waved and started walking toward her. She had no option, did she, other than to meet him halfway? Considering she hadn't been able to stop thinking about the man since she'd seen him again, she sure as hell hoped he found the nerve to ask her out.

He stopped in front of her, slapped his hat on one long, lean thigh— shifting his weight nervously from one booted foot to the other. "Hey Cyn, I was hoping to see you today."

She lifted her arms to indicate her surroundings. "There was a good chance you would as long as your daughter-in-law is here on this floor."

He passed one hand through his hair and looked up and down the hall. "Is there some place we could go to talk for a bit?"

Her breath hitched and she couldn't help but hope for a favorable outcome. She pointed to the alcove behind him. "There's a small waiting area right here."

He took four long strides to the room she'd indicated, before turning back to her. "It's empty."

She met him, sucked in her breath at the feel of his hand on the small of her back as he ushered her inside.

"You, uh—you want something to drink?" He pointed to the vending machine.

"No, I'm fine, thanks." She sat on one of the cushioned sofas in the room and patted the seat beside her. "Sit, John Michael. I'll get a crick in my neck looking up at you." She waited for him to sit then placed a hand on his knee, hoping to put him at ease. "Now, what do you want to talk about? Do you have a concern about your daughter-in-law or your grand-children?"

"No, not at all," he rushed in. "I was wondering—I was hoping . . ." He stopped to take a breath and released it slowly. "I've been a widower for fifteen years and I know it hasn't been long since you lost your husband. But, after seeing you yesterday, I was wondering if you'd maybe want to go out sometime? I could take you to lunch or to supper if you have time."

She fought to keep her cool—not easy when her heart was about to thud right out of her chest. She was a grandmother, for crying out loud, not a teenage girl.

"I'd like that."

He gave her a quick nod then stood. "All right, then. It's settled." He walked to the door.

"John Michael."

He pivoted. "Yes?"

She grinned. "Do you have a date or time in mind?"

"Oh! No, I haven't had time to think about it. My mind hasn't quite adjusted to you saying yes."

Cynthia reached inside her pocket for a business card and held it out to him. "This has all my numbers. Give me a call when you're ready."

He walked over to her, took the card. "I'm ready now. It's been so long since I've asked anyone for a date. I guess I forgot how to do it with any kind of finesse."

She laughed. "Don't worry, I'm in the same predicament as you, remember? I understand, completely."

He checked his watch. "Do you get lunch breaks? I could take you some place around here if you'd like. It'd be nice to catch up a little before an actual date."

"I can't take a break until 12:00 and I have a procedure scheduled at 1:00. I'll probably grab something in the cafeteria."

Was it wrong of her to adore the way his face fell in disappointment? "I'd love the company if you'd like to join me. They make a decent meatloaf and their mashed potatoes are passable." Her heart did a somersault at the sudden grin creasing his handsome face. The single right dimple she'd swooned over as a young girl made its appearance—and had the same effect as it had back then.

"That'd be nice, Cyn. Pop and I just came from seeing my mom and I could go for something to lift my spirits about now."

"I didn't see your dad. He's welcome to come also."

"He's in the restroom."

They both turned toward the door as his dad appeared suddenly. He entered the room, stopping short when he saw Cynthia seated on the couch. "Hey there, young lady, I didn't realize you were in here."

She rose to greet him. "How are you doing, Mr. J.D.?"

He nodded. "I'm good. I'm looking forward to seeing those babies again."

"There's nothing like new grandbabies to make the world seem a little brighter, huh?"

He gave her a sad smile. "Yeah. We saw Marilee earlier. I was hoping it'd be a good day so I could tell her about the twins. We showed her pictures, but it didn't mean much coming from strangers."

Cynthia reached up to give him a hug. "I'm so sorry, Mr. J.D., John and I were discussing lunch in the cafeteria in about an hour or so. I'd love to catch up with what's been going on."

"Lunch, huh?" He patted his belly. "I woke up late this morning and I'm still kind of full from breakfast. I doubt I'll be hungry by then, but y'all go on ahead. I'll be holding babies until the two of you are done."

Cynthia pivoted to face John. "How about if I swing by your daughter-in-law's room when I'm ready? I've got some work to do until then." She took a step into the hallway and looked back at him. "I think they're finished with the room now. I'll see you gentlemen in a bit." She wiggled her fingers in a wave and left them.

She caught Bee's eye at the nurse's station and gave her a thumbs up. "Lunch. One hour." Bee whooped—lifted her chubby arm and Cynthia slapped her hand in a high five on the way back to her office. "Thank you, Bee."

"You are so welcome, sugar. Now see?" She chided her other co-workers. "If y'all would leave it to me—I'd have all you ladies hooked up in no time. But, nooo. Nobody wants to listen to Bee!"

Cynthia grabbed a side salad and placed it on her tray. "Maddie, I'll have the meatloaf and the snap beans—no gravy on the meat loaf, please." She placed the plate on her tray and slid it down the line.

John Michael passed up the salads and chose a side order of fried okra. "I'll have the meatloaf and mashed potatoes, extra gravy, with the turnip greens instead, please." He got to the desserts and chose a slice of apple pie. He pointed at a slice of coconut cream with meringue. "Could I get one of these in a to-go container, please?" He waited for it then slid his tray next to Cynthia's. They both asked for sweet tea at check out. John paid while Cynthia found a table for them in the semi-crowded cafeteria.

When John met her at the table Cynthia eyed the pies longingly. "I miss desserts. Is that slice for later?"

He checked out her tray. "I can get you a slice."

She held one hand in front of her face. "No thank you, sugar goes straight to my hips. My metabolism has slowed to a crawl."

"It looks to me like your metabolism is doing fine." He pointed his fork at the clear plastic container. "It's for my dad. He can't eat sweets much, but he deserves a treat today." He looked up when he felt her gaze on him.

"Was it bad?"

He shrugged. "It's always bad when Mom doesn't know who we are. Nine times out of ten we're strangers to her. Still, Pop goes in hoping for the one day she recognizes us—*those* are the days that keep him going."

He paused, took a sip of tea. "Today was especially difficult. She couldn't remember her own name, which happens a lot. But today, she thought her name was Jenna." He glanced up at Cynthia's gasp. "I know. Talk about a spear in the old man's heart." He shook his head. "Pop barely missed a beat. He said Jenna was a beautiful name and kissed her hand like an old southern gentleman."

"He is an old southern gentleman." Cynthia's voice was thick with tears.

John handed her his napkin. "Honest to God, Cyn. I don't know how he does it."

She sniffed and dabbed at her eyes. "He probably said the same thing about you when your wife passed away. What happened, if you don't mind me asking?"

He reached for the pepper shaker. "Beth died during a surgery to remove a ruptured appendix—complications from the anesthesia."

"How awful for you."

"She had turned thirty-eight a couple of months earlier. I was a widower at thirty-nine, with a sixteen year old son."

"So that makes Zachary thirty-one or so?"

"Yep, he and Cat are the same age." He began mixing his gravy into his mashed potatoes. "It's not like you can prepare yourself. We were in shock, both Zach and I. Hell—everyone was—her parents, her siblings, the whole damn town. Beth was a teacher at Lake Erin Middle School and it threw her students for a loop. It was a freaking nightmare."

"I'm so sorry, John."

He lowered his fork and lifted his gaze. "And your husband?"

"It was a heart attack—very sudden. You've heard of those 'widow makers' right?" She used her two forefingers to point at herself. "I'm living proof they exist. Could I have the black pepper, please?"

She shook the bottle over her meatloaf. "Gene was a few months shy of his fifty-fifth birthday. He was in great physical shape, ran two miles at least three times a week. He was the battalion chief for the Tonka City fire department."

She cut a slice from her meatloaf, her face blank, not revealing a thing. "Every time he went to a fire there were dangers of cave-ins, collapsing floors, smoke inhalation, equipment malfunction, explosions; any number of things could go wrong. He pulled up at his last fire and stepped out of his truck. I was told he clutched his chest and fell to the ground. They tried everything to revive him. Nothing worked. Like with Beth, the entire town was in shock."

John kept quiet through an awkward but brief silence.

She shook her head. "The funeral was very dramatic—an impressive showing of uniformed firefighters—he was very good at his job. He was a good father, and . . ."

She stopped to take a deep breath before continuing. "He'd been a wonderful husband throughout our marriage—I adored that man. By the last morning of the wake I was ready to crack. I kept staring at his coffin, thinking I couldn't possibly survive losing him—" She lifted one finger, pointed up in the air. "But God and Gene found a way to help me get through it."

He picked up on the touch of sarcasm and leaned forward slightly. "What happened, Cyn?"

She sipped her tea thoughtfully. "I was sitting there talking to my sons, when this young woman, clearly distraught, pushes through Gene's co-workers to stand in front of me. A petite little thing, with short, red hair and this punk-rock-spikey cut streaked in bright blue. I asked who she was."

Cynthia stared straight ahead as though reliving the moment.

"She stood there, tight-lipped and silent. At first I thought she was some love child of Gene's, but she looked nothing like him, and his features are so dominant in my kids. Then Charlie Jefferies, my husband's best friend, pushes through the crowd to approach us, and he's got this panicked look on his face, right? So I look around at the rest of the guys from the department, and not one of them could look me in the eye. That's the moment I realized she must have been Gene's girlfriend."

"Oh God. You found out about his girlfriend at the funeral?"

She nodded. "She and I had an illuminating discussion after I kicked everyone else out of the room. Her name was Tamara Sullivan, and it turned out she'd sold me my last wireless phone plan. I remembered choosing my own phone, but rather than risk choosing one Gene wouldn't like, I made him go to the store to pick out his own phone."

John groaned, suspecting the outcome.

She nodded, gave him a tight-lipped smile. "When I mentioned that had been two years earlier, she gave me this smug, satisfied expression—said 'I bet you're wishing you'd have picked out that phone yourself right about now, aren't you?'"

He sat back suddenly. "Damn, Cyn, what'd you say to that?"

She kept her gaze on her plate and cleared her throat, the barest twitch of her right brow her only tell. "I may have slapped that smug look right off her face."

"You—you slapped her?"

"I may have." She dabbed her mouth with a paper napkin and set it aside.

John stifled a laugh. "You—may have?"

"Yes—and it may have been a fairly hard slap."

"How hard?"

She stopped to meet his gaze. "It may have sounded like a gunshot in the room. And I may have threatened her with a restraining order if I ever saw her face again."

"Good for you."

She sighed and rested her crossed arms on the table surface. "Did I mention she was twenty-five years old—the same age as our daughter?"

John couldn't keep the disgust from his hissed reply. "Son of a bitch."

Her chin lifted. "Those were among my very last words to my dead husband." She picked up her fork, used it to point at John. "Never underestimate the benefits of deep seated anger. It makes it so much easier to deal with the death of a cheating spouse."

"Wow. I—I don't quite know what to say."

She sent him another tight smile. "Try facing your children after an episode like that. I'm talking total shock—total disillusionment for all of us. Suddenly, I became *that* woman—the one who didn't hear until her husband's funeral that he'd cheated on her. If there'd been a way I could have left town immediately, I would have."

She stabbed at her green beans. "It took me a year to sell the house and train my replacement at the hospital. All three of my children were upset with me at first for leaving Oklahoma to move back to Louisiana. The boys got over it, of course, said they understood. My daughter is still furious with me. She's found a way to absolve her father of all blame, as I suspected she would. Instead she's heaped it onto me."

John frowned. "That doesn't seem fair. You'd think, as a woman, she'd be a little more empathetic."

She gave him a one shouldered shrug. "She's never had a cheating spouse, and I pray she never does. But, after what I've experienced, her unreasonable anger with me is nothing I can't handle."

He linked his fingers as he sat there studying her. "You seem extremely well-adjusted for what you've been through."

"I fully expected to have some kind of mental or emotional implosion. I even went to a therapist, thinking surely she'd uncover some anger issues, some deeply-hidden resentment waiting to emerge—something to make me go ballistic on a few people."

John had to laugh at the image. "Did she find anything?"

She joined in his laughter. "No, can you believe it?"

"I doubt anyone would have blamed you if you had."

She speared a cherry tomato with her fork. "What good would it have done? The only one I could have blamed was dead and buried."

"Well, it proves you're from strong stock, Cyn."

"You know, you're the only person who's ever called me that. Everyone else called me Cindy or Cynthia." She popped the tomato into her mouth.

"I'm a little surprised. It seems natural. It's always rolled off of my tongue so easily." He took a bite of the tasty meatloaf and they ate in silence for a few moments before he picked up the conversation with a total change of subject. "What was it like being a transplanted Cajun in Oklahoma?"

The corners of her eyes creased with amusement.

"It took some adjusting at first. The real test came when I married into a family whose people had been there for over a hundred years. Those folks were set in their ways, let me tell you. Within a few months, I realized it was mostly my in-laws who were so tough to crack. Everyone else seemed friendly enough."

John had made quick work of finishing his lunch. He pushed the plate away to attack his apple pie. "I'm sure you eventually worked your way into their hearts."

"It took a little time for my mother-in-law to accept me working towards a career. She thought I should have stayed home to take care of her baby boy."

John dug his fork into his slice of apple pie. "And how'd baby boy feel about it?"

Cynthia washed down her last bite of meatloaf with a sip of tea. "He was all for me getting an education and having a career. It was his suggestion to put off having children until I was more than half-way through school. I was twenty-five when our first son was born. Our daughter came two years later and youngest son in another two years."

"That's a good size family for someone beginning her medical career. You must have been stressed."

"Kids are stressful no matter what career you're in. I mean, the responsibility of raising those little lives is massive, am I right? But, Gene and I pulled together to make it work." She stabbed at the last of her green beans and lifted her fork. "That's why I was so shocked at the funeral incident."

"Did you ever talk to any of his co-workers, find out how long they'd known?"

"Once I got home, a couple of his buddies, Jimmy J. and Charlie, showed up at the house wanting to discuss it."

"Must have been an interesting conversation—"

"It never took place," she interjected. "I had no desire to hear them or anyone else attempt to justify his actions to me, or why they all lied for him."

"You've got resolve. My curiosity would have made me listen to what they had to say."

She stopped, stared at him. "What difference would it have made? There is nothing anyone could have said to make what he did the slightest bit acceptable. I told them it was too damn late to use me to clear their consciences—then I shut the door in their faces." She lifted her glass of sweet tea to sip from the straw.

John grinned at her and lifted his glass as well. He reached across the table, touched his rim to hers. "Well done, Cyn. For what it's worth, I agree with you. There's no room for infidelity in marriage."

"Thank you, John Michael."

He dug his fork into his pie again, lifted one brow to send a glance her direction. "You know, you're the only one who called me by my full name all during high school when everyone else called me John or Johnny."

"I love the sound of John Michael together, don't you?"

He swallowed and cleared his throat. "I only thought of it as a way to distinguish myself from my dad and grandfather. Hell, my Paw Paw didn't pass away until I was thirty. For a while, there were three John Ferguson's in Lake Erin. It was crazy. I sure as hell wasn't going to add to the insanity by adding a fourth when I had a son."

"So you named him Zachary."

"Yes, because I wanted him to have some kind of individuality."

Cynthia clucked her tongue. "Such a rebel, going against tradition."

John chuckled. "You think so, huh?"

"Absolutely."

"There are times when it's a good thing. Other times, eh, not so much.".

Finished with her lunch, she pushed her plate aside and pulled her drink closer. "So, have you thought any more about when this date should take place?"

"How about Saturday evening?"

Her eyes crinkled with laughter. "Works for me. You want to meet somewhere?"

He fidgeted in the seat. "I know it's been a while since I've done this, but don't guys pick girls up for dates anymore?"

"I'm sure they do. Would you prefer to pick me up at my place?"

He gave her an enthusiastic nod. "I would. I promise I'll get you back whatever time you need to be home."

Cynthia glanced at her watch and pushed back from the table. She gave him a mischievous wink. "Are you afraid Mama's gonna give me a curfew if she sees I'm going out with you?"

"You never know." When she stood, he followed suit, grabbed both their trays. "You need to get back to work."

She nodded. "I really should. I have to prep for a procedure. So, listen, I've already given you my card with my numbers. Call me when you get a chance and I'll give you Mom's new address in Jennings. I'd started looking for my own place, but she liked having me around and asked me to stay. I figure I'm playing catch up and giving my siblings a break. I'm finally able to pull my fair share of Mom duty."

"Lucky me. I get my pop all to myself—and he is one stubborn old coot."

"If he's anything like Mom, he can't seem to grasp why he shouldn't be doing some things he used to do."

"Exactly—especially with his cataracts."

"And the surgery these days is so low risk, with high success rates. There's really no excuse not to have it."

John held up one finger. "Ah, but there again, he'd have to admit he had a problem to even think about any kind of corrective surgery."

"Like with the prostate."

He gave an abrupt nod. "You got it. I've tried to explain it to him. Something that started out the size of a walnut is probably the size of a lemon now, but he won't listen to me. Maybe you can talk some sense into him."

She checked her phone and slipped it into the pocket of her lab coat. "I'd be glad to give it a shot next time I see him. Thanks for treating me to lunch, John Michael. I'll see you Saturday and don't lose my card." She started backing toward the exit. "I'll be waiting for your call."

Chapter Three

It took every bit of John's patience to wait twenty-four hours before calling Cyn to set up the dinner date for the following weekend. That left him the rest of the week to worry about going on his first date with anyone other than the woman he'd married in well over three decades.

On Friday afternoon, he managed to open his front door, even loaded down with several bags. He dropped four on the kitchen counter and walked straight to the laundry room with the last two bags.

"What'cha got there? Some new duds for your hot date?"

John didn't bother turning to answer his father. "I had some shopping to do. It was time for a new pair of jeans and I happened to come across a couple of shirts on sale so I picked them up. No big deal." *Keep telling yourself that.*

"*Sure* it isn't." His pop's chuckle rumbled in the air like the old Harley John had ridden around on just out of high school. "I hope you made a trip to the pharmacy while you were out shopping."

"I did," John said. "I needed some new blades for my razor."

The old man walked away, clucking his tongue as he shook his head. "You're making a huge mistake if you shave. Today's women prefer a two day growth of beard on men."

John pulled off the last tag from the jeans and threw them in the washer. "How the hell would you know?"

"All the women's magazines say so, and so do the ladies on the morning talk shows. They think it's sexy."

"Save it, Pop. I'm not going on a first date looking scruffy." John removed the collar cardboard and pins from the shirts before dropping them in with the jeans. He threw a detergent pod in the machine and started the cycle.

His dad turned at the distinctive click of the machine's timer kicking in. "Did you throw those in all together?"

"Yeah. Why?" John glanced back at the washer. "They're all dark colors."

"Hmph. Your mother chewed my butt big time once for throwing a pair of new jeans in with a batch of her clothes. It turned all her brassieres and underwear light blue." His eyes crinkled with laughter. "She got me back, though. She purposely threw a new red shirt in with my T-shirts and tightie whities—turned everything the prettiest shade of pink you ever saw."

"They'll be fine."

J.D. grunted. "You know best."

John waited until his dad walked away before stopping the washer. He pulled out the two shirts and set them in the large utility sink, leaving a trail of soapy water on the laundry room floor. He wiped up the spill with a dirty towel, grumbling to himself. "Old fart's got me second guessing myself." His dad's low laughter from the doorway had him groaning in irritation.

"What else did you pick up from the pharmacy section?"

John threw the towel in the bin and turned toward his father. "Nothing else. Why?"

"Not even prophylactics?"

"Why would I need rubbers on a first date?"

J.D.'s eyes widened. "Women are a lot looser than they used to be. There's been a *movement*."

John couldn't keep the grin from his face. "That's something. John David Ferguson keeping tabs with the women's movement."

His dad released a huff of laughter. "Well you have to these days or you'll offend somebody. Used to be the only kind of movement I was interested in was a bowel movement."

John lifted one hand, praying his pop would stop before he got into too much detail. "I guess you heard all about that on the talk shows, too?"

"No, from watching TV. Kids today got no damn sense of morals."

"Well, Cyn and I aren't kids anymore."

"Compared to me, you are."

"Geez, Pop. We're not having sex on the first date."

"What if she offers? You'd turn it down?"

"No. Yes. I mean she wouldn't offer because she's not that kind of lady. And if she would, I'd say no, because—she—well, she wouldn't."

J.D. frowned at his son. "You having some problems in your nether regions?"

John glared at him. "I am *not*."

"Are you sure? If you are, your doctor can give you some of those little blue pills. There are a few different ones out there on the market now to combat the E.D. That's short for Erectile Dysfunction, you know. Back in my day, we just said can't get it up. Either that or the dead soldier syndrome." He frowned slightly. "These days they've got acronyms for every damn thing. ED, VD, STD, PTSD . . . I guess the medical profession can't be bothered with saying all those long words. And the media—well they do their part to make it sound cool. That bullshit gets on my last damn nerve." His eyes suddenly sparkled with laughter. "I guess I should've said that BS gets on my LDN. But the point is if you got a problem down there they can help you out."

John turned and walked away. "I'm not having this conversation with you, Pop. Not now. Not ever." His old man wouldn't let it go.

"It's nothing to be ashamed of, you know. Of course the side effects of those pills sound pretty damned hellacious if you ask me—"

"Which I didn't."

"But I guess some guys think it's worth it to have their soldiers standing at attention again."

John turned, both arms raised, and frustrated out of his mind. "Would you put a cork in it?"

J.D.'s eyes widened even further. "A cork? That would be for a whole *nuther* kind of movement. Those folks even have their own parade. I don't think they call them corks though. They call them plugs or some such nonsense."

John's hands fell to his sides. "You're killing me, Pop."

"I'm trying to help, Son. If you *have* erectile dysfu—"

"For the last damn time, I don't have E.D.!"

J.D. harrumphed and turned on his heel. "Well, why didn't you say so in the first place?"

Saturday trudged along achingly slow, until it was finally time to leave for his date. John dressed quickly then slipped on his good boots.

"Hmmm. . ."

He looked up from a last second touch-up to his tan Tony Lamas, to cast a look his father's direction. "What—now?"

"Maybe you should have worn a suit, or at the very least, some nice slacks."

He straightened to his full height in order to stare down at his father. "Cyn's known me all my life. She already knows I'm not the suit and tie type. It's a little late to start pretending to be something I'm not."

"You don't think she's gonna be wearing her hospital scrubs and lab coat on the date, do you? She'll probably get all gussied up for this. Seems like the least *you* could do is put forth a little effort."

"That's why I shaved. So I'd look like I put forth the effort. You wanted me to go looking grubby."

"Scruffy, not grubby. Somebody named Cosmo said *scruffy* is equal to *sexy*."

"Cosmo is a magazine, not a person. It's short for Cosmopolitan."

"Cosmopolitan? Those women drink those in the *Sex and The City* program your mother used to watch."

"It's also a magazine, and it sounds like you watched it too."

"Well, sure. Tit for Tat. She sat through my old *Gunsmoke* and *Have Gun Will Travel* episodes. I sat through *Sex and the City* and the HGTV programs. It's called compromise."

John nodded. "Yeah, Pop. I seem to remember practicing a little of that in my eighteen years of marriage."

J.D. ignored his sarcasm-laced comeback and handed him a piece of notepaper folded in half. "Here you go. Take a look at these on the way over there."

John unfolded the paper and scanned it. "What the hell is this?"

"It's lines. You know, kind of like pick-up lines, but there are several you might be able to use during the evening. They came from—"

"A talk show, I know." John stifled a guffaw of laughter as he read from the sheet. "You look hotter than a Mexican tamale?"

"I came up with that one myself. C'est bon, huh?"

John re-folded the paper, would have dropped it in the trash bin if his dad wouldn't have been watching. He stuffed it in the front pocket of his jeans instead. "Yeah, Pop. Thanks."

He finally left the house, his father's old-man-cackle and final comment still ringing in his ears. "Have fun, but be careful. If you can't be careful, name it after me!"

In the ten minutes it took to drive from Lake Erin to Cyn's mom's place in Jennings, John was well on his way to working up a nervous sweat. By the time he knocked on the front door, he felt like a green teenager picking up his first crush. The fact was, Cynthia *had* been his first crush, and it hit home in a way he hadn't expected.

He fidgeted with his collar then re-tucked his shirt into the back of his new jeans.

The door opened and Ms. Bess Robicheaux stood there, her face lit up at the sight of him. "Johnny, it's so good to see you."

"You too, Ms. Bess. You're looking good." He reached down to give the woman a hug.

She waved off his compliment. "Oh, pshaw—for my age, you mean? Old Father Time is trying like hades to make me old. I'm too darn stubborn to give in. I keep hoping if I wear the old fart down, he'll leave me alone."

John laughed, thinking this woman and his mom could have been cut from the same cloth, from looks right down to their sense of humor. "If anyone on this earth is capable of sending him packing, it's you."

"Come on in here. Cynthia should be out in a few minutes. How are J.D. and your mother? It broke my heart to hear about the Alzheimer's—Marilee and I spent a lot of time together over the years. She called me a couple of months after Paul passed away, so upset. She'd just heard the news, said your father hadn't wanted to tell her when it happened because she was so ill at the time. She was fighting her own battle with the darn ole chemo."

"Yes ma'am. Pop asked me not to tell her when it happened. He wanted to keep her positive."

"And it must have worked, because she sure beat it."

John Michael nodded. He didn't doubt one bit his father's uplifting attitude helped push his mother through those dark days. He may be an ornery old coot for everyone else in the world, but for his wife, J.D. Ferguson had been nothing but indulgent and gentle. He turned slowly, taking in his surroundings. "You've got a nice little place here, Ms. Bess. When did you move to Jennings?"

"Two years ago. After Ham passed, Allie and her husband kept bugging me to sell the house and move closer to them. I was dead set against it, of course."

"Someone must have been mighty persuasive."

"I held off as long as I could, but then I slipped down my icy porch. No phone around and my neighbors were either out of town or at work. I drug myself up the steps and called an ambulance. I was all bruised up."

He sucked in his breath. "I hope you didn't break anything."

"Luckily, no. But it set things in motion. Long story short, I sold the family home and bought this place. It's smaller, but easier to take care of and only a few blocks from Allie and her family."

"And now, of course, you've got your other daughter here. How's it working out—having two women in the same household?"

Her smile brightened her face. "I adore having her here. She's at work all day, but it's nice having her come home in the afternoons." She looked up as Cynthia entered the room. "I'm so thrilled to have my daughter back where she belongs."

Cynthia gave her mother a quick, one-armed hug. "I'm glad to be back here with you. I didn't realize how much I missed living in Cajun country until I came home." She grinned at John. "Hey, you."

He had to swallow the lump in his throat in order to answer. "Hey." He took in her appearance, suddenly wondering if he should have listened to his father.

She smoothed down her floral print dress, adjusted some kind of light-weight, lace cover up tied in the front to accentuate her breasts. "What's wrong?"

He sent her a lift of a single brow. "To be honest, I'm wondering if I'm underdressed. You look wonderful, Cyn." The look on her face told him he'd definitely said something right.

"You're not underdressed at all, John Michael. You look wonderful, too."

"Are you sure? Pop nearly convinced me to bring my jacket and a tie. I'm kind of wishing I had now."

Was he kidding?

She dabbed daintily at the corner of her mouth with her pinkie, in case she'd begun to drool. He'd looked good in the hospital, wearing faded jeans and a dark blue T-shirt. But here, closely shaved and looking like he'd stepped right off the centerfold of a *Sexy Contemporary Cowboys* calendar—she fanned herself mentally. A hell of a lot could be said for a pair of new, good-fitting jeans on a man of John Michael's stature. The short sleeved dress shirt, tucked neatly into the waistband of said jeans only added to the package. Her gaze raked in his appearance, from his tan leather belt, all the way down to his matching boots. She always did have a thing for men in western boots.

"You look nice, John Michael." *That may have been the granddaddy of understatements considering the drool-worthy figure standing before her.* "*Extremely* nice."

"Thanks Cyn. Pop went on so much about me wearing a suit and tie he had me doubting myself."

"Good grief, in this weather? It's too hot for all those layers this time of year down here."

John lifted one hand and let it fall to his side. "Well, that's what I thought, but he had his own ideas, and plenty of them, I assure you. Are you ready to go?"

Cynthia took the elbow he extended, looped her hand around his well-developed bicep, sucked in her breath at the feel of it. "Absolutely."

Several minutes later, with both of them buckled in his truck, which he claimed to have cleaned up for the occasion, he broached the subject of his father again.

"You know, Pop was even trying to convince me not to shave yesterday and today. He insisted women preferred a two-day growth of beard over clean shaven." He stopped, rubbed a hand along his chin. "Said women today found it sexy. I happen to think anything with that much sparkle to it should be a piece of jewelry. If it's not, it needs to come off. There's getting to be quite a bit of silver in my beard."

She cocked her head at him. "I admit I like a smooth, clean shave on a man. Then again . . ." She left the comment hanging. With his lean, masculine build, dark hair peppered with silver, and Ferguson blue eyes—she suspected even on his worst day, this man looked better than the average fifty-three year old male.

He raised a single eyebrow. "You mean I could have saved a little time? Shown up looking scruffy, and you would have gone out with me anyway?"

She pursed her lips then nodded. "Possibly."

Grinning, he started up his truck. "I'll keep it in mind."

"You do that, Johnny Boy." She slapped her hands lightly on her thighs. "So, where are you taking me tonight? I hope it's someplace special since it's my first 'first date' in thirty-five years."

His head drooped forward as he released a long sigh. "Guess I'll have to cancel our reservation at Mickey D's." He looked up at her, his handsome grin giving him an almost boyish look.

"Definitely no Mickey D's. In Oklahoma, I'd find myself craving fresh seafood—shrimp and oysters and stuffed crabs, if you're looking for suggestions."

He laughed. "Well, I don't imagine fresh seafood is readily available in Oklahoma."

"No, there were plenty of wonderful Mexican restaurants and steakhouses, but nothing that served anything much other than farm raised catfish that was fresh. The seasoning up there is a little different, too."

"Nothing quite like Cajun cooking, is there?"

"You won't get any argument from me. So, where are we going?"

He cocked his head and gave her a one-eyed squint. "It's a surprise, but I've got reservations."

She adjusted her seat belt. "It must be quite a drive. It's a little early for dinner reservations."

He grinned at her. "The reservations are for 5:15. It's only twenty minutes from here."

"You've got me all kinds of curious now. Why so early?"

"It'll be packed by 5:30. You'll see."

She settled in for the drive, deciding to learn more about this man. "So, are you running Lake Erin Feed and Supply with your dad, now?"

"Oh, no. Pop's been retired. I was running the place alone for twenty years. Bethie's life insurance paid off our mortgage and all of Zach's schooling. I bought a few rental properties that have paid for themselves over the years. Now they're adding to my income. I never had time for fancy trips, or anything frivolous, so I've built up a sizeable nest egg.

A couple of years ago I asked Zachary if he wanted to take it over and he jumped at the chance. Now I have time to do the things I love."

"Such as?" she probed.

"I have a couple dozen head of cattle, and since I was able to build the greenhouse I'd always wanted, I tend to my plants and vegetables. I start all the seedlings Zach sells in the store during planting season. And I can harvest produce a lot longer in a controlled environment."

"Do you sell your vegetables at a farmer's market or anything? I try to support those places as often as I can."

"No. I just grow them for the pleasure of it. What I can't eat, I give away to friends and family."

She grinned. "Sounds like you stay busy."

"I do, but it's the kind of busy I love."

"And Zachary's keeping the family tradition alive with the store."

"Four generations and counting. I'm still in Lake Erin, so I'm available to help out if something comes up with Zach."

"Like infant twins?"

He nodded. "You got it. I expect I'll be running the place for a month or two."

"Sounds like a good life, Mr. Ferguson."

"Well, I'm not a doctor or anything."

"Stop that. It's a very respectable living."

He nodded. "Thanks, Cyn. We've always thought so."

She turned in the truck seat to study his profile. "So, why didn't you ever ask me out in high school? We used to have this flirty kind of relationship—and then we didn't."

He sobered instantly. "Bad luck, I guess. Yours was the first face I saw after my folks told me about Jenna. I tore out of that office and there you were. Your eyes big and questioning—your face kind of flushed."

"I was running a fever."

"I know, Mom told me once I stopped running long enough to accept what happened. I must have run ten miles. When I got too exhausted, I stopped and walked back home. The thing is, for the next two years, every time I saw you it brought me back to that moment."

"I'm sorry, John Michael."

"No, I'm sorry, Cyn. You didn't do a damn thing wrong. As a matter of fact, my mom had such a soft spot in her heart for you afterwards . . ."

"Because of the hug?"

He nodded. "Even as distraught as she was, she could feel you were feverish. As sick as you obviously were, you took time to show her how much you cared. Your simple act of kindness has always meant so much to her."

"I'd like to see her again, John Michael. Do you think I could?"

He nodded. "I don't see why not. Even though you haven't changed much, don't expect her to recognize you."

"Where is she? I could go one day after work."

"She's at Extended Care Facility on Lake Street."

"I know exactly where it is. I'll try to stop by one day this week." They exited off of I-10 Eastbound, and eventually drove north on one of the curviest little roads she'd seen since she'd been back in Louisiana.

Cynthia peered out through her passenger side window. "This reminds me of the Oklahoma boonies, without the hills. If it was dark outside and you were wearing a ski mask, I'd be a little worried right now."

John Michael laughed. "Being as I've never skied a day in my life, I'd say you'd have reason to be. We're almost there. As a matter of fact—you see the big, white sign up there?"

She squinted to see the sign, wondering if she'd remembered to bring her glasses. She rummaged through her purse, thankful to find them. Surely she'd have to read a menu. She found her lip gloss, and breath mints, both bound to come in handy if his restaurant of choice offered decent seafood. What if it turned out to be a steakhouse? Coming up empty on the floss picks, she made a mental note to stay away from steak.

"Our destination."

She looked up as they pulled into a nearly empty limestone parking lot. The huge roadside sign boasted two large letters—D.I.'s—in a bold red against a stark white background.

"D.I.'s . . . I haven't heard of it. Is the food good?"

"Yes—and so is the entertainment. It's the reason we have to get here so early." He parked his truck before grinning at her. "How do you feel about listening to Cajun music from a live band while we eat?"

She clapped her hands and shrieked with excitement. "*Please* tell me you dance, John Michael. I don't think I could bear it if you told me no."

His rumble of laughter reverberated around her, but he'd only commit to a slightly cryptic reply. "I guess you'll have to drag me out on the dance floor to find out."

As he stepped from his truck, Cynthia tried to recall if she'd seen a spare panty liner in her purse—unless he had two left feet she planned to keep his good looking butt out on that dance floor. Amazing how time shifted a girl's priorities when it came to the contents of her purse.

He opened her door and she stepped onto the parking lot, paused to observe the sprawl of a neatly painted wooden structure that spoke of more than one expansion throughout the years. "Seems like I'd know about this place, but it could be because I spend most of my days in stuck inside a Lake Coburn hospital. How long has it been in business?"

He gave a low whistle. "I want to say the actual restaurant has been running since sometime in the late 80's, but I can remember going to eat boiled crawfish in their barn a decade earlier. Five bucks for all you could eat—and let me tell you, I did on quite a few occasions."

She looked at her watch. "It's only a little after five o'clock. Are you sure they're open?"

He chuckled as four other vehicles drove up simultaneously. "Trust me. We're right on time." He walked her up the steps to the wooden porch and ushered her inside. A young woman greeted them at the entrance.

"Hey Mr. John, it's good to see you. We have your table ready for you."

"Thank you, Danette."

They were seated in the section nearest the open dance floor. One look at the wooden floor slats, worn slick and smooth from decades of dancing, told her everything she needed to know. This was Cajun country—when the music is good, people dance. She was in for a fabulous night.

"I've never danced to Cajun music, but I'm a good student if you're willing to teach me."

"You're in luck," he said. "I hadn't danced in years until my son's wedding last year, but it all came back to me."

"Kind of like riding a bike?"

He nodded. "Only, I need at least one beer in me to get the nerve to step out there. Not a good idea on a bike, I'd imagine."

She watched the band starting to move their instruments to the raised platform. "I may need at least a couple to loosen up." She shook her head. "I've been away far too long."

He reached across the table and placed his hand over hers, brushed his thumb lightly over her knuckles. "All that matters is you're back."

Her heart skipped. Drawing in a deep breath, she picked up a menu with her free hand, without pulling her other hand out from under John's. "So what's good to eat here? Everything looks delicious." *Including you.*

"I've had nearly everything on the menu. It's all good. The crawfish are still in season, so I'm having the crawfish platter. You can't go wrong with the fried tails and etouffee."

"Do they taste anything like fried shrimp?"

"Nope. Get the shrimp and you can try my crawfish tails. I don't mind sharing with you."

She nodded and studied her menu.

"You can keep looking, but I doubt you'll find anything that looks as good as you do tonight."

She closed her menu and stared at him. "For someone out of practice at dating, that's a pretty good line."

John Michael's face broke out in a huge grin. "Did it work? Pop gave me a whole list of them to try on you. I said it as a joke. I figured you'd fall out of your seat laughing at me."

"You're kidding, right?"

"I am absolutely serious." He pulled a slip of paper from his pocket and unfolded it, pointing to one in particular. "What do you think of this one? Apparently, it's his creation."

"You look as hot as a Mexican tamale?" She burst into laughter. "Your dad is such a trip."

"You have no idea. Every day is a new adventure."

"So you don't really think I look as good as anything on the menu?"

He ducked his head sheepishly. "Well, as it turns out, that one's kind of true. Pop lucked out, but I'm not sure I want to tell him."

"Oh God, this is hilarious. I can't wait to tell the gang at the hospital on Monday morning."

"You mean everything I say and do tonight will be scrutinized by your co-workers on Monday?"

"Sure. It's the female version of kiss and tell."

"But we haven't kissed yet."

"No, but there'll be plenty to whet their appetites. Bee practically had us married off once she discovered we knew each other. She's the nursing staff's version of one of those little old Jewish Matchmaker ladies—except she's not Jewish."

"Bee—is she the one with the . . ." His voice trailed off as he pointed to his hair.

"Yes, Bee's the owner of the silver wig that always seems to be on slightly crooked. She calls it Tonto, says it's her sidekick so it deserves a name. As a matter of fact—" She held up her phone to take a picture of him. "Smile for the camera so I can prove to her I actually got out of the house this weekend. She won't leave me alone, otherwise."

He sat still long enough for her to snap the picture. "She seems like a character. So tell me about the rest of them."

"The other two RN's assigned to our wing are Nan and Maggie, both sweet girls. And then there's Kevin."

"What's up with Kevin?"

"Everything but his height, apparently. He's not much taller than me and has asked me out at least once a day since I've been there." She sipped at her water as John grunted his disapproval. "He reminds me of one of those irritating little dogs . . ."

"What?"

She tapped her nails on the table top. "I don't want to say. You'll get the wrong impression about me."

He laughed. "Are you serious?"

She smiled. "Yes. Thirty years around firefighters tends to jade a lady."

"Just say it, Cyn."

"Okay, Kevin reminds me of one of those little dogs you can't get to stop humping your leg."

He grinned and nodded. "My wife's best friend had this huge golden retriever. Anytime he was in the vicinity, he'd try to sniff at Bethie's—you know."

"Oh, I hate that!"

"So did Beth. It irritated her so bad, she threatened to stop going for visits. I taught her how to lift her knee into the dog's chest when he approached and got him to stop."

"Gene kicked our friend's dog into the swimming pool for the leg humping thing several years ago."

Their laughter subsided by the time a waitress came to take orders. Cynthia smiled at John. "I think I'll try the small crawfish platter, with a baked sweet potato, plain, and light vinaigrette on the side for my salad."

"I'll take the large platter, loaded baked potato, bleu cheese dressing with my salad. Oh, and a bottle of Coors, please." He pointed to Cynthia. "What'll you have?"

She rested her arms on the table. "Sounds good to me, but make mine a light."

Their waitress made her exit but came back immediately with two beers.

John twirled his beer bottle on the table. "So, I don't have to worry about this Kevin fellow putting the moves on you at work?"

"I can't promise he'll stop trying, but I can tell you it'll never happen."

Laughter accompanied his nod of approval. "Frankly, I'm shocked you don't have guys clambering after you, Cyn. You're a beautiful woman."

"Well, thank you, sir. But I could argue the same about you. With your looks and being on the market a lot longer, I can't believe the ladies haven't plied you with their womanly charms all these years."

He grinned. "A couple of years ago, this woman kept sitting by me in church. I mean, even if there were entire pews available around me, she'd sit right next to me."

She giggled. "Blatant stalker tactics. Anyone I know?"

"No. Hell, I didn't even know her. I mean, she was a good looking woman, but frankly, she bugged the hell out of me. I skipped a couple of Sundays in a row, hoping she'd get the message."

Cyn sipped from her long neck bottle. "Did it work?"

"Sure did. Next time I went, she sat somewhere else. I was thrilled."

"So, it's been—what—fifteen or so years for you? Why did it take you so long to get back into this 'dating' thing, John Michael?"

He rested both elbows on the table, his gaze piercing in its intensity. "Honestly, after Beth died, I threw myself into working at the feed store and Zachary to keep going. Between the two, I was busy enough to keep from thinking about it too much. Zach needed me at home and he was so involved in everything. Football, baseball, basketball, track, and FFA—you name it and he was in it."

She nodded. "Sounds like my oldest son. It can keep you hopping."

"Yes, and it did. His mother had always been the one to attend all of his games. I mean, I made most of the home games and track events, but only a few of the away ones. After she passed, I made it a point to be at every event until he graduated high school. He played baseball in college, too—stayed in the dorms—so four more years of attending his games. Dad broke his hip a few months after Zach's college graduation. There were complications and a long recuperation period. As soon as he got better, we discovered mom had cancer."

"Oh God . . ."

"Yeah." He released a long drawn out sigh, as though about to tackle the hard part. "A four year stint of surgeries, chemo treatments, radiation therapies, remissions, reappearances, and the final remission, thank God. A hard fought battle but she won. A year or two later she started having mild episodes of dementia, and eventually we got the Alzheimer diagnosis. I don't know, Cyn—I guess there was so much going on all the time I got used to going through it alone. Or . . ."

"Or what?"

"Or maybe I was waiting for you to move back home."

She smiled at his lopsided grin and reached out her hand. "Let me see your dad's list again."

He shook his head. "You're not gonna find that one on there. I just came up with it." His smiled and slapped his hand over his chest. "Comes straight from the heart." He paused before continuing. "Ca c'est bon?"

She turned her head to the side, giving him a curious look. "Meaning?"

He laughed. "Was it good?"

She cleared her throat and made herself sit up straight. "I'll let you know by the end of the night."

They were comparing their parents' escapades with ladder climbing— Bess's refusal to stop picking figs, to J.D.'s addiction to cleaning the gutters— when the waitress arrived with their food.

"Lord, this smells wonderful!" She closed her eyes, savoring the aromas of golden fried crawfish and rice, covered in more of the crustaceans smothered in a savory, seasoned gravy. The sweet smell of the perfectly baked sweet potato wafted up from her loaded plate. She took a bite of the gravy covered rice and groaned. "Oh, my goodness. This is fabulous. I'm so glad you suggested it." She was still raving over her first taste of fried crawfish when the band kicked off the first set.

John Michael pointed discreetly to a middle-aged couple on the rapidly filling dance floor. "Keep your eye on those two. They're regulars here and both excellent dancers."

Cynthia watched, fascinated with the energetic dance moves of a Cajun jitterbug, and then a two-step. When the third song started up, she nodded. "I'm ready to try."

By the end of the first song she had it. When they kicked up a waltz she followed his lead easily enough. Soon they were gliding as gracefully around the floor as couples who'd danced together for years.

She sat down, slightly out of breath. "That was so fun. I can't believe I've never learned before. It's so easy."

"It's not that easy for everyone, Cyn. You're a quick learner." He finished off his last few bites of etouffee while she dug into her fried crawfish.

She closed her eyes as she chewed and swallowed, savoring the deliciousness. "The best part about eating this *here* is I get to burn off all these calories immediately."

He sat back and seemed to study her. "I don't know why you're so preoccupied with calories. You're beautiful just as you are. For whatever no-good reason your husband did what he did, I promise it wasn't because you lacked in the looks department."

She put her fork down, wiped her mouth with her napkin. There it was— the sure-fire constriction of her heart every time she thought of Gene and Tamara. "I never had a problem with my looks before, John Michael. Lately, since seeing you, the vision of that woman—" She still had to swallow the bile that rose in her throat at the thought of her. "That twenty-five year old *young* lady, with her perky breasts, tiny little waistline, and no stretch marks on her belly from carrying three ten pound babies—"

He reached out to grab both her hands. "Stop. I mean it. She may have been twenty-five, but to do what she did, I guarantee she was no lady. You are beautiful, Cyn—inside and out. Don't let the actions of two selfish people make you doubt yourself."

She squeezed his fingers. "Thank you. I had no idea you'd be so good for my ego."

"Besides, have you stopped to consider I may have the same doubts about my own body?" His mouth twisted in a sardonic grin. "Once Zach took over the family business I haven't done nearly as much heavy lifting." He leaned back in his chair and patted his belly. "I'm afraid I've gone soft."

She lifted her brow, but bit down on her lower lip, attempting to hold back the threatening grin.

"Oh—not there—uh—not what I was talking about. I mean—" He gave up on the explanation and groaned.

She burst into laughter. "Sorry, I told you I've been jaded from thirty years of being around firefighters."

He joined in and held out his hand. "Shut up and dance with me?"

"Absolutely." She pushed back her chair and took the hand he offered. She stood, crooked her finger. When he leaned in she pulled him close to speak over the sound of the drums and accordion kicking up the melody. "Just so you know. You have no reason to be concerned about your looks. As for the other issue—"

He cut her off quickly—spoke over the music into her ear. "Just so *you* know—you have no reason to be concerned about that."

She pulled back to study him, her lips pursed. "Is that a fact?"

He nodded and gave her a wink. "Absolutely."

After three hours of dancing, Cynthia finally sat down and confessed. "My feet are killing me. If you ever bring me here again, please remind to wear comfortable shoes."

John grinned, thinking he'd definitely make a return trip to D.I.'s with Cyn anytime she was willing. "I will—on both counts. You ready to go?"

"I think I am."

He escorted her through the dining room, still crowded with customers, and people seated on benches near the entrance and waiting for a table. They stepped outside where, despite the humidity of an early June evening, it was still noticeably cooler than the heat of the crowded building—even with its continuous blast of air conditioning so necessary in the south.

The comparable quiet of the outdoors was in stark contrast to the noisy interior of the building. "Whoa!" Cynthia stopped suddenly on the porch. "You don't realize the noise level until you get out of it, do you? My ears are ringing."

"It's a rocking little place." He placed his hand on the small of her back as they hit the steps. His boot had just landed on the concrete walk when they came face to face with an old classmate of theirs.

"Johnny Ferguson! What are you doing here?"

"Robin? Are you Robin White?"

Cynthia's question had the woman leaning so far forward on her too-tall heels John was afraid she'd topple over from sheer momentum. He groaned inwardly as Robin stuck out one of ten long fingernails, all decorated with zebra stripes and studded with rhinestones sparkles. Three of her five fingers on the one hand were loaded down with bling—huge, gaudy looking rings—no doubt booty from the two husbands she'd taken to the cleaners.

She squinted at Cyn. "Yes, but who are you?"

John was glad to make the re-introduction. "You remember Cynthia Robicheaux, Robin. She's Cynthia Ellender now. She hasn't changed a bit since high school."

Robin cocked her head, fluttered fake eyelashes before pursing blood red lips. "I vaguely remember the name. Did you get knocked up and drop out senior year?"

Cynthia frowned. "I did not. I graduated. Moved to Oklahoma, and became a pediatrician."

"*You're* a doctor?"

"Yes."

"One of those women who chose a *career* over a family?" Robin spit out the comment like a poisoned dart.

"Well, I did marry and have three children along the way. My husband died eighteen months ago."

"Oh." Out of ammo for the moment, Robin turned her attention to John. "So, are you two a couple now? I must admit, if I'd known you were on the block again, I'd have called you."

"This is our first date." John focused his gaze on Cyn. "Hopefully not our last, though." He turned to Robin again. "We were just leaving. You take care, Robin."

"Likewise, Johnny." She pulled him close for a hug, taking full advantage of the chance to mash her boobs up against him. Pulling a card from the side pocket of her purse, she slipped it deep into the pocket of his jeans and leaned forward to whisper in his ear.

John jerked back from the feel of her teeth scraping his ear lobe and urged his date along. "Let's go, Cyn."

She waited until he'd helped her into the truck before speaking. "What the hell was that about?"

"I have no idea. I haven't spoken more than a dozen words to her since high school." He closed her door, walked to his side of the truck, and climbed inside the driver's seat. He pulled out the card she'd shoved into his pocket, glanced at it before he ripped it in half and dropped it into the ashtray.

"What did she give you?"

He scrubbed at his earlobe. "Other than the urge to decontaminate and file a restraining order, you mean? Her business card."

Cynthia pulled the card from the ashtray. "With all her contact information, no doubt. What the hell does she do for a living, anyway?" She pieced the card together and read from it, before bursting into laughter. "*She's* an interior designer? Good grief. I haven't seen anyone wear that much eye makeup since I went to a KISS concert in the seventies." She put the card back into the ashtray and clucked her tongue. "Well, if you're in the market for one, I know drag queens with more class and way better taste." She turned to face him again. "What did she say to you?"

"For a good time, call 555-SLUT." He grinned as Cynthia burst into laughter. "Not really, of course, but she may as well have."

His date seemed to think on the situation before turning to him. "You aren't the least bit curious—or tempted to call her?"

John turned to face her full on. "Listen, Cyn. I wasn't tempted in high school, and she was plenty obvious about what she wanted then. I'm even less tempted now. I will not be giving her a call—ever."

She smiled and gave him a quick, but satisfied nod. "Good answer, John Michael."

He drove her home to the mellow sounds of an easy listening radio station playing some of their old favorites. He sang quietly along to Paul Young's version of *What Becomes of the Broken Hearted,* stopped suddenly when he caught her watching him. "What? I like this song."

She rested her elbow on the window and ran her fingers through her hair. "I was thinking I wished you could have known me then, like just out of high school."

"I did know you then."

"I mean date me, know me—before the necessity for Spanx, support bras, and bi-focal lenses—"

He pulled out his glasses from his shirt pocket. "Mine are tri-focals—I've got you beat. Not sure about those spanks though. It sounds a little kinky; like something Robin would be into." He wiggled his eyebrows, hoping to get her to laugh.

It worked.

"It's a support undergarment, like a girdle but much thinner—and stronger. I don't know how they do it but those puppies work wonders."

"Are you wearing one now?"

"No."

"Then you obviously don't need it. And now that you mention it, I heard two guys at the pharmacy talking about wearing those spanks things to keep their guts sucked in." He slapped his belly. "I'm opting out. If I wore those, I'm pretty sure I'd get a midnight visit from the man-card police to revoke mine."

John was feeling pretty damn good about their first date by the time he pulled into her mom's driveway a little before 10:00 p.m.

Cyn unfastened her seatbelt and turned to face him. "I had such a good time tonight. Thank you so much for asking me."

"Thanks for coming with me, Cyn. I can't believe how much fun I had with you." John stepped out of his truck, went around and opened the door for her. He took her hand to help her out, kept it as her gaze locked onto his. "Maybe we can do it again?"

She slipped her arms around his waist, smiled as he wrapped her tightly in a bear hug. "You have my number, John Michael. All you have to do is call."

Chapter Four

Monday afternoon, Cyn approached the nurse's station, humming to the same tune she'd had running around in her head since her date with John Michael.

Bee's head popped up at her approach. "Oooh, girl! I love that song. You've got good taste in music." She cocked her head. "What's up with you? You've been positively chipper all day long." She froze suddenly, pointed a finger at Cynthia. "Wait a second. Didn't you have a date this weekend?"

Cynthia flipped through her phone's photos then raised it to display the picture she'd snapped of John Michael.

"There he is. Mr. Tall, Dark, Sexy as Hell himself. Mm, mm—he is one fine specimen of a man if ever I saw one. Look at that beautiful smile and those pearly whites, would you? Where'd old blue eyes take you?"

"Dancing, Bee. He took me to a place called D.I.'s. Best food ever and it had a live band playing Cajun music. We danced for hours."

"Uh huh—I know that place. I love their boiled crawfish."

"Maybe next time we go I'll try them boiled."

"You sound pretty confident there'll be a next time."

Cynthia gave her a wink. "I am." She turned and walked off with Bee's comment of "The girl's still got it!" ringing in her ears.

She'd barely finished the paperwork for the release of the Ferguson twins when her desk phone rang. "Dr. Ellender."

"Hey, Doc Ellender, it's Bee—wanted to let you know your new boyfriend's in the house."

"Ah, he mentioned he might be coming by today to help his son load up everything. Thanks Bee."

She picked up the twins' release papers and headed to their mother's room. It took some effort not to search out John Michael's face upon entering the room. Instead she concentrated on communicating with the new parents on what to do when they got the babies home.

John's gaze stayed riveted on Cyn as she addressed his son and daughter-in-law. Damn she looked good today.

"How's the new mama feeling?"

"Wonderful, Dr. Ellender. Bored and ready to go home with my babies and my husband."

"That is certainly understandable. You've been in here a little longer than we expected. Your low iron count and the twins jaundice kind of held the three of you up. But their bilirubin level is perfectly normal. They're released to go home."

John Michael waited for Zach to share a tender kiss with his wife before approaching Cynthia.

She turned her gaze on him then. "Hey there, Paw Paw. How are you?"

He grinned, nodding at her. "I'm good. How about you?" He lifted a finger when his cell phone chirped. "Hang on, Cyn, it's my dad." He stepped out of the room to answer. In seconds, he returned, wearing a wide grin. "Zach, Pop says mom is her old self today. We could stop there on the way home, right?"

Zach's face lit up. "Sure we will. God, I hope she's around long enough to see the twins and still know us. Can I speak to Paw Paw John?"

John Michael handed the phone to Zach and returned to Cynthia's side. "How are those feet of yours?"

"I was sore yesterday but I seem to be over it today. Wonderful news about your mom. I'll call the attending to rush Cat's release so you can all get over there."

"Any chance you'd want to come with us?"

"I'd love to, but I don't want to intrude on family time."

Her hopeful gaze warmed his heart. "I'd like you to be there, Cyn."

She smiled, nodded. "I'm off in an hour. I'll meet you all over there. Let me go call for her doctor."

John grabbed her hand, squeezed it lightly. "Thanks Cyn. I appreciate this." He watched her walk away then turned to see Cat and Zachary staring at him, their faces covered with smug grins. "What's up with you two?"

Cat chuckled under breath. "Maybe we should be asking what's going on with *you* two."

Zach cleared his throat. "Paw Paw John told me I should ask how your hot date went over the weekend. Dad, are you dating our pediatrician?"

"I took her to D.I.'s Saturday night."

Cat's head dipped curiously. "And . . ."

"She'd never had fried crawfish and she loved it. And she'd never danced to Cajun music, and she loved that too." He lifted his hands. "We had a nice time. I'm not sure what else I can say."

The couple exchanged amused glances and both turned back to face him.

Cat stood to pick up her daughter, who was starting to fuss. "Will you be taking her out again, Poppa John?"

He rested his hands on his hips and smiled at baby Cassandra in Cat's arms. "I think so."

Zach stepped forward. "Well, have you asked her yet? She won't wait forever, you know."

John turned to his son. "I didn't come out and ask, but it was implied we'd be seeing each other again."

"Maybe you should give her a call and make some concrete plans."

John grinned at Zach. "I saw her for the first time in thirty-five years less than a week ago and I've already had lunch with her and taken her out. Not to mention she's going to meet us to see mom after work. Besides, I should be taking advice from a guy who let the love of his life walk away for twelve years before telling her how he felt?"

Cat elbowed her husband. "The man's got a point."

Zachary shook his head. "Not applicable. I had to wait for said love of my life to realize no other man could possibly measure up to the standard I'd established."

"Yes, Zach-Attack. You were my benchmark, I admit it. But leave your dad be." She turned back to her father-in-law wearing a grin. "You're doing fine, Poppa John." She cuddled her daughter and cooed. "Paw Paw Johnny's got some smooth moves, doesn't he Cassandra?"

He approached her and leaned over to kiss the top of her head. "Why thank you, Cat."

She reached out for his hand. "I want to see you happy. It's time you had a little fun."

He squeezed her hand. "I agree, and I'm doing my damnedest."

Cynthia tapped lightly on the door of room 124. It swung open and John Michael stood there, beaming down at her.

"Come on in here, Cyn. Someone wants to see you."

Cynthia entered the room slowly, with no expectations of what she'd find. There was Ms. Marilee, seated in an overstuffed chair, holding both her great grandchildren. Her husband sat on one side of her, while her grandson, the happy new father, sat on the other. "Well now, don't you look right at home holding those great grandchildren of yours?"

"Cynthia, you come sit right in front of me where I can get a good look at you. These old eyes aren't what they used to be." She clucked as Cyn did as she was told. "Oh, you're every bit as beautiful as you were in high school, sweetie." Her eyes teared-up slightly. "You look so much like your mother. How is she, dear?"

"Mom is wonderful. She mentioned she'd love to come visit you, if it's okay?"

Marilee's eyes lit up. "Oh, I'd love to see Bessie again. Please tell her to come."

"I'll let her know. I'm not sure if you knew, but she moved to Jennings a couple of years ago, and I'm staying with her."

The older woman's gaze travelled from her face, upward to where John Michael stood beside Cynthia, then back to her. She beamed at Cynthia, nodding slowly. "You know, your mother and I were so close. We always hoped the two of you would end up as a couple. I adored my daughter-in-law, of course. Beth was a wonderful person."

"I don't doubt it, Ms. Marilee, and she and John Michael gave you a fine grandson in Zachary."

Marilee nodded. "I wish she and Paul, Cat's dad, could have seen their grandchildren before they left this world. These two are something, aren't they? But they're so heavy. My arms are tiring."

Zach reached over and took both babies from her, but stayed beside her where she could see them.

"Oh, thank you, Zachary." Marilee leaned forward in her chair to take Cynthia's hands in hers. "Don't let too much time get away from you. It's important to make the most of whatever amount of time God sees fit to give us on this earth, you know."

Cynthia nodded her agreement; her heart hurting for this woman who'd already had so much taken from her but still found a way to be positive.

"That's why I keep my journal." Marilee took a pink floral book from her lap and held it up. "Every time I'm myself again, I write in it. When my John told me about the birth of our twin great-grandchildren, I wrote them in here. And you're in here now too, Cynthia."

Cynthia's eyes watered as she looked up at John Michael. It took some effort on her part to clear them before she turned her gaze back to his mother. "I'm honored to be in your journal, Ms. Marilee."

Marilee stroked the floral cover softly, lovingly. "I read this when I'm not myself. Sometimes it helps me to remember. Sometimes it doesn't help at all. More importantly, when I'm gone for good—when I can't make it back from wherever it is I go when I leave here—I want my John to read it. It's a guide, you see."

"A guide? Like a map?" Cynthia asked.

Marilee's eyes sparkled with a mixture of joy and sadness. "More like an instruction guide." She gave Cynthia a wink. "J.D. would never admit to it, of course, but he loves it when I tell him what to do. It keeps him from having to make a decision."

Laughter bubbled up from Cynthia's belly, until she was wiping tears from her eyes. "Ms. Marilee, you haven't changed a bit. You sound so much like my mom."

"Your mother and I shared some good times, dear. She was always there for me when times were rough. You laugh like her, you know."

Cynthia wiped a wayward tear from the corner of her eye. "Would you mind me taking a picture with you?"

"Oh, not at all. Come on over here. We took tons of them before you got here. A couple more won't hurt."

Cynthia pulled up the camera app on her phone and showed John Michael how to work it. They posed for a couple of shots. Afterwards, Cynthia took Marilee's face in her hands and kissed her cheek. "I'm so glad I got to see you."

Marilee smiled at her as she patted her hand. "I am too, dear. Come back soon."

Cynthia rose and stood beside John Michael again. "Yes, ma'am, I will. Next time I'll bring my mother."

Marilee's broad smile began to fade as her brow creased in a slow-forming frown. "Your mother, dear? And who is she?"

"Bess, Ms. Marilee. My mother, Bess Robicheaux."

Marilee shook her head. "I-I don't know any Bess. And I don't know you. Who are you?"

John Michael sucked in his breath, his body tensing suddenly. When Cynthia reached for his hand he grabbed at it like a drowning man would a life preserver.

Marilee looked around the room, growing more flustered by the second. "I-I don't know any of you. But I feel as though I should." Her gaze landed on her great grandchildren. "Oh, what adorable . . . oh—they're like tiny little people. What's the word I'm looking for?"

"They're our babies," Zachary said, answering her question.

"Yes. Babies. But why are they here? Why are any of you here?"

J.D. got to his feet slowly. "It's time to go, everyone."

"Oh, I'm sorry. But I think you should." She looked down at her polyester pants and silk blouse. "I'm not presentable enough to meet—" She paused, as though searching her mind for a particular word. "To meet . . ." She looked around, growing more frantic, but still clutching her journal tightly to her chest. "I think you should go."

J.D. spoke in a soothing tone to his wife. "Now, now, we were just leaving. I think we may have walked into the wrong room. But, it's okay—I assure you, ma'am. We're all harmless." He picked up her room phone. "Would you like me to call your nurse for you?"

Her panic seemed to lessen at his reassurances. "My nurse? Why, yes—if you don't mind."

John Michael's gaze stayed glued to his father as J.D. called for the nurse and continued to soothe his wife. During those few minutes Cynthia's gaze remained locked onto *her* John. The features of his face tightened at the torture of seeing his father lose his wife one more time.

The worst of it, obviously, had to be wondering if she'd ever return to them. She tried to pull her hand from his so she could join Cat and Zach in the hallway with the babies. John Michael held tightly to it, keeping her there with him in the room's doorway—his gaze remaining on his father.

Finally, Marilee calmed. Although clueless as to her husband's identity, she at least didn't seem upset by his presence. By the time he left the room, Cat and Zach had already left for their own home with the twins.

J.D. tried to smile through his obvious heartache. "She's fine now. I don't like to leave her upset. It's not good for her health or mine. There'll be another time."

John Michael reached out to him. "Pop . . ." He gave his father a one armed hug, never relinquishing his grip on Cynthia's hand.

"I know, Johnny. I know." J.D. returned his son's hug, gave him a pat on the back before he pulled away. "We can only do what we can do."

"I know, Pop, but I can't help worrying about you."

Cynthia wiped her eyes and sniffed. "Are you okay, Mr. J.D.? Physically, I mean?"

He reached out to give her a reassuring pat on her shoulder. "I'm fine, Cynthia. Really, I am. There's no need for either of you to worry about me." He looked down, rubbed the back of his neck with one hand.

"I used to explain to her who I was, who she was, give her a rundown of our life and her disease. But she'd get so upset. Sometimes she'd be paranoid and tell me I was lying to her. Other times she said she believed me but didn't seem to care one way or the other. Most times, once I was finished she'd ask me who I was again."

He took a deep breath and released it. "Sometimes, she stares blankly and doesn't say a word. It seems easier for us all when I say we came into the wrong room. She doesn't seem nearly as uncomfortable with the story." His gaze settled on their linked hands and he grunted, giving them a nod before turning away. "I've got to hit the head, and then we can go, Johnny."

"Sure, Pop."

Cynthia waited until he'd disappeared into the men's room before releasing the half-sob she'd been holding back. "Oh, God. John Michael—I'm so sorry." She turned into him, looping her free arm around his waist. He hugged her back tightly, folding her hand close to his chest. They stood there in the middle of the corridor, as though posed for a slow dance.

"I don't know how he does it, Cyn." His voice broke as he rested his chin on her head. "How do you let your wife go—over and over again—and still come out of it with a positive attitude?" He cleared his throat. "Every time he goes through this I have a whole new respect for him."

"I know. He's obviously a strong man who still loves his wife very deeply. As parents, they've both set the best examples their entire lives and are obviously still doing it. You've paid attention and show them the respect they deserve by following their lead. You show it, John Michael. In the very life you lead, in the way you treat them and others. It shows."

He took a deep breath, pulled back to meet her gaze. "Thanks Cyn, for those words, and—well, for being here. It means a lot to me. It's easier having you here."

She placed a hand on his face. "Do you have any idea how honored I was to be a part of it? I got a picture with her to show my mom. She'll be so thrilled."

He nodded and managed a smile. "We got a four generation picture out of this visit, Cyn. That's something no disease can take away from us."

Chapter Five

The next morning, John Michael stood at the feed store's counter, going over a list of inventory at the computer. He glanced up from the monitor at the sound of the door opening and swooshing shut. The cloud of perfume reached him first—heavy, sweet, and far too concentrated—a smell so alien to the store where he'd spent a good portion of his life. He faltered at the sight of Robin standing before him, barely managed to keep from high tailing it out of the room.

"Johnny! I didn't expect to see you here. Somebody said you'd retired."

"I did—I'm filling in here for my son. He and his wife brought home their new twins yesterday and they need some quality time together."

"Grandchildren, huh?"

He couldn't keep the grin from his face. "You bet."

She grimaced, as though she found the thought repulsive. "I don't have any of those little beasties yet. And if and when I ever do, they'd better be prepared to call me something other than Grandma. I am *nobody's* grandma."

"I've been looking forward to being a paw paw for years."

She gave a feminine grunt as she jutted one hip out and clicked her zebra striped nails on the surface of the sales counter. "Well, if it's any consolation, you sure don't look like a grandfather. I refuse to say Paw Paw—that sounds so archaic—so back woods."

He turned his attention back to the computer monitor. "I want mine to call me Paw Paw Johnny. And I will cherish every archaic and back woods second of it. Because my wife didn't live long enough to see her grandchildren, and my mother doesn't remember who she is ninety-five percent of the time, much less that she has great-grandchildren."

Obviously determined to change the subject, Robin rested her arms on the counter. She leaned forward, baring her significant cleavage to his line of sight.

"You might want to buy a bigger size shirt, there, Robin. You seem to be falling out of the one you're wearing." He pointed to a rack. "We have some denim work shirts in women's sizes hanging right there."

She threw her head back, sniggering as though she found his suggestion highly amusing, then dabbed at the corner of one eye.

John cringed at the sight, expecting her to gouge out an eyeball with her ridiculously long nails.

"I had no idea you were dating again, Johnny. If I'd known you were ready to get back into that particular saddle, I'd have thrown my hat in the rodeo arena earlier. I love a good ride."

"Well, thanks Robin, but I doubt I could keep up with you."

"Oh honey, my cousin the pharmacist has got something to fix you right up."

"Not exactly what I was talking about. I'm fine—there."

"I bet you are," she purred and reached out to scrape a long nail over his arm. "So, are you and Cynthia a couple now, or what?"

John gritted his teeth, seeing where this was headed. More than ever, he wished he could say yes. But he hadn't heard it directly from Cyn's lips, and he wasn't the type to out and out lie to a lady—or—person. "Um, I hope to see her again, but we've only had the one date you saw us on."

She straightened, her breasts practically bursting forth from their meager confines of latex animal print in a display of brazenness that would do a Bourbon Street hooker justice. "So, the barn door's still open for other fillies."

"Well, not exact—"

She spun on her high heels and headed out the door.

He was still waving away the cloud of perfume she left behind when his dad walked in from the back room.

"Okay, the bedding plants are inventoried, and so are the—good God, what is that smell?"

John pointed to the red Cadillac pulling out of the drive. "Robin White, an old classmate of mine. The smell is whatever she drenched herself in before she waltzed in here."

"Smells like a *putain*, to me."

John sent a sidelong glance at his father. *"C'est toute la meme chose."*

"Geez—since when does someone like her come into this place? Did you set up a cheap perfume counter in here?"

"She's under the assumption I'm dating again."

"Well, you are, aren't you?"

"Yeah, but—not her."

"Is it exclusive between you and Cynthia?"

"I don't think so. Not yet, anyway."

"Well then . . ."

John widened his eyes at his father. "You didn't get a look at her, did you?"

"Nope."

John shook his head. "She'd chew me up and spit me out. I can't stay far enough away from her."

J.D. chuckled. "I get your point, Son."

Unfortunately, Robin didn't. By closing time of that afternoon she'd made two return trips, clearly determined to bribe him with gifts of food. She'd done the same every day for the rest of the week. No matter how many times he said he wished she wouldn't go to the trouble, she waved him off and kept it coming.

By Friday afternoon he'd brought home lasagna, pot roast, cookies, three sheet cakes, and two pies—none of which had even been sampled by John the younger.

J.D., on the other hand, was of the opinion that any food he didn't have to cook was better than no food at all. He finished off the last bite of his latest slice of sweet potato pie. "I wonder if her apple pie would be any good."

"I have no idea."

"Maybe you should ask."

John glared at his father. "The only thing I'm going to ask is for her to stop. I don't like all this. I don't like it at all. She won't take no for an answer."

"Hell, don't ask her to stop. String her along to keep it rolling in."

"Pop, do you hear yourself?"

His dad shrugged and pushed his plate away from him. "I guess you're right." He rubbed his belly. "She's kind of a crappy cook, isn't she?"

John shrugged. "I have no idea. I haven't touched anything she brought."

J.D. frowned. "Why not?"

"I've been too afraid she put a roofie in it or something. I'm terrified I'll wake up with her in my bed and not remember a thing."

"A what?"

"A roofie—it's a drug." Rather than take the time to explain, John waved it off. "Never mind." He picked up his ringing cell phone, grinned when he saw Cyn's name flash across his screen. "Hey there, pretty lady. What's up?"

"Mom and I are in Lake Erin and I thought we could stop in for a visit."

John jumped up, immediately began tidying his kitchen. "Come on over. Please keep in mind we're not the best housekeepers and I've been pulling Zach's hours at the store."

"No problem. We're leaving the cemetery now. Be there in about five minutes."

John ran around throwing away junk mail and trying to de-clutter the living area as best he could in five minutes. J.D. loaded the sink full of dirty dishes into the dishwasher and set it to washing.

John opened the door before either of the two women had a chance to knock. He hugged the older woman briefly. "Come on inside, Ms. Bess." He turned his attention to Cyn, giving her an even tighter hug. "I'm glad you called. It's nice having you drop by like this. Were you two visiting Mr. Ham's grave?"

She nodded. "It was Dad's birthday today. We brought a new silk arrangement for his vase. Mom and I found Jenna's and Beth's graves and I took a couple of roses from the arrangements and put them on their headstones. I hope you don't mind."

"Of course not. That was sweet of you. Come on in the kitchen. Pop put some fresh coffee on if you ladies would like some."

Bess turned at the mention of his father. "J.D.'s here, too?"

John nodded. "He stays here during the day most of the time—not too fond of being alone in his big old house." He scratched his head. "He's where he is the majority of the day—in the bathroom with his enlarged prostate."

J.D. entered the room grumbling. "I heard that."

"It's no secret, Pop."

J.D. walked toward Bess and stopped. "It's good to see you, Bessie."

"You too, J.D. I'm so sorry to hear about Marilee. My old friends have had more than their share of hard times. How've you been?"

He nodded. "I'm good. Fit as a fiddle."

John rolled his eyes and coughed the words *prostate* in one hand and *cataracts* into the other.

Bess's eyes sparkled with laughter. "J.D., you know Marilee wouldn't want you neglecting yourself. If you've got health and vision problems, they'll only get worse with time if you don't stay on top of them."

J.D. sent a glare his son's direction and waved off Bess's comment. "Now, I know you didn't come here to discuss my health issues. I've made a fresh pot of coffee and we have a ton of desserts."

The two women entered the kitchen first and stopped in front of the snack bar filled with sweets.

Bess waved a hand over the multitude of trays. "Which one of you gentleman has taken up baking?"

J.D. snorted. "Neither. One of us has a suitor and it ain't me." He wagged his eyebrows at his son.

Cynthia turned on him, her brow raised in question. "Oh? Is it serious?"

John gave her a sheepish look. "No."

She put her head back and laughed. "It's Robin, isn't it, John Michael?"

J.D. nodded. "That's her—Robin—somebody. She smells like a—"

"Pop!"

J.D. lowered his voice and whispered in dramatic fashion. "Like an ol' *putain*."

John Michael shook his head. "Oh yeah, like nobody heard *that*."

"Well, it's true," J.D. insisted.

Bess reprimanded her old friend through her chuckles. "J.D., that's not Christian. What would Marilee say?"

"Marilee would tell that old whore to quit stinking up the store and to stay away from her son."

Bess burst into laughter. "Knowing her as well as I do, you're probably right."

"I know I am. Sit down. What's your poison—pecan or sweet potato pie? Carrot cake?"

"The cake looks interesting. I'll try it." Bess thanked John Michael as he set a cup of coffee in front of her.

Cyn took the opportunity to sidle up to him. "So Robin's staking her claim, huh?"

"Stop, Cyn. Please."

She chuckled, obviously enjoying his discomfort. "So which one of these do you recommend?"

He shook his head. "Ask Pop. I haven't touched them."

"You haven't?"

"Hell, no."

"You afraid of cooties?"

"He's more afraid of roofies," J.D. interjected. "Whatever the heck that is."

John glared at his father. "Good God, Pop. You can quit talking any second now."

J.D. leveled one of his don't-mess-with-me gazes at his son. "Now Johnny, you know you burned that bridge the second you uttered the words prostate and cataracts. Payback's hell, ain't it?"

John groaned as Cynthia's hand flew over her mouth to stifle her laughter.

Bess cleared her throat and put a forkful of cake in her mouth. After a moment, she set the fork down and took several sips of coffee before pushing her plate away.

"What's wrong, Mom?"

"Well, it's not bad, per say. It's just not very good."

Cynthia turned to John Michael's dad. "You see, Mr. J.D.? *That's* how you criticize someone's cooking the Christian way."

J.D. gave her an enthusiastic nod. "I'll be damned. I've been doing it wrong all these years."

Bess tried the other desserts with the same results. "The poor dear—she really isn't a good cook, is she?"

Cynthia stopped laughing long enough to add. "Now Mom, you know it isn't southern unless you end it with 'Bless her heart'."

The room resounded with John Michael's laughter. "I threw a huge container of lasagna and a burnt pot roast to the chickens, yesterday afternoon. The stuff's still sitting out there."

J.D. shivered. "You know it's bad when the chickens won't eat it."

"Oh, you poor things." Bess's gaze moved from the father to the son. "The two of you are coming over to our house tomorrow for a good supper, along with a dessert that won't turn your stomachs."

J.D. turned to his son. "I'm game. How about you, Johnny?"

"I'll be there." He leaned over to whisper in Cyn's ear. "If it's early enough maybe we could do something after supper?"

She nodded, her eyes sparkling with encouragement. "Sounds good to me."

The same evening, around eight p.m. sharp, John Michael's name flashed across the screen of Cynthia's phone. "Hello there."

"Hey, Cyn. You got a few minutes to talk?"

"I sure do, what's up?"

"This whole thing with Robin has me bugged. I want you to know I haven't encouraged her at all. I hate to be rude, but . . ."

"But you may have to resort to it at some point?"

"Exactly. I guess I didn't want you thinking I was leading her on in any way."

"I wasn't."

He paused. "Does it bother you?"

She was quiet for a moment, weighing her response carefully.

"Cyn?"

"I'm here. I was wondering how to answer without sounding presumptuous."

"About what?"

"Well, it shouldn't really bother me. It's not like we're dating exclusively."

"But it does bother you?"

"A little, I admit."

"What if we *were* exclusive?"

"Then I'd definitely be bothered." She paused. "John Michael, are you asking me to go steady?"

"If I did, would you accept?"

"Absolutely not. We haven't even kissed yet. It could have a major impact on my answer."

"It's as good as done."

She laughed into the phone. "You're mighty sure I'd say yes."

"If your answer is based on a kiss, I'm not worried." He waited through her pause of silence. "What are you thinking, Cyn?"

"I'm not sure I should say."

"Come on."

She bit the inside of her lip to keep from laughing.

"You know you want to tell me," he urged.

"Okay. Well, a certain amount of confidence in a man can be downright sexy." She could practically see the sexy little uni-dimple forming in his confident grin.

"Oh yeah?"

"Uh huh. But anything over the top is borderline pompous jerk."

"O-oh . . ."

She pictured him again, deflating like a leaky balloon before her eyes. "Mom likes to get her cooking over with early. We'll see you both at 5:00 p.m. tomorrow, John Michael." She ended the call before he could answer.

He pushed back from the table. "Ms. Bess, the roast—everything—was delicious. Thank you so much for this."

"You're very welcome, Johnny."

J.D. patted his belly. "It sure was. I haven't eaten good home cooking since Marilee . . ." His voice faltered. "It—it's been a while." He threw a glance in John Michael's direction. "Too bad your stalker isn't a better cook, huh, Johnny?"

Cynthia rested her elbows on the table, linked her fingers under her chin as she gazed at John Michael. "Yeah, too bad."

His mouth twisted as he shifted in his chair and cleared his throat uncomfortably. "You've had the last of it, Pop. She came into the store this morning with something and I told her I wouldn't accept it."

Cynthia sat up straight in her chair. "Did you?"

J.D. leaned forward to face his son. "You did? What was it?"

John Michael rested his forearms on the table and smiled at Cynthia. "Yes, I did, and it doesn't matter what it was because I didn't want anything from her."

She pursed her lips then gave him a slow nod.

Bess cleared her throat. "How long has Marilee been in extended care, J.D.?"

"It'll be a year August 1st, but in all honesty, she should have been there a good six months earlier." He wiped his face with one hand and shook his head. "I couldn't see it then, but I do now."

Cynthia didn't miss the look passed between father and son. "Did something happen?"

"I'd say so," J.D. grunted. His mouth tightened, accompanied by a series of rapid blinks.

"Mom nearly burned the house down one day."

Cynthia leaned forward in her chair. "Oh no! What happened? Was anyone hurt?"

John turned to face Cynthia. "No, but it could have been really bad. Dad was sick, sleeping in his recliner. Mom was feeling pretty good so she decided to cook. In the middle of it she got—lost."

"Lost, like in the recipe?" Bess asked.

"No ma'am. She didn't know where she was. She walked right out of the house. I got a phone call from the Sheriff's Department. A deputy who's known her all his life picked her up walking along the highway. He brought her home, but she was hysterical because she didn't recognize the place the deputy insisted was her home. Meanwhile, the dishtowel she'd dropped near the lit stove burner had caught on fire." He looked up at Cynthia's horrified gasp. "Luckily, the smoke alarm had already wakened Pop. He was still trying to put out the fire when the deputy arrived with mom."

Cynthia covered her mouth with one hand. "Oh my gosh. That could have been—"

"Yeah—so much worse than it was, but it was the turning point. Once mom was herself again and we told her what happened, she insisted we bring her someplace."

Bess sniffed and reached out to place a hand on J.D.'s arm. "I'm so sorry. I hadn't heard. It must have been difficult for her—to leave the home she's been so happy in all these years. It had to break her heart to leave you, J.D."

His head drooped forward. "I'm not going to sugar coat it. It was a hellacious day. Only day tops it was the day we lost Jenna." He slapped his thigh suddenly. "But, at least I know I can see Marilee. She may not always know me or even who she is, but she usually lets me sit and talk with her. And sometimes she does know us—for a bit."

He shrugged at the woman who'd called his wife a friend for so long. "When I start to feel sorry for myself, I think of friends I've lost, like good old Ham—and my daughter-in-law, Bethie—and how young she was when Johnny and Zach lost her. It has a way of putting things into perspective for me real quick."

Cynthia sniffed and blinked back a tear. Here was this wonderful man, losing a little more of his wife every day, but still finding a way to see the glass half full. She reached across the table to squeeze his hand. "You're a good man, Mr. J.D., a really good man."

He met her gaze, his eyes misting for a moment before he shook his head and gave a low grunt. "I could have been better, little lady. I can promise you. But, as far as Marilee is concerned, I've tried never to disappoint her. Hopefully, I succeeded."

Bess dabbed at her eyes and sniffed delicately. "You did, J.D. Your wife adores you, and always has. She's bragged on you for years."

He cocked his head. "Had she? Don't know if I knew that."

"Absolutely. She always said you spoiled her for any other man. Ham begged her once to stop—said you were making it difficult for the rest of the men in town to measure up."

He issued a low chuckle. "I tried my damnedest, Bess. I'm glad she felt spoiled all these years. It wasn't so easy the first several years we were married. But, she never complained, even during the lean years. Marilee looked at everything as though it was a new adventure."

John Michael crooked his neck, gave Cynthia a sidelong glance. "Speaking of adventures, how would you like to catch a movie in Lake Coburn tonight? The new WWII flick looks interesting."

Her eyes lit up. "I'd love to. I love movies. I'll sit through anything. A big screen with surround sound, a small popcorn, a bottle of water, and I'm a happy camper." She checked her watch. "What time?"

"There's one at 7:00 I think we could make, but I'd have to bring Pop home right now and double back to get you."

Bess sat forward. "I can bring him home so you don't have to. Or better yet, leave him here and pick him up on your way home. I don't mind having him around. We can catch up or watch some TV."

John Michael's brow arched in question as he turned to his father. "Pop, you okay with that? If not I can bring you home now and we can catch the 7:30 feature instead."

His father shrugged. "If Bess can stand me for a few hours, I don't mind sticking around. You two go on and have some fun that doesn't include babysitting your old parents."

Bess pointed a finger at him. "Speak for yourself, J.D. I'm not old—I've matured—like a fine wine."

J.D. lifted one hand. "My mistake, Bess. You go ahead and call yourself mature. I don't have a problem with calling myself old. I earned every one of these gray hairs."

Cynthia pushed back from the table. "You want me to clear these dishes and load the dishwasher before I go, Mom?"

"No, no! You two get on outta here. J.D. and I can clean up."

Mr. J.D. nodded and waved his hand. "That's right. We got this covered."

"You sure, Pop?"

J.D. raised an eyebrow at his son. "What did I say?"

John Michael lowered his head in an obvious attempt to hide a grin. "I hear you. We'll leave as soon as Cyn's ready to go."

Cynthia touched his arm softly as she turned. "I'll only be a minute, John Michael, and then we can head out."

John Michael exchanged a look with Cyn when the man seated three rows in front of them answered yet another phone call. Grumbles and comments from those seated around him had gone unheeded, or worse, answered with a crude return. Patience had gotten him nowhere with this jack-ass, and John was at the end of his rope. "Inconsiderate son of a—" Remembering his manners, he left the rest unsaid. He let it go another few seconds until the guy had the nerve to laugh loudly at whatever he heard over the phone, despite his girlfriend's repeated efforts to shush him.

John rose from his aisle seat and took two long steps to the big mouth, and stood staring down at him. "Hey. You're gonna have to get off of that phone, buddy. The rest of us came to enjoy this movie."

The young guy looked up. "You need to calm down old man. This is important."

Old man? John's hands fisted as he leaned over, ready to show him what kind of damage an old man could do. Before he could say anything, Cyn spoke up.

"Excuse me, but there are rules we're all supposed to follow in here. Why is it you think the rules don't apply to you?"

The man swung his head around to check her out. John Michael's gut clenched as the punk licked his lips and gave a primal grunt. He spoke into the phone. "Hold on, a-ight? Got a ho here wid a big mouth an' a old man 'bout to get himself busted up."

John's icy comeback cut through the grumbles from nearby patrons. "You're going to apologize to this lady, and then go outside to finish your phone conversation so the rest of us can get our money's worth and watch this movie in peace."

"You need to shut up old—"

John grabbed the guy by the collar, jerked him to his feet.

"Hey, man! Don't touch me!" The guy, shorter than John by at least four inches, tried unsuccessfully to wrench himself free from the iron grip on his collar.

"Apologize to her, now."

"You can kiss my —"

"Yo! Shut up, punk." A huge man, six and a half feet tall if he was a foot, and half as wide, approached and stood before the trouble maker. "I just dropped twenty-five bucks so my wife and I could watch this movie and you haven't shut up since you got here. Truthfully, if this man hadn't called you out when he did, I was about to."

The punk shook off John's grip. "This mo fo put his hands on me, man. I ain't havin' it!"

"You do realize I, along with everyone else in the theater," the giant emphasized his point by waving his finger around, "heard what you called his lady, don't you?"

"She raggin' on me."

"She spoke the truth, punk! You're the only ignorant fool holdin' a phone conversation when everybody else here's got enough sense to turn their phones off. Man, get on outta here before I let this man go off on you like he's itching to."

John Michael stepped forward, becoming aware that, at some point during the three-way exchange, the movie had paused. "Not until he apologizes to this lady."

The punk snorted. "You trippin', *old man*."

The big man poked his thick finger in the guy's chest. "You're the one *trippin'* if you think you're walking outta here without doing what he says."

The punk, even puffed-up like a rooster, barely reached the big man's chin. "What you gonna do if I don't? You gonna take a white man's side against a brother?"

"You ain't my brother, and I ain't gonna do a thing but step aside and let this man give you what you deserve. Dude looks like he's worked hard all his life—I'm thinking he'd finish you off in about ten seconds flat."

A young woman approached, wearing the khaki pants and navy polo shirt required of this particular theater's employees. "Excuse me, I've called security and they'll be here any second. You gentlemen can leave now or be escorted out."

Several people spoke up, pointing at the troublemaker, every one of them insisting he was the only one who needed to leave.

She gave him a stern look. "Sir, you're going to have to leave."

"If I do, you gonna give me my money back."

The big man got in his face. "You're the one who needs to give us all our money back. I doubt I'm the only one who missed the first fifteen minutes of the movie because you're in love with the sound of your own voice. Now tell both these ladies you're sorry, and leave before I drag you out into that parking lot and finish what this man started." He leaned over to get in his face as the security guard arrived.

Apparently, the punk didn't have the personal space or the ability to bow-up in the giant's presence. "Ah-ight. I apologize to you—" he nodded once in Cynthia's direction then turned to the female employee. "And you, too." He threw an ugly glare in John Michael's direction and pointed a finger at him. "But this ain't over, old man."

John Michael made two fists, the work-hardened sinewy muscles of his arms tight and ready for a fight if needed. "Oh, you better hope it's over."

The mall's burly security guard stepped forward, looking as though he'd judged the situation correctly. "It's over unless you want me to call the Lake Coburn PD for a pick up."

The big man took a step closer to the punk's face. "Nah, he's going—ain't you?"

The punk tried to hold his ground, made an obvious effort not to back up at the giant's threatening stance. John suspected it was in an effort to save face in front of the woman who'd accompanied him—and who'd remained quiet during the entire exchange.

"Yeah man." He reached out his hand to the young woman. "Come on, baby."

The woman shook her head and slapped his hand aside. "I ain't ya baby, and what the *hell* you talking about gettin' *your* money back? *I'm* the one paid for your ticket. Like I paid for the phone that got ya no-good behind in trouble, because *you* ain't any better at keeping a job than you are at keeping ya mouth shut." She pointed at the theater worker. "Don't you give him a dime."

Several people around them snickered as the theater worker shook her head. "No ma'am, I won't. Let's go, sir."

The punk contemplated for a full second before turning his back on her. "Fuh-get you." He stopped, turned back. "Give me the car keys."

The woman crossed her arms. "To *my* car? You can walk your broke ass back to your mama. I work fifty hours a week to pay the note on my car, and I don't do it so you can ride around in it." She stood then and waved her finger in his face. "Im'a tell you something else, too. If you leave outta here and key it or mess it up in any way, I'm gonna hunt you down and have your no-good, useless carcass thrown in jail, you hear me? Don't you *touch* ma car." She seated herself again. "Good riddance," she said, then raised her hands. "I'm sorry y'all. I tried to get him to shut up."

He turned with a wave of his hand. "Fuh-get all y'all, man. I don't need this!" He walked off in a huff, followed by the security guard as the theater exploded in applause and cheers at his departure.

The uniformed woman walked to the front and addressed the crowd. "We'll put the movie back on for y'all, folks. Sorry about the interruption."

Someone in the front row threw in a question. "Don't suppose you could restart it, could you? He walked in talking right at the start and didn't shut up the entire time."

She shook her head apologetically. "No sir, but we'll back it up a bit."

John Michael turned to the big man. "I didn't need your help, but I sure did appreciate the reinforcement, man." Straight-backed, with his chin up he offered his hand. "Thank you."

The man shook his hand. "It was the right thing to do, my man. He was out of line."

The two parted, each going back to their spots.

John Michael lowered himself into the seat next to Cynthia. He glanced over to see her watching him. "What?"

She slipped her arm through his and gushed as she fluttered her eyelashes. "Who's my big, strong hero?"

He adjusted his collar uncomfortably. "Stop it," he groaned, catching her low chuckle as the lights dimmed and the picture started up again.

John held the theater's exit door open for Cynthia—kept it open for the approaching couple. He nodded at the big man who'd recently backed him up. His wife, who seemed to be in her last trimester of pregnancy, gave him a bright smile.

He placed a friendly hand on the man's massive arm as he passed. "Thanks again, man."

The man's smile widened. "No problem, sir." He leaned in closer. "Besides, if I hadn't stepped up, I'd have had to fight my wife off of him. She's been waiting for this movie for months."

John laughed as they stepped through the door into the brightly lit corridor. He extended his hand again. "John Michael Ferguson."

The big man took less than a second to contemplate before offering his own hand. "Ferguson, huh?"

John nodded, realizing the man was remembering the Michael Brown incident in Ferguson, Missouri. "Yep. No relation."

A deep chuckle resonated from the giant as he gave John's hand a hearty pump or two. "I'm Jordan Brown."

John grinned. "It's nice to meet you, Jordan."

"Jordon. *Michael*. Brown."

John froze. "Seriously?"

The big man nodded. "Yep. No relation." He shrugged and grinned at John, revealing large, straight, white teeth. "What are the odds, huh?"

"Pretty slim, man." He turned to Cynthia. "This is a friend of mine and my beautiful date for the night, Cynthia Ellender. Cyn, this is Mr. Jordan Brown."

Cynthia extended her hand. "Nice to meet you, Jordan and . . ."

The pretty, petite woman beside him took her hand. "I'm Lydia, and it's nice to meet you Cynthia. For a while there I thought we were going to be bailing these two out of jail. Can you believe that guy, talking on his phone like he was in the middle of Wal-Mart?"

"I know! I don't know why some people think they don't have to follow the rules."

"I swear that made me so angry. Jordan finally got up because I was about to say something."

Jordan placed a hand on his right side. "It might have something to do with the bruises from her elbow jabbing into my ribs. She's been breaking my arm to see this movie for three weeks. I thought for sure the troublemakers would have come and gone by now." He looked at his wife and shook his finger at her. "I swore after the last time we wouldn't come here again."

She caught hold of his finger in the crook of her own and pulled it down. "I know, you're here because of me, and I appreciate it."

"What happened the last time?" John asked.

"A couple showed up here with two kids, looked about three and four years old. They let those two run around here like some wild animals—kicking the back of my seat, running up and down the aisles, screaming and talking like they were in a daycare. Got on my last nerve."

"I hope you had them thrown out."

"We sure did. And the worst thing about it was those little ones shouldn't have been in there in the first place." Lydia's eyes widened. "All those zombies and monsters terrified me."

Cynthia covered her mouth. "And they brought their children?"

Jordan leaned forward, speaking in a conspiratorial whisper. "I thought white folks would've had more sense."

John Michael's reply was accompanied by a snort of laughter. "Yeah, well I've learned stupid people come in all colors, shapes, and sizes."

Jordan nodded. "Now that's a righteous statement if I ever heard one, my man." He gave John's shoulder a hefty pat.

Cynthia leaned closer to the man's wife. "I loved the movie anyway, Lydia. What did you think?"

"I enjoyed it, once we got to watch in peace. Oh . . ." Lydia reached for her side, made a face as her husband's worried look reached her. "I'm okay, Jordan. It's nothing."

Cynthia leaned forward. "How far along are you?"

"Nearly thirty-six weeks. I can't wait for him to come."

"A son." John nudged Jordan. "Gonna have fun with that one, huh dad?"

"Oh yeah, man. I got plans. He's gonna be outdoors with me. I ain't letting my kid keep his nose stuck in some stupid video game all day long. And when he's old enough I'm gonna keep his butt so busy he won't have time to get in trouble. You got kids, John?"

"One son, and he and his wife gave me a set of twin grandbabies." John shook his head as he thought of the two adorable babies. "Man, you think kids are great. Wait until you hold your first grandchild."

"Twins! That sounds like a nightmare."

"Nah, they handle those babies fine. Besides—" he gave Lydia a sideways glance. "You sure there aren't two in there?"

Jordan's laughter boomed in the theater's emptying lobby. "Oh man, don't you be cursing me. I can barely handle one at a time."

Lydia grabbed hold of his arm. "Just think, Jordan, twice the dirty diapers." She laughed at her husband's dramatic cringe. "The first time he tried to change our daughter's poopy diaper, I thought he was gonna be sick. I mean, really— there he was; six foot six and two hundred and seventy-five pounds of muscle— dry heaving over his baby daughter's diaper. It was pitiful, I tell you. Pitiful!" The three of them laughed as Jordan made convincing gagging noises.

Cynthia pulled a business card from her wallet and handed it to Lydia. "Take this. If you have any problems, call me. I'm a pediatrician."

Lydia studied the card. "This is where I'm delivering."

"Then you'll probably see me there. I'm off a couple of days a week so call me if you don't see me around."

"I sure will, and thank you." She checked her buzzing phone. "Ah, Jordan—the babysitter has an emergency. We need to get going." She palmed her phone and turned to John and Cynthia. "It was a pleasure meeting you both, and I *will* hang on to this card."

A couple of goodbyes and two handshakes later, John helped Cynthia into his truck.

"What a sweet couple. I sure hope Lydia delivers when I'm on duty."

"You gave her your card, so . . ."

"Oh, I think she'll have other things on her mind when the time comes."

He buckled himself into the driver's seat and lifted her hand from the center console. "I have a feeling we'll see those two again."

About halfway home on I-10 Eastbound Cynthia leaned forward to gaze out of the windshield. "Look at all those stars. With all the lights and trees and roofs blocking the view you can barely see the stars at Mom's place."

John Michael grinned. "Are you in a hurry to get home?"

"Not especially. Why?"

"You'll see." He took the next exit, hit the service road and turned onto a smaller, parish road. Her gasp of delight had him smiling as he pulled up beside a huge pond, the full moon reflecting brightly from the glass-like surface of the water. John backed up his truck to the pond then parked it. He climbed out and met her at the passenger door. "Come on, I have a feeling you're going to appreciate this."

He lowered the tailgate of his truck and helped her up before seating himself beside her.

"How's this for a view?"

She stared out at the glistening surface of the pond, then lifted her gaze skyward and smiled. "It's beautiful out here. How do you know this place?"

"I've helped a friend of mine work cattle out here for years." He pointed to the south. "His place is about a mile down, just past the ridge of trees."

She arched her back to stare at the sky. "Look at all these stars, would you?"

"Not a thing out there to block your view."

"No kidding."

John Michael reached up to point at the moon. "The moon's waxing and it's only a crescent so there's not enough light to compete with the stars tonight." He lowered his arm and rested it on the truck bed behind her.

They sat there, surrounded by nature—bullfrogs croaking, crickets chirping, the fluttering of wings as a hawk or owl hunted for its supper, and the water making gentle lapping noises at the shoreline. The moment was peaceful, beautiful, and it didn't surprise him when Cyn reached for his hand and draped it over her neck. She gasped as a shooting star streaked across the sky.

"Make a wish, Cyn." John Michael watched as she closed her eyes. She turned, lifted her gaze to his. He lowered his mouth to hers and kissed her, softly, gently. When he pulled back and looked down at her, she was wearing a smile. He touched the corner of her mouth with one finger. "What are you smiling at?"

"It's nothing."

"Doesn't look like nothing. What?"

"I was thinking I'd never had a wish come true that quickly before."

"Yeah?" He nodded and chuckled, before planting another kiss on her, this one with a little more tongue and a significant rise in heat level.

He pulled back, feeling slightly breathless, his heart pounding as he rested his forehead against hers. "So, Dr. Ellender—have I passed your test?"

She grinned and nodded. "Mm. With flying colors, Mr. Ferguson."

"Does this mean we're going steady?"

Cynthia lifted one shoulder in a dainty shrug. "Until something better comes along."

He pulled back, frowning. "Really?"

Her eyes crinkled with laughter. "No." She pulled him by the collar and went in for another kiss. Moments later, it was Cyn pulling back, breathless and panting. "You know, I've always told myself I was remembering my first kiss from you as more than what it was. I mean, we were both gawky kids. No way could you have perfected your kissing technique first rattle out of the box, right?"

John stepped down from the tailgate, laughter rumbling deep in his chest. "Well, I'd like to think I've learned a few things over the years. Maybe I'm a little rusty." He stood in front of her, stepped between her legs, the height of the truck putting Cyn's face level with his.

She reached up, taking his face between her two palms. "You're missing my point, John Michael."

He leaned forward, kissed her forehead. "What's your point, Cyn?" He placed a gentle kiss on the tip of her nose.

"I'm trying to tell you even at thirteen, your kiss made my toes curl. It's only improved with time."

He ran one hand up the back of her blouse to her neck, his fingers cupping her skull to pull her closer. He started a trail of soft kisses, starting at her left ear to the crook of her neck, and then on to the smooth as silk skin of her shoulder. Her guttural groan had him smiling as his mouth followed its own trail back to her luscious lips. His arms lowered to her butt and he pulled her closer, voiding any gaps between them.

She reciprocated, lifting her arms around his neck to embrace him as he kissed her again. The feel of her foot curling around his calf, urging him closer, had him wondering how she'd feel about sex under the stars.

A buzzing by his ear and a sudden slap to her neck brought him back to the harsh reality. This wasn't some love scene from a sappy romance movie. This was late spring in south Louisiana . . . replete with enough mosquitoes to carry off a small child.

"Looks like the bugs found us," he growled. "Damn, that didn't take long."

"It was bound to happen." She slapped at the mosquitoes covering her arms. "Oh my goodness. I'd forgotten about the perils of parking in Louisiana."

He brushed off a couple of the blood suckers from her face, then his own as he helped her down from the tailgate. "Parked a lot, did you?"

"Some. Probably not as much as you did, but apparently enough to remember *this* part of it."

"Only not with me."

"Nope. Never with you."

He grinned as he walked her back to the truck and opened the door for her. "Can't say that anymore, can you?"

She laughed as she slapped at another mosquito. "No, I guess not. Now get me the hell out of here before I need a blood transfusion. If I pass out before we get to the emergency room, I'm B positive."

He laughed as he started the truck, and got them quickly back to the paved road. They drove with the windows down until all the bugs that had followed them into the cab had been blown out.

Cyn's laughter surrounded him, light and carefree, as she flipped open the lighted visor mirror and tried to smooth down her hair, then gave up and fluffed it instead.

Suddenly, the strangeness of the situation hit him. For the first time since Bethie died, he had a woman sitting beside him in his truck. He waited for a pang of guilt but it never came, finally decided he'd let enough water pass under this particular bridge. A decade and a half was a hell of a long time to be without female companionship.

He wasn't only thinking about sex. Sure he missed the hell out of it, but he missed other things more. Like talking to a woman about the day he'd had, falling asleep in bed in the middle of a conversation, holding her in his arms, or dancing in the kitchen for the fun of it—all the things he and Beth used to do.

It dawned on him then. He'd never taken his wife to the spot he'd taken Cyn. For some reason, it made him a little sad. But then, shouldn't he be working on new experiences rather than reliving old experiences with a new woman? He turned, caught Cyn gazing up through the passenger window at the night sky.

Definitely.

He turned his attention back to the highway, warmth creeping into a part of his heart that had remained empty and cold since losing his wife. For the second time since seeing this lady again he had to ask himself . . .

How in the hell had he forgotten about Cynthia Anne Robicheaux?

Chapter Six

Bess opened the door to her home and held it until her daughter entered the house. The Sunday church service had been enjoyable, and they'd stopped off at the new Chinese restaurant in town and filled up on shrimp lo mein, and pepper steak with onions, along with a couple of side items.

Cynthia placed the to-go boxes in the fridge and straightened, patting her belly. "I'm stuffed."

Bess had to agree. "I am too, but it was delicious, and we've got enough leftovers for supper tonight."

Cyn threw her keys in the catch-all bowl by the back door and smoothed down her blouse. "I think I'll have a salad or soup tonight and save mine for lunch tomorrow at the hospital. I can already feel the walnut shrimp going straight to my butt."

Bess waved off her daughter's complaint. "What butt? Thank goodness you were blessed with your father's DNA when it comes to body shapes. All the women in his family stayed tiny. If I live to be eighty or older you'll be able to roll me around like the little blueberry brat on the Willie Wonka movie you made me sit through the other day."

Cynthia laughed. "Oh, stop. You look wonderful, Mom. Sorry about the movie, but it was one of the kids' favorites when they were little. I couldn't help myself when I saw it was on. I had the urge to reminisce a little."

Bess rolled her eyes. "At least it was the older version. The newer one was a little creepy, don't you think?"

"Yeah, well, Johnny Depp has a knack for making his roles a little creepy, doesn't he?"

Her mother stopped in the hallway to face her. "Speaking of Johnny—"

Cynthia stopped and made a face as she raised her thumb and forefinger. "I was *that* close to getting away with it."

Bess gave her daughter a hearty laugh. "Dream on, *ma petite femme*. You and Johnny stayed out in his truck quite a while after he brought you home. I was tempted to flash the porch light like your father did when you were a teenager."

Cynthia frowned. "Don't you dare. I'm fifty-three years old. Besides, we were only talking."

"Really, Cyn? With a man as nice looking as John Michael, all you could do is talk?"

"Well, we talked most of the time anyway. Ah-ah." She lifted one finger. "Don't ask and I won't have to lie to you." She finished by "zipping" her lips shut.

Bess rested her hands on her hips. "I was wondering if he was as good a kisser as he was at thirteen, that's all."

"Sure you were." Cynthia pretended to go through her purse then stopped suddenly and faced her. "For the record, he was fabulous then and he's even better now."

Bess stood there, staring at the daughter who'd gone through so many changes in the past year and a half. Not only had she lost a husband, but she'd been slapped in the face upon his death. What an awful thing to happen before you put your husband into his eternal resting place.

As much as she hated to admit it, she was almost grateful to her son-in-law. If he hadn't broken his wife's heart, Bess may never have had this opportunity to get her daughter so fully back into her life. She may have chosen to stay among the friends she'd made there, in the home where she'd raised all three of her children. But the cheating so-and-so had caused Cynthia to cut her ties with the past, and no mother hen had ever been so glad to have her baby chick back home.

"Well, you may be fifty-three, but you're still my little girl, and I want to see you happy again before I die."

Cynthia rounded on her. "Don't say things like that, Mama. You've still got at least a good twenty years left, as active as you are."

"Oh, I imagine I've got a few left in me—not sure it's as many as twenty, though." Bess stopped, the corners of her mouth drawn in the frown that made her the spitting image of her own mother. She replaced it with a smile when she felt her daughter's hand on her shoulder.

"You all right, Mom?"

She nodded, blinking away tears. "I've lost so many of my friends the past few years." Her eyes grew moist as she shook her head slowly. "And there's poor Marilee, sitting in that place, not knowing from one day to the next who she is. It breaks my heart."

"Would you like to go see her today, Mom? I could bring you—right now if you'd like."

"Oh . . ." she spoke breathlessly. "Could we, please? I'd so love to see my old friend again."

"Sure. Let's get into something more comfortable for the drive over. Maybe bring her some of those tarts you made yesterday."

Bess knocked on the door to Marilee's room, pushed it open after hearing a soft "Come in." Her old friend sat there, dressed and ready for company. Whether or not she'd recognize her, was still up in the air.

Marilee rose from her seat. "Oh, hello. Can I help you ladies? Perhaps you're in the wrong room?"

Bess stood frozen in place, unsure of what to say. The feel of Cynthia's light touch on her arm gave her the courage to speak. "Hello." She took a tentative step forward. "I'm Bess Robicheaux, and this is my daughter, Cynthia. We're going around visiting some of the residents. Would you mind if we sat and talked for a bit?"

Marilee beamed at her. "I'd love it. I don't get many visitors here—or, I don't think so, anyway. What did you say your name was?"

"I'm Bess, dear—and your name?"

"I'm—I'm . . ." Her voice trailed off suddenly.

Bess stemmed her urge to cry, keenly aware of the pain poor J.D. must go through every time his wife saw him as nothing more than a polite stranger. "Are you Marilee, by any chance?"

"I—I believe I am." She looked around her room as though she were trying to assess her surroundings. "Sometimes—they have to tell me my name. Sometimes I'm a little lost." Her gaze returned to Bess. "But, I could use some company, so if it doesn't bother you, it shouldn't bother me, right?"

Bess smiled, amazed how even in the throes of dementia her old friend still retained her sense of humor. Whether Marilee realized it or not, she'd possessed her own unique wit, and for as long as she'd known her, had made good use of it.

Her first visit with Marilee was the most difficult for her. She spent an hour talking with her, must have had to repeat her name, as well as their reason for being there, at least four times. Finally, she'd given her daughter "the look" indicating she was ready to leave. She'd been on the verge of tears all the way home, vowing silently not to go back. It was too difficult seeing her that way.

By the next morning, she knew she would make more return trips. Something told her Marilee was still inside the polite shell of a woman she'd once been. As long as there was a chance to see her again, she'd keep trying.

Three days later, she made the second trip alone and it was easier. For a split second, she thought she saw a hint of recognition on the woman's face. It vanished instantly, leaving Bess to reintroduce herself, using the same story as before. That time Marilee handed her a spiral bound notebook.

"Could you sign this, please?"

"Well, certainly. What's it for, Marilee?"

"It's so I can keep track of my visitors in case I forget your name."

Bess released a low chuckle as she signed her name. "This doesn't surprise me one bit. You always were a smart cookie and *always* so organized."

"Was I?"

Bess stopped and met her intense gaze. "Yes, dear. You've always been organized."

Marilee blinked several times, put her hand to her chest, and smiled. "You knew me before?"

Bess reached out, placed a hand on Marilee's shoulder. "Yes, dear. We're very good friends, you and I. We've been through a lot together."

Marilee seemed to study her for a moment. "I know I'm in this place because I occasionally forget who I am. I wish I could remember every memory I've lost. I wish I could remember you. You seem . . . important to me somehow."

Bess sighed as a single tear made a track down Marilee's fair cheek. She gave her friend a sad smile and a gentle hug. "At our ages, some things are best left forgotten, old friend."

She waited two days before making another trip to see her, again with no trace of recognition from Marilee. She "signed-in" as a visitor, none the less. The following Monday's visit got exactly the same result. Three days later, Cynthia suggested she take J.D. along, since John Michael would be filling in for Zach at the feed store all day.

Bess agreed, whole heartedly. "I'm more than happy to take him but we really need to talk J.D. into having his cataract surgery. Once a man loses his independence, the rest goes to hell in a hand basket. It about killed your father to have me cart him all over the place once he got too weak to drive."

"I agree. Maybe you can talk him into it on the way over." She kissed her mom on the cheek and headed to the door. "Later Mom, and drive carefully."

They made one stop at a nearby florist so John could pick up a bouquet of Forget-Me-Nots for Marilee. When he got back into the car, she eyed the flowers.

"That's why those flowers are always in her room. I'd wondered."

"They've always been her favorite flowers, but now they have a special meaning, don't they? I always come here for them. This place keeps them in stock for me, as much as they can, anyway."

By the time Bess pulled into a parking spot at the facility, they were deep in conversation about his cataracts and whether or not to have the surgery. They met at the front of the car and she gave his arm a pat.

"I'm telling you, it's a piece of cake, J.D. After you're done, you'll wonder why the heck you put it off for so long."

J.D. scratched at his chin. "I suppose you're right. Come on. Let's go see if the lovely Marilee knows us today."

Bess watched as J.D. hesitated at the door long enough to close his eyes and take a deep breath. He knocked and waited for her invitation to come in.

Bess would never forget the look of immediate recognition on Marilee's face as she got her first sight of her husband.

"J.D., you're here!" The two of them met in the middle of the floor like long separated lovers.

He cupped her face in both his hands. "Of course I am, *ma femme*. Why wouldn't I be?"

She lifted one hand to his cheek. "How long has it been this time?"

"Four weeks or so." He pulled her hand from his face and placed a kiss in her palm, then planted a kiss firmly on her mouth.

Bess watched the exchange, amazed at the intensity of her old friends' feelings for one another. She turned to leave them alone, but stopped when Marilee called out to her.

"Bess? Bessie, is that you?"

Bess turned to face her. "It's me, *mon vieux*. I hope you don't mind me tagging along."

"Oh no, not at all. Come here, old friend!" She held up the spiral notebook. "I've seen how many times you've visited while I wasn't myself. They're all in here."

Bess approached then found herself wrapped in Marilee's warm embrace. "I've missed our talks, Marilee."

"I know you have, but I'm here now. Let's sit. Where's our boy today, J.D.?"

"He had to take Zach's place at the store today, hon. I'll call him to come by, if . . ." His voice trailed off.

"If I'm myself long enough, you mean? It's all right, honey. I'm just glad to have the two of you here."

They spent the next hour talking about Zach's new family. Marilee's face lit up when she heard John Michael and Cynthia were seeing each other.

"Oh, I'm thrilled. Johnny's been alone for too long. He's a good man."

"Yes, he is. I believe he and Cynthia make a lovely couple."

J.D. gave a low rumble of laughter. "It's almost like they're teenagers again, honey. You should see them together."

"Tell them I'm hoping for a visit from the two of them. Oh wait a minute." She pulled a floral notebook from her desk and flipped to the last page. "They've come already. I remember now." She turned to Bess and pointed to a small photo album Cathryn had put together for her of their visit with the twins. "I have pictures with her. She's a beautiful young woman, and you're right. They do make a lovely couple."

When J.D. excused himself to use the restroom, Marilee grabbed Bessie's hands in her own. "Bess, can we speak candidly for a bit?"

"Sure. What's on your mind?"

"The thought of leaving J.D. alone in this world breaks my heart, Bessie. I've been praying someone would come along to make this all easier for him."

Bess shook her head slowly. "He's not alone, sweetie. He's got Johnny and maybe Cynthia, as well as Zach and his beautiful little family. He'll never be alone."

"It's not the same as having someone, Bess. J.D. has always been a man who thrives on companionship. He needs someone to spend the long, lonely evenings with. I'd love it if you'd be that someone for him."

Bess shook her head. "I don't want to hear this, Marilee. You're still *here*."

"But not for much longer, old friend. I can feel it. You and Ham were always good friends to J.D. and me, Bess. Now that Ham's gone, I'd love it if you and J.D. could find some happiness in the days you both have left."

"You make it sound as though J.D. would have an easy time forgetting you, Mari. Surely, you must know how much he cherishes you."

"I don't want him to forget me, but to learn to live without me. I know he cherishes me. He always has, as much as I've loved him. But I'm not here for much longer, Bess, you must realize how rapidly this disease is progressing. I can see how well the two of you get along together."

"Oh Mari, don't ask this of me."

"Please, Bessie, this is so important to me. *Promise me* you'll find a way to convince him not to mourn me. Not to live out the rest of his life a lonely old man without someone around to make him live. I can't bear leaving this world knowing he'd be alone—he'd stop living. Please, Bess. Give me some peace of mind. Tell me you'll be there for him."

Bess held Marilee's hands tight. "I can promise you this. If, at any time, J.D. needs me—I'll be there for him."

Marilee's shoulders drooped in sudden relief, her face instantly free of all signs of worry. "Oh, you can't know, Bess. You can't know how *relieved* I am. Sometimes the effort is too much—coming back to this place, knowing I'll lose it again. Because sometimes when I do, I remember more than I want to."

Bess squeezed her friend's hand, to let her know she understood.

"Sometimes all I can remember is my sweet Jenna and the pain of losing her. I know because I write it all down, you see. And sometimes I remember leaving the time before, because some days, to me, it's only happened a few seconds ago, even though it's been days or weeks. When I'm about to leave, I see it on J.D.'s face. It's always there, the heartbreak of having to lose me all over again."

Bess sniffed and wiped her eyes, her heart breaking for her old friend as she pulled her close for a hug. "Oh sweet, sweet Marilee, you've always been such a good friend."

Marilee pulled back and patted her friend's hand. "No more than you have been to me, Bessie. I feel so strongly about this. I couldn't trust just anyone to my J.D. I know that she-devil LaVyrle Fruge has already come by to check out the situation because she signed my book. I need someone to boot her butt to the curb if she goes sniffing around. The poor man would die of some kind of awful venereal disease if he spent too much time around the old floozy."

J.D. walked in on the two women as they were doubled over with laughter. "What are you two old hens cackling about?"

Bessie rose from the sofa and smiled at him. "Nothing you need to know about. I'm going to find some coffee so you two can have some time together."

Marilee's gaze followed Bess out of the room, the remnants of a smile still on her face. When they were alone she opened her journal and began to make some notes.

"What do you write in that book of yours, Marilee?"

She lifted her smiling face to his. "I'm leaving you a recipe, sweet man."

"I hope it's something quick and easy. Johnny and I aren't exactly what you call geniuses in the kitchen."

She waved him off. "No, no. It's more of a—a guide—yes, it's a guide. And it's not time for you to read it yet. This is for when I'm not here any longer." She looked up. "When I'm not me anymore, John—do you understand?"

He couldn't do anything more than to nod. She scribbled a few more lines then looked up, a frown creasing her brow. "I'm afraid it'll be soon, dear husband."

J.D. shook his head. "I don't want to hear such foolishness, *mon coeur*—"

She put a finger to his lips. "Stop, we both know my time is near. I hope, when it happens, it happens quickly, for your sake. Right now, while I still can, I want you to know how much I've adored being your wife all these years."

He kissed her gently on the lips. "It can't be any more than I've enjoyed being your husband."

She gave him a bright smile. It started to fade. "My husband. . ." She returned to her journal, scribbled frantically for a minute, then paused, wrote another word or two until her pen drew a long, straight line before her hand came to rest.

She blinked several times, and then looked up at him, her eyes wide with panic. "It's—it's—I . . ." Her voice trailed off as she gazed frantically around the room.

He patted her hand, hoping to reassure her. "Sh, sweet lady. It's all right. You're completely safe here. Let me get someone to help you."

J.D. rose and went to the door to call for her nurse. He stepped aside as the woman went in to calm her patient. He sagged against the wall, overwhelmed by a heaviness of heart that left him feeling exhausted and filled with an unusually sharp sense of utter hopelessness. Even then he swore he could hear Marilee's gentle chiding.

Don't give in to despair, old man—it'll only send you to an early grave.

He shook his head. He was way past the risk of an early grave, wasn't he? Eyes closed, lips moving in silent prayer, the soft sound of a woman clearing her throat jarred his attention. He looked up, seeing Bess standing there, holding a cup of coffee. He wiped his eyes, somewhat ashamed he'd forgotten they'd come in together.

"Has she left you again, J.D.?"

All he could do was nod.

"I'm sorry."

He pulled a handkerchief from his shirt pocket and wiped his eyes. "It's a cruel disease, Bess. But we had her for a little while, didn't we?"

She looked up through her tears and gave him the saddest of smiles. "Yes, we did." She walked to him, placed a reassuring hand on his shoulder. "I have no words of comfort for you. All I can say is I'm here for you if you need to talk, *mon vieil ami*. My shoulders are strong, and I still have my hearing."

He chuckled and gave her hand a gentle pat. "We are old friends, aren't we? And I appreciate the offer. It's always less difficult with someone else around to talk to after one of these—episodes."

"Find yourself a therapy group, J.D. Believe me, I thought I was ready to handle it when Ham passed on. For months you watch them endure the suffering, trying to make it as comfortable as possible for them. Somehow, you fool yourself into believing it'll be easier once they're gone, right? You'll be ready." She blinked several times and cleared her throat. "It doesn't seem real at first. The company leaves, and the children and grandchildren all go back to their own homes, their own busy lives. Then you're left sitting alone in a big old house and it hits you, I mean really hits you hard. He's gone. Nothing you can do will ever bring him back." She shook her head. "Only others who've been through it can understand the pain, J.D.—the deep, bone-chilling sense of loss. Trust me on this."

He nodded. "Maybe you're right." He gave one last look at the room housing his wife. She'd calmed relatively quickly compared to some previous incidents. Small blessings, he supposed.

Well hell . . . he'd take 'em wherever he could get 'em.

Chapter Seven

J.D. entered the room full of strangers at the Community center. He looked around, surprised at the varied ages of the people gathered there.

"Quite a shock to see so many younger people at a group like this, isn't it?"

He turned at the deep, bass of the male voice, recognized a large man he'd seen once or twice at the facility where Marilee resided.

J.D. gave him a brusque nod. "I was thinking I'd better ask someone if I'm at the right place. This is the Alzheimer's Support Group, right?"

The man grinned, his big white teeth glowing from skin as dark as Marilee's old fashioned fudge, his skin wrinkled from years of living. He leaned forward, lowering his voice a decibel or two. "It looks like you and I are here to represent the seniors in the room."

J.D. chuckled and offered his hand. "I think you're right." After introductions, they each got a cup of coffee and found a seat near the front.

By the end of the hour long meeting, J.D. had heard several different versions of the same story. The heartbreak of seeing loved ones—spouses, parents, siblings, friends, and even adult children—slowly retreat to a place beyond recognition and reason. Never much on public speaking, J.D. somehow felt comfortable enough to stand and tell an abbreviated version of how it felt to be losing his beloved wife to the disease. He learned Alzheimer's had no respect for barriers—be it genders, race, religions, or even age. One woman his age had lost her fifty-seven year old daughter to the disease.

J.D. walked away from his first meeting with an entirely new appreciation for "group therapy" and feeling grateful to an old friend for the suggestion. Once Johnny dropped him off at his house, he took the opportunity to call her with the news.

Bess settled down in her overstuffed reading chair with the only afternoon cup of coffee she allowed herself. She took one leisurely sip before setting the cup down to answer her phone.

"Bess, this is J.D. I hope I'm not disturbing you."

"No, not at all. Is everything all right with Marilee?"

"As far as I know, it is. I'm calling to thank you for suggesting the Alzheimer's group. I attended my first meeting today and it was every bit as much help as you said it would be. I never realized there were so many people out there going through the same things I am."

"Eye-opening, was it?"

"Absolutely. The idea I could actually take comfort from hearing other people's experiences . . . I learned a lot about myself, as well as this awful disease. Why, there was a woman our age at the meeting who lost her *daughter* to Alzheimer's. The poor thing started showing symptoms at fifty-three years old and it advanced rapidly."

Bess's heart clenched at J.D.'s comment. "How awful for her. It's horrible enough to be struck down after a long, full life, but to have those terrifying symptoms when you're so young."

"I know. It's heartbreaking." He paused, and when he spoke again his tone took on a lighter note. "I even got a business card with the name of a good eye surgeon. The guy who gave it to me said the cataract surgery is a breeze and he regretted waiting so long to have it."

Bess stared at the phone in her hand and rolled her eyes before putting it up to her mouth again. "Haven't I been telling you this all along?"

He chuckled. "Yeah, I thought your feathers might get a little ruffled."

She clucked her tongue. "Hmph . . . men! You won't believe anything until you hear it from someone who is probably every bit as hard headed as you are. Stubborn old goats."

His laughter rang out over the phone. "Most likely—I guess us stubborn old goats will eventually seek each other out no matter where we are. I'll talk to you later, Bess."

"Goodbye, J.D." Bess gave her head a slow shake as she hit the end call button on her cordless phone. She couldn't help but smile at the old coot's news. No doubt he'd see a doctor now and have the surgery necessary to get his driving privileges back.

Her smile faded suddenly. The last few times she'd needed to run errands, she'd called him to see if he wanted to come along for the ride. He'd jumped at the chance, saying how much he hated depending on his son to drive him everywhere since he had other things to do. Bess couldn't deny it had been nice to have a little male companionship again.

It's funny how she'd never enjoyed driving until Ham had grown so ill. Once she'd been forced to take over the wheel, she discovered how much she enjoyed it. Thinking back on it, she believed it gave her a slight advantage—the tiniest bit of control over a totally uncontrollable situation. The down side, of course, was the cost to her husband. Even as *she* had begun to feel more in control, poor Ham had started to lose all hope.

She supposed losing the ability to drive made men feel emasculated in some way. Lord knows their egos couldn't handle stopping for directions if they were behind the wheel. She'd known her husband to waste a half a tank of gas rather than admit to being lost on their last road trip before his diagnosis. He'd been so stubborn.

She had to wonder how it would affect J.D. once they reinstated his license. Would he still want to accompany her if she called him? Or maybe *he'd* call her asking if she wanted to go along for the ride. They could always take turns driving, assuming he'd want to spend more time with her.

She shook herself from her thoughts and remembered Marilee's request. As usual, it overwhelmed her with feelings of guilt. The poor woman was still around, and if a miracle cure suddenly appeared and Bess had her way, Marilee would be the first in line. Prompted by the thought, she closed her eyes and whispered a prayer for her old friend. She wiped at the trace of tears. They always appeared when she thought of Marilee and her illness.

"Your will be done, Lord. Your will be done." She followed with a quick sign of the cross, something she'd picked up as a small child after seeing her paternal grandmother do the same.

It was strange how memories from her childhood stood out vividly as she got older. She could remember the first time she'd crossed herself in front of her mother, a staunch Baptist. She couldn't have been more than four years old. The simple act had annoyed her mama to no end, especially since she'd never gotten along with her mother-in-law. But Bess had adored her Grandma Guidry, even if her mother hadn't.

She'd always looked at it as a sign of respect, both to her "Gram" as well as the God who probably didn't give two hoots about religious differences. She figured the good Lord would let anyone into heaven if they acted right and treated others kindly.

Besides, Marilee and J.D. *were* Catholics, and she knew they'd appreciate any extra help she could give them.

She caught her reflection in a small stand mirror she kept on the table next to her reading lamp. An old woman she barely recognized stared back at her.

She passed her hand through hair every bit as snow white as her father's had been when he'd been an old man. "Who's the old person now, huh, Bess?" Her fingers slid lightly over a face well-worn with laugh lines, as well as wrinkles in other places.

"Hmph. Serves you right for even thinking twice about another woman's husband, old lady." *But what if said woman begged you to?* She turned away from the mirror, suspecting it wouldn't make much of a difference to her conscience. She couldn't help but wonder if the good Lord had any protocol set up for situations such as this.

John Michael entered his dad's house without knocking, found the old man where he was most of the time—in his recliner watching the tube. "I brought you some tomatoes from my greenhouse, Pop. I've got a nice crop this year."

His pop kicked down the footrest of his recliner and struggled to get out of his chair. He inspected the contents of the bag. "That's some good looking tomatoes, right there. Bess will be happy. She's been on my butt about eating healthier. Telling me I need to eat more fresh vegetables."

"There's nothing wrong with eating right, at any age."

"No, but every time I see her she sends me home with a batch of fresh fig tarts, or some kind of pie to go along with her healthy advice."

"But at least hers is good, right?"

"Yep." J.D. rubbed his belly. "And you know how I feel about wasting good grub."

John chuckled at his father's comment as well as his accompanying cheesy grin. "Well, I know how you feel about wasting *any* grub—good or not."

J.D. nodded. "I'd argue with you if I could figure out a way to prove you wrong. But, seein' as I can't, I guess I'll keep quiet."

John grinned and stuck a finger in his father's chest. "Now, that *would* be nice for a change."

J.D.'s chest rumbled with laughter. "Where you going all spiffed up?" He wagged his brows. "Or do I even need to ask anymore?"

"You shouldn't, but you've never held your tongue before, have you old man?"

"You and Cynthia got a hot date?"

"We're going to the movies and then dinner."

"The movies again? After the last fiasco?"

"We're trying a different theater tonight. They revamped the old Queen Cinema in Eunice. A co-worker of Cyn's has been before, says we'll love it."

"Well, try not to pick any fights or anything. I can't make the drive to bail your butt out of jail. Not yet, anyway."

John snorted. "You sound as though you've done it before."

"No—you spared me that indignity when so many others your age seemed to think it was a cool thing to do. What got me at the time was how their parents downplayed the incidents, like it was some kind of rite of passage."

John Michael remembered those instances well. His most vivid memory, however, was his dad's warning after some friend of his had done something stupid. J.D. had pulled him outside for a "talk". It had consisted of one burly finger in his face and two sentences, each of them heavy with a thinly veiled threat. "Don't even think about it, boy. I brought you into this world, and I can take you out again."

He'd believed him.

"Are you taking your sweet girl dancing again tonight?"

His father made what he probably thought was a couple of smooth dance moves in his day, making John laugh. "Be careful, old man. You might throw out your back with those moves."

J.D. shot him a glare. "Your mom and I used to do a lot of dancing back in the day."

"When dinosaurs roamed the earth?" He got a weathered finger wagged in his face for that one.

"Nobody likes a smart-ass, Johnny. I bet I could still teach you a thing or two."

"About dancing?" John shook his head. "Hm. Doubtful, Pop."

J.D. frowned. "Why is it you young kids always think old people have nothing to teach?"

"I don't think that at all. I only said you can't teach me anything *new* about dancing. Most of what I learned I picked up from watching you and Mom. Then Beth and I took lessons and we passed y'all up in moves."

"Well, you're never too old to learn." His eyes lit up suddenly. "Last night I watched a documentary on one of those cable channels. It was all about some spot on a woman's private parts—"

John lifted both hands in front of him. "Aw damn—what have you been up to now?"

J.D. cocked his head and stuck one hand out. "Hold on, now. Let me finish."

John gave his own face a one-handed swipe. "I'd really rather you didn't."

"Now this could be important to you, son. This particular spot—they call it a G-spot after some guy named Gutenberg I think, who discovered it was there—well, it sounds pretty important with women today."

John Michael groaned. No way would the old man let up on this. His jaws were clamped into the subject matter pretty firmly, it seemed. "I think his name was Grafenberg, and he was a German gynecologist who did the studies on it in the 1950s."

"Yeah, Grafenberg—he had a hell of a job, huh?"

"Well, it wasn't exactly his *job*, but rather something—never mind." He may as well quit now—no way would he ever come out ahead in this matter. "Anyway, I have a sneaking suspicion it's been important long before today." He nearly laughed at the bewildered look his dad gave him.

"You think so? I'd never heard of it before."

"Well, I did."

"Really? Do you know how to find it? What to do with it?"

John stared at his dad, struggling to hold back the laughter. "I know where it is. Believe me. I'm good, Pop."

J.D. leaned forward, spoke in a near reverent whisper. "They say it controls whether or not a woman reaches her peak—you know—during the act. It's supposed to give them a deeper, stronger—"

"I know, Pop!" John covered his mouth with one hand to smother the guffaw threatening to explode any second. He cleared his throat loudly, somehow managing to control himself. "That's what it does, all right." He fidgeted under his father's watchful stare.

"And you *know* about it already?"

John Michael could only manage a nod.

"Hmph." J.D. gave him a look hovering somewhere between admiration and awe. "Maybe *you* should have given *me* the birds and the bees talk." He shook his head. "There's a disadvantage to coming of age before the sexual revolution." He shrugged. "Of course, your mother never complained."

John Michael placed a hand on his dad's shoulder, praying for the right come back to put an abrupt end to this nightmare of a conversation. "Just because it didn't have an official name doesn't mean it wasn't there all along. Maybe you found it, only you didn't know it."

J.D. seemed to ponder his comment and finally nodded. "Yep, must be it."

John gave him a huge nod. "Yep, it must be. Later, Pop." He spun on his heel, hitting the door before his old man found a way to expound further on the subject at hand.

It took barely ten minutes to get to Ms. Bess's place.

His date for the evening pulled the door open before he could even knock, sounding a little breathless. "Come on in, John Michael. I'll be ready in about two minutes."

He gazed in appreciation at Cyn, who looked lovely in a sleeveless dress— what Beth used to call a sundress. It was the perfect choice for the first week in

July. It hugged her waist and the neckline was cut low enough to give the barest hint of cleavage. The bright yellow color set off her green eyes—all in all, quite a becoming sight. "I don't know what you could possibly do to improve what I see before me, but you go ahead. We have plenty of time."

She gave him a sheepish smile and rubbed her hands over her bare arms. "You're sweet, but I always feel a little self-conscious in sleeveless dresses."

"Honestly, Cyn. You look great. I don't know what the heck you're talking about."

Bess entered the room. "I told her the same thing, Johnny. Maybe *you* can get her to see reason."

"Hey, Ms. Bess." John bent his long frame to give her a hug and then straightened. "Here you go." He handed her a plastic bag. "I brought y'all some fresh tomatoes."

"Oh, thank you! They're beautiful."

"Yes ma'am. I've had a good crop this summer." He stopped to look down at her. "Do I have you to thank for Pop making an appointment with an eye surgeon?"

Bess gave her head a brisk shake. "Actually, he got the card from a man he met at the Alzheimer's group. The old coot wouldn't listen to me."

"But you're the one who kept on him to find the group so you're indirectly responsible. Regardless, I was thrilled to hear it. I'm hoping it'll give him back his independence. Speaking of which, are you two scheduled to go visit Mom again anytime soon? He couldn't stop talking about how glad she was to see you."

She seemed to falter a bit before widening her smile. "I told him I'd be glad to take him any time he needed me to. It was so good to see her."

"Were you able to have an actual conversation with her, Ms. Bess? Was she lucid for long enough?"

She nodded. "Oh yes. She was her old self for a good hour or so. I left for coffee to give them some time alone and by the time I got back she was . . . gone again."

He wiped his hands on his jeans. "Yes, ma'am. It's rough on him. You don't know how much it means to me having you there for him."

Her eyes turned liquid and her smile faded. "I saw first-hand how hard it is for him when she—when she leaves him. But I felt so blessed to be there and to speak to my old friend, even for little while."

John focused on Cyn as she re-entered the room, adjusting a short-sleeved, light green, lacey pullover she'd slipped over her dress. He could see it was light-weight, which was important in this heat. If it gave her an added boost of self-confidence, he didn't have a problem with it.

Her negative self-image bothered him, though. She obviously had no idea how beautiful she was. He figured he had her dead husband to thank. She had no idea how difficult it was for him not to rail on the guy. But he was the father of her children and it wasn't his place. He'd seen it so many times in couples he'd known. Cheating spouses did a hell of a job on the faithful one's self-esteem. But he hoped like hell *Gene* was in a position to see his wife enjoying the company of man who wouldn't dream of hurting her by turning to another woman. What a dip shit.

He shook himself out of his musings and turned his attention back to Ms. Bess. "I went to see Mom a couple of days after you and Pop did. I guess I was hoping the sight of me would jog her memory."

Bess stepped forward. "Oh, and did it?"

"No ma'am. I stopped by again this afternoon, hoping . . ." He shook his head. "She—she wasn't—it wasn't good."

The silence grew thick and heavy in the room. Cyn placed her hand on his arm and finally spoke. "I'm sorry, John Michael."

He nodded and took her hand. "You ready to hit the road?"

"I am." She turned and gave her mother a hug. "Bye Mom. Don't wait up for me."

Bess patted her daughter on the back then waved her off. "Oh, I won't. I trust Johnny to take good care of *ma petite femme.*"

Cyn turned to him, her eyes sparkling mysteriously. She gave him a look—a good combination of "He'd better" and "I know he will". Her eyes darkened suddenly, heating him from the inside out. In that moment, he knew she trusted him every bit as much as her mother did, and it pleased him to no damned end. After what her ex had done to her, he'd damned sure keep it that way.

He led her to his truck and helped her up onto the seat, working hard to avoid staring at her cleavage—and was rewarded with a healthy glimpse of smooth, bare thigh as she slid across the leather to settle into the bucket seat. He closed her door and walked around to settle in behind the wheel. Within seconds, they were on their way.

Her voice sliced through his thoughts like a bass boat through the smooth surface of the Mermentau River.

"Do you want to talk about it, John Michael?"

He turned, realized he'd been lost in thought for a couple of minutes. "Talk about what, hon?"

"Your last visits with your mom, maybe? Were they bad?"

John nodded. "She never even acknowledged I was there for either visit. As a matter of fact, I doubt she knew she was there. It's the worst I've seen her, Cyn. The doctor said it's a sign she's slipping into the next stage of the illness. From here on out, we *may* see her slightly lucid on occasion, or she may never come out of it. He couldn't say for sure. Each person's illness and symptoms proceed at a different pace."

"Oh God. Has your dad seen her like that?"

"No, he hasn't." He swallowed, remembered well the overwhelming sense of hopelessness he'd felt as he'd stared down at his mother. "She just sat there, Cyn, a trickle of drool running down one side of her mouth. It's like she's slipped around a corner and disappeared from sight." He slapped the steering wheeling lightly. "I got the distinct feeling that we won't be seeing her, as herself, ever again."

He blinked several times and reached across the console for her hand. She didn't seem to mind. At a time like this he'd give his right nut for his old truck again. No console separating him and Cynthia—only one long bench seat so she could slide over and sit close to him for comfort. Too many damn consoles in this world—and they came in many different forms: smart phones, video games, television, computers, texting, social networking and emails. All the ways technology had removed human touch, human to human communication.

He released a long, low sigh and squeezed her hand tighter. "Let's talk about something more pleasant . . . like the bubonic plague or something." He spared a glance away from the road to catch her sad smile. "I'm okay. Really." She nodded and he faced the road again wondering what to say to lift them from the suddenly dismal mood. He found himself smiling at the memory of his recent conversation with Pop.

"What are you grinning about over there?"

He faced her, deciding they'd reached a point in their relationship where it was safe to broach a particular subject matter. "My dad. It seems he's watched a few talk shows and documentaries recently and has turned into this advice-doling-expert on the subject of sex."

Her laughter rang out in the truck cab. "Seriously? Am I going to have to limit his contact with my mother?"

"When I was leaving to pick you up for our first date, he asked me if I had any condoms." John held up his hand to stop her from commenting. "Even worse, I passed by his place on the way over here, and he starts telling me all about *G-spots*—as in their locations and roles in a woman's body."

Laughter, riddled with snorts and giggles, both his and hers, filled the cab. It took a bit of earnest effort on both their parts, but they finally caught their breath after a minute of side-splitting laughter.

"Oh my goodness!" she gasped. "I don't think we should let those two go anywhere without adult supervision."

"Oh, I think your mom's safe enough with him. He admitted he'd never heard of the G-spot until he saw the program. I was forced to tell him I knew all about it. He seemed quite impressed because I knew where it was and what to do with it."

She faced him, her eyes filled with new interest. "Oh, really."

He gave her an enthusiastic nod. "I think I've attained rock star status in my father's eyes."

"Hmph."

John glanced over at Cyn. She turned toward the front wearing a sober expression. "What does that mean?"

She shrugged one shoulder. "Mm, maybe something along the lines of 'I'll believe it when I see it'—or rather, feel it."

Feel it? More than a little shocked by her suggestive play on words, he couldn't help but wonder how serious she was. The corners of her mouth twitched invitingly. Once again he found himself longing for a bench seat. It'd be so nice to have her tucked neatly into his side right about now. "You know, Cyn. Maybe it's wishful thinking on my part, but that sounded an awful lot like a challenge."

She faced him slowly, her mouth twisted in a one-sided grin. "What if it is?"

He pulled to a stop at the intersection of LA 26 and US 190, checked left and right and to the rear, verifying they were alone on the roadway. He turned to face her fully, his groin tightening suddenly at the look on her face.

"Well then, I'd have to say—challenge accepted."

Her gaze narrowed slightly as she seemed to gauge his sincerity. Slowly, she offered her right hand. "It's a deal, then—too late to back out now, John Michael. I take my challenges very seriously."

John Michael's eyes darkened to a shade of even deeper blue, if it was possible. Her heart beat a rapid cadence in her chest as he reached for her hand. He took it in his own, softly stroked her palm with his thumb. Thankful she'd taken the time to apply her favorite scented lotion, she sucked in her breath as he bowed his head and kissed the surface above her knuckles. As if that wasn't enough to get her juices flowing, he flipped her hand slowly and placed an even softer kiss on her open palm. As a bonus, he lifted his smoldering, sexy as hell gaze to meet hers—and winked.

Holy . . . How could one, sweet gesture turn this man into something simply irresistible?

She swallowed, tried to replenish the moisture suddenly sucked dry from her mouth and lips. "I, um, did the wink mean you were kidding? I've already told you, I take my challenges very seriously." *Not to mention I'm dying to see if you really know what to do with a G-spot—mine, in particular.*

"I accepted, didn't I?" As though hammering his point home, he placed a soft kiss on the inside of her wrist.

Oh. My. God.

He looked up, checked his rearview mirror. Cynthia assumed he saw a vehicle approaching, but couldn't say for certain since she couldn't tear her gaze from his profile. He put on his right signal and looked both directions before turning east onto US 190. Once on the highway, he glanced in her direction and gave her his devilishly handsome grin.

"You tell me when you're ready and I'll start making the plans to prove my case."

Ready? Hell, she was ready now. Like, right now. She couldn't remember the last time she'd been this ready. And he'd done it with a single look, a simple gesture, a few words. She found herself squirming in her seat. Good grief-a-mighty, was she ever ready.

Suddenly, she imagined herself in that old cartoon with the two tiny figures—one on each shoulder.

The little red devil was screaming and gesticulating wildly at her. "*Now* Cyn! Tell him you want it *now*! Tell him to turn the truck around and drive straight to his house so you can get this challenge underway. Right. Damn. *Now*."

Of course, the tiny, angelic, white-garbed figure, complete with iridescent wings and glittery halo, spoke up in a calm voice. "This will wait. All good things come to those who wait. You don't want him to think you're easy, do you? There's plenty of time to work out these feelings of yours. You're an adult."

Cue the Devil: "Exactly! You're both mature adults. Your husband sure had his fun—at your expense, too. Come on Cyn, you know you want to. Cyn wants to do a little SIN-ning of her own. You *deserve* this."

Cue the Angel: "If he really cares for you, he'll wait. Your first time together should be because you both love each other, not to retaliate against your dead husband's act of betrayal."

"Uh—Cyn? Are you okay over there?" John Michael snapped his fingers in front of her face.

She blinked, took a deep breath and faced the front. "I'll—I'll let you know by the end of the night."

"It'll take you until the end of the night to know if you're okay?"

She glanced in his direction. He rewarded her with another grin. "No. I'll let you know *when* by the end of the night."

He nodded slowly. "I gotcha. Sounds good, Cyn."

Good? Good was a trip to the movies and dinner. What she was hoping for was a little bit of *awesomeness.* Okay, a hell of a lot of awesomeness. And she suspected it had nothing to do with her dead husband—and everything to do with the wonderful man seated beside her.

She squirmed in her seat again, at the moisture flooding her girl parts. Slowly, she turned to face John Michael again. Without taking his eyes off the road, he reached out, his palm up. She placed her left hand in his and squeezed.

He pinned her with his heated gaze, wincing slightly as he pulled his hand back to grasp the wheel. With his left hand, he made an adjustment of his own while performing his own rendition of the old bucket-seat-squirm-dance.

He felt it too. Sweet, liquid warmth pooled at her core, adding to what already existed there. *Amazing.* "Good grief," she groaned.

"I know," he countered. "It's gonna be a long night."

"A hell of a long night," she agreed. Cyn couldn't find a bit of humor in the low growl he emitted. But she did get a clear image of her little red devil and her winged angel meeting in the middle, each conceding to the other. Maybe this wouldn't happen tonight, but it was definitely due to happen.

She met his smoldering gaze, still exhibiting some discomfort, but no less intense.

Maybe she was building herself up for a huge letdown, especially since she expected nothing less than fireworks. She groaned again before turning to stare out of her passenger window, strongly suspecting this man wouldn't rest until he'd delivered.

After all, today was the third of July . . . maybe she'd get her fireworks a day early.

They pulled up at the theater with the brightly lit double marquis illuminating the street.

Cynthia gaped through the truck's windshield. "It's a throwback to a scene from a fifties movie."

"Yep. Seems like it should be advertising "The Blob" or something, doesn't it?"

She laughed. "It does. I've got a feeling this is going to be a nice experience."

John paid at a window built at an angle to the street—one of two on either side of the three glass doors. No touch-screen kiosks placed intermittently to buy tickets with a credit card. Other than the old man working the window, and a few other cars, there was no sign of anyone else yet.

Cynthia waited for him to push the door open for her and entered the theater lobby, hand in hand with John Michael. She stopped, immediately transported back in time to her childhood.

The lobby floors glistened, the light tan linoleum tiles brought back to life with buffers and tons of wax. She lifted her gaze, immediately drawn to the various pops of glass and chrome accents that designers of today called "retro". In this building, it looked more like they'd refurbished all original working parts. Wooden benches lined the walls, and she could practically see herself as a child sitting on one, waiting impatiently for the movie to start.

"It's like taking a step back in time, isn't it?"

She turned to John Michael, agreeing wholeheartedly with him. "We're coming back here."

He grinned, his eyes sparkling with excitement. "Definitely. I can hardly wait to see inside the theater."

After purchasing two small popcorns and drinks, they entered one of three separate theater areas. Cynthia uttered a gasp of appreciation. "They got this right too, didn't they?"

"Yep. It's just like the old days."

They made themselves comfortable in the small theater, eventually joined by a couple dozen other people. They made small talk until the feature started then settled back to enjoy the show. Not once during the movie were they interrupted by someone talking, or a phone ringing, or a brightly lit screen of someone texting, or children running around, or anyone else who thought *they* were too special to follow the rules made for everyone.

Two hours later, Cynthia exited the theater first and dumped their trash into the bin outside the door. "What a pleasant experience."

John Michael gave her a wholehearted nod of agreement. "I'm all for making this our theater of choice. How about you?"

"I agree. I'll be sure and thank Hannah for suggesting it when I see her Monday. She'll be pleased we love it so much. The owners are friends of her family." She stepped through the heavy glass exit door John Michael held open for her, and slammed into a wall of heat that was heavy and dense with moisture. "Good grief, I hate this humidity. It's about the only thing I didn't miss all those years in Oklahoma."

"Your husband never considered moving down here?"

She frowned. "Oh, no. His mother would have had a conniption fit."

"It was totally acceptable in her eyes for you to be separated from your family though?"

Cynthia pictured her mother-in-law—strong, sturdy, salt of the earth, and firm, but always loving. "She didn't have daughters, so she probably couldn't see it from my parents' point of view. She decided long ago having daughter-in-laws around was her reward for raising all those rowdy boys."

His hand on the small of her back, he reached for the passenger door of his truck to open it for her. "Were your in-laws good to you?"

"Oh, absolutely. I never had a cross word with either of his parents, and they stayed out of our business for the most part. I'm so glad they'd both passed on before Gene. The entire mess, his infidelity, it would have devastated them. I doubt either of them could have accepted that kind of behavior from their son."

"I don't know how anyone could." He crossed around to the driver's side and settled in beside her. After buckling his seat belt, he faced her again. "Has your daughter's attitude toward you softened any? I know you said she was having difficulty blaming her dad for anything."

"I've called her dozens of times since I've been here. I try to get her to skype or some kind of video chat call. She keeps making excuses, then finds a way to end the call quickly. Truth be told, it's been that way since Gene died, even when I was still in Oklahoma. I don't know what to do about it. I saw my sons over the Easter holidays, but Trini bowed out of seeing the rest of us." Her chest tightened at the thought of her sweet granddaughter, Zoe. "I miss my granddaughter so much. She's almost two years old and she's growing up not knowing me." She blinked back the sudden onslaught of tears.

John started the truck and pulled out onto the street. "Maybe it's time for a visit."

"I agree, but when I broach the subject, she always says it's a bad time." Her tears finally won out as she fumbled around in her purse for tissues. His hand came into view holding a crisp, white handkerchief. "Thank you. I'm sorry, I don't normally do this."

"Don't apologize, Cyn. I know I promised a movie and a good meal after, but are you still up for the restaurant?"

She dabbed at her eyes. "Well, I'm hungry, but I'm afraid I don't feel like being out in public right now."

He reached out to grab her hand and squeezed it tightly. "How about we order a pizza for pick-up and head over to my place to talk or watch a movie?"

She swiveled in her seat to face him. "Really? You wouldn't mind? I'm sure you had something much nicer planned for tonight."

"We're together, Cyn. I can't think of anything nicer." He handed her his smart phone. "Pizza Palace is already in my phone list. Order a large pan, one-half loaded and the other half with whatever you want on yours. We'll have to pass through Jennings on the way home, anyway. By the time we get there it should be ready."

He held the door open for Cyn to walk into his home. She looked around and nodded, seeming somewhat surprised at its extraordinary neat condition. "Were you expecting company?"

John Michael shrugged. "One can always hope." The truth was he'd spent most of the day cleaning in case they ended up here tonight.

She nodded, and smiled at him, her eyes still a little red from the short bout of tears she'd allowed herself at the thought of her granddaughter. His breath hitched when she caught her lower lip in her teeth, giving her a vulnerable look. He wanted to kiss away any sadness, any heartbreak caused by her cheating dead spouse and selfish daughter—no doubt a trait she picked up from her father's DNA.

She looked around, fidgeted uncomfortably. "At least you didn't say expect."

He set the pizza and his phone on the counter, grabbed a couple of plates from the cabinet. "I never expected a thing and I still don't." He headed for the fridge and peered inside. "I've got Coke, canned tea, and bottled water. Or maybe you'd like a beer with your pizz . . ." Hands wrapped gently around his waist, cutting off his question. Cynthia pressed her body against his back, laid her face softly between his shoulder blades. He grabbed her hands, pulled her arms tighter around him and let his head fall back to rest against hers.

His eyelids drifted shut. The simple act of closeness, of the companionship sorely lacking in his life, had him releasing a long, slow sigh of satisfaction. Her next words had his eyes snapping open again.

"Maybe you should."

"Wh—what?"

"Expect it. Maybe you should expect it."

"Well. I'm—I'm not quite sure what to say."

"Why?"

He sucked in his breath. "It sounds a little like one of those loaded questions. You know, like "Have you stopped beating your wife?" Seems like anything I say could get my ass in a crack. Until you give me the word, the best I can manage is to hope." He held his breath throughout her prolonged pause.

"Word."

He released his breath slowly and turned in her arms to face her. Cyn's green eyes showed no hint of teasing. "Spell it out for me, please, so there's no chance of miscommunication." Her smile had him sucking in his breath again as he tightened with need below the belt.

"I want you, John Michael. Here, now, before we fill up on pizza and beer. I'm starving. For you."

"Well, all right, then." He kicked the fridge door closed with his booted foot and dipped his head to capture her mouth with his own. She unbuttoned his shirt, scraped her nails gently over his chest.

He sucked in his breath sharply. Cyn emitted something similar to a low growl in the base of her throat and his groin tightened painfully. "Oh. God." He looked around. No way would this happen in his kitchen. He grabbed her hand, pulled her down the hallway into his bedroom.

Cynthia jerked open the button of his jeans and pulled his shirt out and off of him in one, smooth move. She turned her back to him. Wordlessly, he pulled down the zipper of her dress, baring her back to him. He slowly eased the dress from her shoulders, baring them to his touch. She groaned low in her throat as he dipped his mouth to her neck, placed a trail of kisses along her collar bone.

She turned slowly to face him, let the front of her dress fall forward. The swell of her breasts drew his hands to the delicate lace bra covering them. He cupped them both, his palms filled with the soft weightiness. Her turn to suck in as his thumbs made slow circles through the silky material, causing her nipples to pebble.

How long had it been? Too damn long. He couldn't believe it. This was happening. Tonight. Here in his home. The next thought burst forth, unheeded, and sure as hell unwanted.

In the home you shared with Beth.

He pushed it aside. This had nothing to do with his wife. Absolutely nothing. He dipped his mouth to the creamy smoothness of Cyn's neck.

She'd want me to find someone.

He knew it in his heart. His gaze landed on their wedding picture. It gravitated to the first family picture they'd taken when Zach was a baby. It landed on the last, taken many years later, a few months before she'd been taken from them.

Guilt washed over him like oversized waves from a Category 5 hurricane attacking the Cameron Parish coastline. He lifted his head, eyes clenched to shut out his surroundings, dipped his head to Cyn's neck again, trying to get back to the moment for her sake.

"John Michael, stop."

Her words brought him to an abrupt halt. He pulled back, but kept his head lowered. He couldn't look at her—too ashamed he couldn't follow through with this.

She placed her hand gently on the side of his face. "I understand. You have nothing to apologize for."

He met her gaze, expecting to see sympathy, or sorrow, both of which he didn't want or need from her. What he saw was an acute awareness of what he was feeling. She understood.

"Not here," she said. "I should have realized before."

John wiped his face with one hand before pulling her dress up to cover her shoulders. He turned her slowly to zip it up then turned her back around. He started to apologize, but Cynthia placed her finger on his lips.

"Don't bother. I couldn't have, either."

His expression must have conveyed his doubt.

"You're looking at someone who had to cross three state lines to escape her baggage, remember?"

He leaned in to place a light kiss upon her lips. "I guess you're right."

She lifted one shoulder. "I suspect we'll both know when it's time."

He wrapped her tightly in his arms for a hug. "Thanks for giving me a little leeway."

"We've only been dating for a month, John Michael. Besides, something tells me you're going to make it worth the wait."

He released her, and then cupped her face gently in both hands, wanting her to leave here tonight with something to look forward to. He kissed her thoroughly, ending it with several nips to her lower lip. He graduated to her earlobe, gently scraping with his teeth, thrilled as she shivered noticeably. More determined than ever to prove her right, he spoke, his voice raspy with genuine need.

"Something tells me you're right on the money."

Chapter Eight

It had been a week since the bedroom "incident". She'd had to work the next day, on July 4th, but she and her mom had joined him and Mr. J.D. to watch the fireworks display out on the lake. The next Friday John Michael called her, begging for help.

"I've got stuff in my walk-in closet from before Beth passed away, Cyn. I really don't know what to do with everything but I want a fresh start around here. I'm willing to pay you in grilled T-bones for your time if you're willing to help."

The seriousness of a "fresh start" and all its implications was enough to have her jumping at the chance to help.

So far, the opportunity had been eye opening, giving her the chance to get to know his "Bethie" on a somewhat intimate level.

"What about this, John Michael? This looks like something extremely important." Cynthia handed him the sealed box from a side shelf, deep in his walk-in closet.

He studied it, his face blank. "I have no idea what that is." He took out his pocket knife to slit the taped edges of the box. "Let's see."

She leaned forward as he lifted the lid, gasped as he pulled back fragile white tissue paper. "Oh, how beautiful."

John Michael sat back on his heels and stared at the contents of the box.

Cynthia lifted a framed photo on the dresser and studied it before turning back to the box. "It's Beth's wedding dress, isn't it?"

He nodded. "Yeah. I'd forgotten it was in there somewhere. She hoped we'd have a daughter to wear it one day, but we only had Zachary." His brows rose quizzically as he stared at her. "If I donate it to Goodwill, maybe someone will get some use out of it."

She didn't even attempt to disguise her horror at the suggestion. "This is a family heirloom, John. You can't get rid of it."

"But we didn't have a daughter and the only son is married already."

"But you have a granddaughter. You never know." She lifted the gown, fingered the delicately beaded bodice with its sweetheart neckline. "Do you happen to know if someone handmade this for her?"

He shook his head. "I have no idea."

She lifted the gown out of the box, checked it for stains or discolorations. "Other than a slight yellowing, it seems fine. You'd be surprised what the cleaners can do now." She reached into the box, lifted a piece of paper. "Oh, look! It says who made it for her and what they paid and everything. You see? Beth knew details like this are important in family heirlooms. You have to keep this, or give it to Zachary and Cat for their daughter."

"You're right. Put it in the Zach pile and I'll get it to him tomorrow with the rest of the stuff."

"I think you should bring it straight to a reliable dry cleaner. Maybe have it sealed up again. Cat won't have time to deal with this right now with the babies."

He agreed and stood. "I'm thirsty. Want something to drink?"

"I'll take a tea if you have any left." Her phone trilled its distinctive ring tone. "Can you grab that for me?"

He brought it to her, his mouth tight. "It's Trini, hon. Do you want some privacy?"

She grimaced at the name flashing. "No, as a matter of fact I'm going to put her on speaker. She's always telling me I'm picking fights with her. You can be my judge, or jury, whatever the case calls for." She pushed the talk button, then the speaker button. "Hey, Trin. What's up, sweetie?" She placed the phone carefully on the nightstand.

"I'm positive Mick is sleeping around on me."

"Well, hello to you, too."

"This is serious, Mother!"

"I didn't say it wasn't, Trin." The sound of her daughter's acidic voice filled the air space.

"I called you because I thought you, of all people, might understand what I'm going through."

"I'm here, Trini. What's going on?"

"Mick is spending more and more time away from the house. I'm sure he's having an affair."

"Well, have you spoken to him about it? Maybe there's some other explanation."

"Oh God. I knew you'd take his side."

"Honey, I'm not taking his side. I'm—I'm just. . ." She looked at John Michael and spread her hands in question. He shook his head. "So, tell me everything."

"I. Already. Did."

John Michael's eyes widened perceptibly.

"Honey, there must be something else. Does he say he's going to a bar after work, or that he's working out with some of his friends?"

"How would I know?"

"Have you asked him why he's spending so much time away from home? Have you asked him where he's going?"

"Of course not! I'm not going to accuse him without proof."

"Well, how do you expect to get proof?"

"I don't know."

"Well, honey. I still think the first step is to confront him. If he's spending too much time away from home, ask him where he's been."

"Oh, my God. You don't believe me, do you?"

Cynthia grabbed two handfuls of her own hair. "Trini, do you really want to know what I think?"

"I called you, didn't I?"

Cynthia closed her eyes and took a deep breath. "Okay, now bear in mind this is only my opinion. I'm not there, so I have no idea what's really going on—"

"Other than taking your own daughter's word, which is what any other *loving* mother would do."

John Michael lifted one hand and turned away, as though he'd heard enough. "Oh Trini, I do love you." *Or I would have given you away by the age of thirteen.*

"So you say."

"Honey, don't let your father's actions poison your relationship with Mick. You have a child together. Your marriage is worth saving."

"Would you have given Daddy another chance?"

"Moot point, dear. I didn't have the opportunity to give him another chance. Now, what I'm hearing from you is not definitive proof, as you said. Your choices are to speak to him about your suspicions or realize you could be a little paranoid because of what happened with your father." Trini's burst of hysterical laughter told her not to expect any kind of reasonable comeback.

"Oh my God. I should have *known* you'd do this—turn everything around so the focus was on *you* rather than your daughter. Haven't you ridden your pity train long enough, Mother?"

John Michael reappeared in the doorway, his expression incredulous as he mouthed the words, "Is she kidding?"

"Are you kidding, Trini?"

"About what? The way you neglected your husband for years until he finally turned to another woman?"

John Michael clamped down tightly on his jaw, shook his head.

"Do you even realize what you're saying, Trin?"

"I believe I do."

"Really? So, I suppose if Mick *is* out sleeping around with another woman, it could only be because you're not giving him what he needs at home."

A moment of silence preluded Trini's muttered "What a bitc—" before the line went dead.

Cynthia placed both hands on her forehead. "Wow. I'm—wow." She looked up at John Michael. "Is it me?"

He reached for her hand, helped her up from where she sat cross-legged on the floor. "It's definitely not you, Cyn. Nothing you said called for her to speak that way to you. I'm grasping at straws here but has she, by any chance, had some kind of head injury recently?"

She released a burst of nervous laughter. "If only it could be explained that easily. I'm afraid my daughter is simply a self-centered brat. I've already told you how her father spoiled her. She talked him out of every punishment I ever gave her for talking back and sassing. She was the perfect child at school and for everyone else. But at home she was—well—you heard it. I'm telling you, if I'd had my way, my daughter would have stayed grounded, with no privileges for at least eight years of her life."

She grabbed onto John's biceps, stared into eyes filled with sympathy. "She hates me. You heard her. My daughter hates me. Honestly, I don't know what to do."

He pulled her close for a hug and she relaxed in his arms. The man always seemed to know what she needed before she even needed it.

"Maybe you should call your boys. They may have some insight as to what's going on."

"They may, but she doesn't have a great relationship with them, either. There was always lots of tension between them. Especially when their punishments held and hers didn't. I could never make Gene understand how his favoritism put a strain on the family."

John grunted. "I never had a daughter, so I can't see it from his point of view. But, if anything, my parents were a little more protective of Jenna. Even though she was two years older, she had a few more restrictions because she was a girl. I remember thinking how it sucked for her, but she didn't complain about it too much though. And after she died, I wasn't in any frame of mind to party and put my parents through another kind of hell. We'd all been through too much. I didn't want them worrying needlessly."

"Of course you didn't. You were a good kid, even back then, and you grew into a phenomenal man—to your parents' credit." She picked up her phone and shook her head. "I love Trini but I hate my daughter's shrewish behavior. We didn't do her any favors. Or Mick either—nobody deserves the brow beating she gives her poor husband." She reached up to give him a quick kiss then retreated onto one end of his comfy couch with her phone.

She'd spent the last five evenings here and had grown quite comfortable at John Michael's place. He walked by with an armload of "closet" stuff to be delivered to one of a few places tomorrow, pausing long enough to give her a wink. She smiled as she dialed her oldest son, Jeremy. Within seconds she was speaking to his girlfriend.

"Hi Lena, this is Cynthia, Jeremy's mom. Is he around by any chance?"

"Hey, Ms. Cynthia! I'm sorry, but he's working out right now. How are you? Is everything okay over there in Louisiana?"

"Oh yes, sweetie. Everything's fine. I received a disturbing call from Trini, though. Have either you or Jeremy spoken to her lately?"

"I haven't, and if Jeremy has he hasn't mentioned it. To tell you the truth, it would be highly unlikely. They don't exactly see eye to eye."

"Doesn't surprise me, hon. I'm not sure if Trin sees eye to eye with anyone."

"Well, it's not for me to say . . ."

Cynthia chuckled, reading between the lines. "It's all right Lena. I don't want to put you on the spot with your boyfriend's mom or sister."

"Thank you, Ms. Cynthia. I'm glad you called though. It saved me from sneaking your number from Jeremy's phone. I'm giving him a surprise party for his birthday, and he'd be so excited if you could make it."

"Fabulous! I know his birthday is the 29th and falls on a Tuesday this year, so when are you having the party?"

"The next Friday evening, so that would be August 1st. I was thinking around 7:30 to give everyone time to get off of work and it would give you all day to make the six hour drive to Little Rock, unless you'd want to fly in. If so, let me know what time to pick you up from the airport."

"I don't mind the drive, but I'll let you know for sure nearer to the party. I—I may be bringing a plus one if that's okay."

"Sure." After a brief pause, Lena added to her comment. "So, is there anything you want to tell us, Ms. Cynthia?"

Cynthia walked to the window, her gaze glued to John Michael arranging boxes in the bed of his truck. "No. Not yet. Like I said, I'll let you know if I'm going alone or with someone, but I'll be there for sure."

"Awesome! Tyler's driving in from Memphis, too, with his girl of the month—we haven't met her, so don't ask. This party will be epic."

"Have you spoken to Trini about the party yet?"

"I've been dreading calling her, but I can't put it off any longer. She's always a little . . ."

"Rude?" Lena's sigh told her she'd guessed correctly.

"I was going to say *brief* to be nice, but rude is probably a better fit."

"Welcome to the club, Lena. She just hung up on me." She decided not to mention the rest of it. "Well, okay. Have Jeremy call me when he gets a chance please, and I won't breathe a word about the party."

"Great talking to you, Ms. Cynthia."

"You too, sweetie. I can't wait to see everyone."

She ended one call and made another to her youngest son.

"Hey Mom. How's it going over there?"

"Hey Ty. Everything's fine. How about you? Is Memphis treating you well?"

"It's great. I love my job and I've even got a new girlfriend. I can't wait for you to meet her."

"Really." This was new. "Are you bringing her to Jeremy's party?"

"Yep. Jessie's a great girl, Mom. She reminds me a lot of you. Strong, independent, and she's got something none of the others had."

She tapped her nail on one tooth. "Oh, yeah—like what?" *Please* don't let the name of some awful STD fly from his lips.

"Morals." He laughed. "Had you worried for a second there, didn't I?"

"Nope."

"Admit it, Mom. You thought I was going to say big hooters or something equally as distasteful."

"No, I can remember a few of your girlfriends with those."

"Yeah, I guess you're right. But honestly, you're going to love her, Mom."

He sounded genuinely satisfied—something she'd never heard from him before. She suddenly couldn't wait for this party. "I'm sure I will."

"Is Grammy Bess all right?"

"She's wonderful. I'm wondering if you've heard from your sister recently. I got a disturbing call from her." His groan said he'd been informed of the subject matter already.

"Not Trin, thank God. But Mick called me all kinds of upset. He says she's losing her freaking mind, Mom—totally paranoid. He's been working late to earn extra cash for their anniversary cruise in September. She's been accusing him of having an affair. Honestly, I think she needs therapy."

"I was thinking the same thing, Son. The thing with your dad threw her for a loop."

"Well, yeah. It did all of us, but no one more than you, Mom."

"When I mentioned it could be why she's so suspicious all of a sudden she accused me of trying to make it about me and not her."

He answered with a burst of laughter. "Of course she did. She's the only drama queen in our family. No one's allowed to be more miserable than Trini. Period. Honestly, if Mick is cheating on her, I wouldn't blame him one b—"

"Tyler! There's no good excuse for infidelity."

His end of the line was silent for several seconds. "I'm sorry Mom. I know how insensitive I must have sounded to you. I wasn't saying you deserved what Dad did. You didn't. He was so wrong. The old man had it too damn good with you. Trini knows the score—but as Dad's pet, she's having a difficult time facing facts."

Cynthia clamped down hard on her jaw, trying to decide which direction to take this conversation. She couldn't bear to have either of her sons know what their sister had said to her. It was bad enough John Michael knew.

Tyler released a long sigh. "I'll shut up now."

Nervous laughter bubbled up from her until he joined in. "I miss you so much, Ty. I cannot wait to see you and your brother. As for Trini, well I love her to death, but she surely knows how to try my patience."

"I suppose we'll have to put up with her like we always have," Tyler added. "Poor Trin. She lost her cheering section when Dad died. It's kind of sad when you think about it."

Cynthia stared at her phone for a moment.

"Mom, are you still there?"

"Y-yes. I guess you're right, Son. It is sad. But I found myself thinking I can't wait to meet Jessie."

John looked up when Cyn sauntered out the back door and stood on the porch, stretching her back. The hem of her white shorts landed a few inches above her knees, and a figure hugging yellow T-shirt accentuated her shapely little body. She wore some thick soled, bling-ed up flip flops she claimed were the most comfortable shoes ever invented. If he didn't know her, he'd have sworn she was forty, at the most. She looked that damn good. She saw him at the grill and smiled as she slipped her phone into her back pocket. She must have had a good conversation with at least one of her boys.

"You look happier."

"I spoke to Tyler. He's met a girl who seems to be a darn good influence on him. And . . ." She held up her two forefingers for emphasis. "He can't wait for me to *meet* her."

He wiped off the grates of his gas grill. "I'm assuming this behavior lands in the extraordinary range for him?"

"Extremely. His previous girls have always been—well, for the sake of decency, they've been for *decorative purposes only*. This gives me hope."

"Yep. That's how I felt about Zachary's previous flings. Thank God Cat had the good sense to come home and grab him up."

"No telling what kind of daughter-in-law you'd have ended up with, huh?"

John shook his head. "I have a feeling he'd have been a die-hard bachelor, and I would never have had the chance to be Paw Paw Johnny." He finished the cleaning process of the grates and sprayed them with a coating of non-stick vegetable oil. "I think Zachary's always known Cat was the only one for him. They'd been friends forever." He grinned at a particular memory. "They had this ridiculous 'friendship pact' during school. She seemed to think it was important, so he went along with it."

Cynthia bubbled with laughter. "The 'We can't date because you're too important to lose as a friend' pact?"

"Sounds about right, but hell, we all knew he was crazy about her. Thank God for Cathryn after Beth died. Many nights she brought my son home safe and sound after he'd pulled a good drunk." He suppressed a shudder. "But, during their senior year, something happened to put the emphasis on Cat's well-being instead of his. Snapped my son out of feeling sorry for himself real quick. It all came out last year."

Lines of concern appeared on her brow. "Sounds ominous."

He took a deep breath. "Still turns my stomach to think about it. She snuck off to a college football game with some friends. It was the Tiger Bowl—Auburn at LSU—they ended up at a bar around the campus after the game. Cat was drugged and . . ." He let the left go unsaid. "She didn't know who it was and didn't want to know."

"So there was no police report or visit to the ER?"

He shook his head. "She told one person—Zachary. Begged him not to tell a soul, knowing he'd never break a promise to her."

Cynthia groaned. "It happens more than you know. Poor Cat. I can't imagine what kind of hell she went through." Her eyes widened suddenly. "Oh wait, wasn't that the owner of the home and business security company? The one vandalizing businesses so he could sell them systems? I remember Mom telling me about the stink—and how he was linked to several rapes." Her hand flew to her mouth as sudden realization dawned.

John Michael nodded. "Jack Stanley. They got him for several counts of arson, attempted arson, and once the smoke cleared, several counts of rape and attempted rape."

"I remember he was caught red handed for arson. Did he confess to everything else?"

"Not without a little goading. Turns out Zach had known for years who'd attacked Cathryn. Just after she left town for college, he and a buddy of his attended a rodeo in Jennings. They ended up sitting two rows above a group of drunks causing all kinds of trouble. When security showed up to escort the idiots out, Zach's friend pointed out the ring leader, Stanley. He said he'd seen the jerk in a bar around LSU after the Tiger Bowl. He said Stanley had been bragging about what he'd done after slipping a roofie in a girl's Coke. Zach put two and two together."

Cynthia settled into one of four wooden Adirondack chairs on the deck. "Now I understand your reluctance to try Robin's cooking."

"Right."

"I'm assuming Zach didn't turn him in, because of his promise to Cat, right?"

"Right. But he did something any man would have done for the woman he loves in a situation like that. He went to the same bar and watched for Stanley. Sure enough, he showed, and Zach saw him slip something into a girl's drink. When the girl stepped out to get some fresh air, Stanley followed her. Zach caught him trying to force her behind the bar. He beat the hell out of him and brought the girl back inside to her friends. She was completely out of it by then."

Cyn pulled herself upright. "Well, it was a good start. Not nearly what he deserved, though."

"Without getting into too much detail, he found himself with one other equally deserving opportunity to kick Stanley's ass." He shook his head slowly. "As a father, I should probably regret my son hospitalizing a man on two separate occasions. But I can't—not when I know what he did to so many young girls."

Cyn reached for his hand, pulled him down to her level to do one of many things he'd missed over the years. He closed his eyes, groaning in pleasure as she tunneled her fingers through his hair. Hair with a hell of a lot more silver in it since Beth had last done that. She ran her thumbs gently over the outside corners of his eyes, both creased and wrinkled from too much sun and the passing of time. Cyn didn't seem to mind either of these signs of aging. Sometimes he had to wonder what the hell this woman saw in him.

"If he'd hospitalized a real man, maybe you could have regrets. But the boy capable of doing all the things you've described—well, he's no man. He's an animal with no regard for another human life. I'd say Zach should have a clear conscience and so should you. You raised a fine young man, and anyone can see how much he adores his wife."

He reached out, slid the back of his hand gently down the side of her face, her fair skin already turning pink in the summer heat. "You think so? I'm well aware a lot of people think we're all kind of back woods crazy here in Louisiana with our gun ownership rights and all, even though the great majority of us use them for hunting deer, ducks, and geese."

"That's not true."

He cocked his head. "It's not?"

She leaned up to kiss him on the mouth. "No. They think all people in Louisiana live in the swamps and eat gators every day." She pointed to the grill. "As a matter of fact, I'm expecting you to grill me up a mess of tiny little baby alligators like Adam Sandler did in—"

John cut her off with his roar of laughter. "Don't tell me you're a fan of *WaterBoy*."

"Oh come on! You mean you're not? Bobby Boucher was a wonderful character."

"It's ridiculous."

"Well sure—it's *supposed* to be ridiculous. But wasn't Kathy Bates funny as hell? Foos-ball is the *devil!*"

He busted out laughing then played along. "Mama, when did Ben Franklin invent e-lec-tri-ci-ty?"

She put her hands on her hips. "That's nonsense. *I* invented electricity. Ben Franklin is the *devil!*"

He kept it rolling by lifting his glass of water to examine it. "Now that's what I call high quality H2O."

She pointed at him, grinning. "I bet you can't tell me why alligators are ornery."

He surprised her with his comeback. "Well, sure. It's because they got all them teeth and no toothbrush."

She chuckled as she poked playfully at his chest with her forefinger. "For somebody who didn't like the movie, you sure know a lot of lines."

He straightened and cleared his throat. "I said it was ridiculous. I didn't say it wasn't funny as hell." He slapped her lightly on the thigh. "It's too damn hot for you out here. Let's go inside and get those steaks ready for grilling. They've been marinating since last night."

He helped her up and followed her to the house, his gaze glued to the graceful swing of her hips.

"You'd better not be looking at my butt, John Michael."

"I wasn't," he countered immediately with a lie.

She turned, the corners of her mouth pulled down in a frown. "Aw. . . Really?"

He grinned. "Yeah, I kind of was. I couldn't help myself."

She smiled, placed both hands over her heart. "Why, that's the nicest thing you've ever said to me."

He burst into laughter. "I clearly have some work to do."

She batted her eyelashes. "Like what kind of work?"

"Like giving you some better compliments."

"Ask your dad. I'm sure he could help you come up with a suitable list."

"No doubt." He wrapped his arms around her, relishing the closeness. "It feels good, you being here, Cyn."

She rested her face on his broad chest. "I'm more comfortable with every visit."

"That's what I like to hear." He kissed her forehead before leaning in to place a gentle kiss on her mouth. "We'll get there, Cyn. I promise."

She reached up to thread the fingers of both hands through his hair and smiled. "There's not a doubt in my mind. We have time."

Chapter Nine

The skies opened up the next Sunday, thanks to the latest tropical disturbance making its way in from the Gulf of Mexico. Dark clouds and rolling thunder accompanied what promised to be an all-day affair of rainfall. Cynthia placed a plate of assorted cheese, crackers, and olives onto the tray and reached into the cabinet for wine glasses. She smiled at the feel of two strong arms encircling her waist.

"Can I do anything to help, beautiful?"

She cocked her head as he leaned in to place a soft series of kisses on her neck. "Mmm—suddenly I'm feeling very appreciative of rainy afternoons." His low growl had her shivering as a slow, sweet heat started in the pit of her belly and spread lower. Amazing how the slightest touch from this man turned her into a quivering mass of give-me-more.

She turned in his arms for a soul melting kiss. If only her mom had planned to spend the night with her younger brother and his family in Lafayette. She'd tried to convince her to do just that, but Bess had insisted on sleeping in her own bed. Knowing her mom, that meant being home no later than five o'clock, or as soon as the weather broke so she could make the forty minute drive home.

Cynthia looped her arms around his neck and reached up to kiss him. "You can open the wine for me, unless you'd prefer a beer. I think there are a couple of bottles left in the fridge." She kissed his chin, which showed a little more stubble today than she was used to seeing on him. She'd convinced him to come over without shaving so she could judge which look he wore better. She had to admit, the silver tinged five o'clock shadow was a good look for him. But then again, so was a nice, clean shave. She sighed, drawn equally to two versions of the same man, and she didn't mind having to compare.

"Have you thought any more about accompanying me to Jeremy's birthday party August 1st?"

He kissed her nose. "Mm, as a matter of fact, it's looking pretty darn good, barring any complications with the old folks, anyway."

She withheld a whoop of excitement. "Are you sure? As much as I'd love to show you off to my sons, I know how much you hate putting too much space between you and your parents, especially with your mom's situation."

"Well, I spoke to Pop. His cataract surgery is scheduled for this Thursday, the 17th. Hopefully he'll have his driver's license re-instated by then. In short, he told me to get the hell out of here."

She beamed at him. "Remind me to give Mr. J.D. a big old hug the next time I see him."

His chest vibrated with his low chuckle. "Will do. By the way, you said you wanted to show me off to your sons. Did Trini and Mick have to back out of the party?"

Cynthia grinned and kissed his chin. "I'm sure she'll be there. But she'll probably spend the entire time finding fault where there is none, as is her way."

"Ah, I get what you're saying." He shrugged. "I'll have to find a way to win her over, won't I?"

He kissed her again, ended with him nipping gently at her lower lip. She arched her back, pressing against him, thinking she wouldn't mind putting off the movie for a bit longer. She took great satisfaction in the effort it took him to push away from her. She admired a gentleman as much as the next girl, but she could hardly wait to see him lose a little control . . . hell, scratch that . . . a *lot* of control.

He reached around her for the bottle of wine. "Cork screw?"

She took a deep breath and fanned her face with both hands. "Mm-hm. Top drawer."

He reached for the drawer. "This one?"

"Uh huh." She turned away and grabbed the tray. "Bring the bottle and those glasses when you get it opened, please. I'll get the movie ready." She left the room, trying to walk with shoulders back, gut tucked in, and backside tightened as she called back to him. "Are you watching my butt again, John Michael?" His laughter preceded his comeback.

"Yep, and it's such a nice butt, too."

She grinned. "Thank you."

"Anytime."

She barely had time to set the tray down on the large rectangular ottoman when the doorbell rang.

Cynthia wiped her hands on her shorts, and padded over to the door in her sandaled feet. She pulled it open, her breath hissing out of her at the sight of the man standing there.

"Hello, Cyndi. You look well."

"Charlie. What are you doing here?"

He took his cap off and shook the rain from it. "I'm afraid I wasn't prepared for this storm, and I'm drenched. But if you let me come in, I'll explain why I'm here."

She stepped aside to let him in, offered to get him a towel, which he declined.

"Look, if you're here to make excuses, I really don't want to hear them."

"Is everything all right in here, Cyn?"

She turned to where John Michael stood a step or two behind her and reached for his hand. "Come over here, John Michael. This is Charlie Jeffries."

John extended his hand. "John Ferguson. You were Gene's co-worker, I believe?"

Charlie accepted John's hand and gave it a firm shake. "And his best friend since first grade."

John's nod was brief but decisive. "I'm sorry for your loss. I'm sure you miss having him around."

His genuine concern seemed to take Charlie by surprise. He took a step back and dropped his gaze. "Thank you. I do. We all do at the station."

"No doubt." John Michael stepped closer to Cynthia.

Charlie's gaze darted from one of them to the other. "Are you two a couple?"

Cynthia lifted her chin. "Yes, we are." *And damned proud of it.* John looped his arm around her waist, almost as though to back up her statement, an unnecessary action, but oh, so appreciated. She leaned into him a little, thankful for his presence.

Charlie nodded. "I'm happy for you, Cyndi. I really am. Is uh . . ." He slapped his damp cap on the thigh of his jeans. "Is there any way we could have a talk?"

She spread both hands. "You're here. So talk."

He grabbed the back of his neck and shot a quick look in John's direction. "In private, I mean?"

John adjusted his stance and shot Cynthia a look that said he'd rather not leave her alone with this guy. "You need some time alone with him?"

"Definitely not." She grabbed his arm, pulled him back beside her and gazed up at Charlie. "He knows everything, Charlie. Anything you say to me, you can say in front of him."

Charlie nodded, a little reluctantly. "Okay then."

Cynthia led both men into the living room. She offered Charlie a seat in the rocker while she snuggled up next to John Michael, never releasing the hold on his hand.

"Here's the deal, Cyndi. Tamara Sullivan was blackmailing Gene to make him keep seeing her. I know you don't want to hear this, but it's true. He tried to get out of it, but she wouldn't allow it. This girl chased him shamelessly. He resisted for two months. I guess she finally wore him down. God knows I'm not making excuses for him, Cyndi. It was wrong, but you have to know the whole story. He slept with her once and felt so guilty afterwards, so awful about what he'd done to you. He never intended to see her again."

She sighed. "Yet he did see her again. He was afraid I'd find out about the one mistake he made with her, so he saw her for nearly two more years? It doesn't fly, Charlie. Not with me." John Michael cleared his throat, his frown telling her it obviously didn't fly with him, either.

Charlie raised his hands. "Hear me out, please. Two months later she starts calling him. He hung up on her and wouldn't answer any more calls from her. A week later, she showed up at the firehouse, made a huge stink, ends up waving a report around saying she's pregnant—and it's his kid. So, he tells her he'll take care of her and the baby, *if* a DNA test proved it was his."

She sat up straight. "Are you trying to tell me my children have a half sibling out there?"

"Long story short, she miscarried—with complications that left her unable to have any more children."

Cynthia covered her mouth. "Oh God. Are you serious?" She endured another prolonged pause from Charlie.

"While she was still in the hospital, Gene asked a doctor friend of his to run a DNA test on the fetus to see if it was his baby—took a few days to find out, but it turned out it was."

Cynthia released her breath in a rush. "And of course, Gene blamed himself for being the cause of her never being able to have children."

Charlie nodded. "Of course, and I believe she was more than happy to use it against him—as a form of emotional blackmail."

"Well, Charlie, based on what I witnessed, it sounds like he was more than happy to accommodate her."

"The thing is, he thought for sure Tamara would tire of him and move on. It turned out she was too desperate."

"No more desperate than Gene to keep me in the dark." Cynthia gave him a tight smile and shook her head. "But Gene was far too intelligent to fall for something so ridiculous. If he continued the affair it was for one reason— because it gave him a thrill."

Charlie's jaw dropped. "Cyndi, you knew Gene better than anyone. How can you say that?"

She lifted her hands and let them fall to her sides. "You said it. I knew Gene better than anyone."

His eyes darkened with anger. "You're wrong about this."

John Michael stepped forward, his mouth tight with fury. "It seems to me you're angry at the wrong person. Your friend cheated on his wife and got you and everyone else in your department involved in covering up his infidelity. I know *brotherhoods* always take care of their own, but I was raised by a belief that every man has to earn respect, and every man is answerable for his own mistakes." He stepped forward, raised one forefinger to hammer his point home. "Your mistake was enabling your best friend to continue with his affair by accepting it."

"It wasn't my place to say—"

"By keeping quiet, you sent the message of acceptance," John Michael insisted, cutting off his lame excuse. "You let him get away with it. Hell, he ran with it and that's on you. If that girl hadn't crashed the funeral, Gene would have gone to his grave with everyone believing he was an honorable man."

Charlie stepped forward to meet him head on. "You didn't know him."

"It kind of sounds like you didn't, either."

Cynthia stepped between the two men, turned to address Charlie. "Go home to your wife and try to forget about all this. Accept it. Gene did what he did for so long because he *wanted* to, whether anyone wants to believe it or not. He wasn't perfect. He wasn't the fine, upstanding man we all thought he was, or maybe he was, but with a single flaw. One hidden corner of his mind that convinced him he had no choice in the matter, when nothing was further from the truth."

Charlie's face fell in utter defeat. "It floors me you think you're so sure about this, Cindy."

"I am sure." She showed him to the door. "Goodbye, Charlie. Be careful driving in this rain." She closed the door on him. Turning, she found John Michael's gaze locked onto hers. Without a word, he opened his arms and she walked to him, relishing the feel of comforting arms around her.

"I'm sorry, Cyn. I tried to keep quiet, I really did."

She closed her eyes and rested her face against his broad chest. "Don't apologize for defending me."

He rocked her back and forth, holding her tightly in the silence of the room for several moments before he broke it by speaking. "If you don't mind me asking, how *can* you be so sure about what you said to him? I mean, the man is dead and he didn't admit to anything, did he? Isn't it possible—"

She pulled away from him and shook her head. "I have my reasons. Believe me, I'm right about this." She wiped a tear from the corner of one eye and clamped her jaw against the pain nagging and pushing at her, no matter how hard she tried to set it aside. She'd be so happy if she could find a way to erase it from history.

He grabbed her hand when she tried to turn away from him, his blue eyes turning a shade darker as he brought his face level to hers. "Tell me, Cyn. If it'll help you to get it out, tell me. You have my word no one else will ever hear it from me."

His sincerity touched her—touched the one place in her heart she'd tried to harden against the pain of her husband's deceit. Judging by the tears tightening her throat, cutting off her breath, she'd failed miserably. He pulled her close, one large hand moving in soft, comforting circles on her back as the fingers of his other gently massaged the base of her skull. Her barrier crumbled and hot tears trailed down her cheeks, soaking the front of his shirt.

He led her to the couch, sat, and then pulled her onto his lap. She buried her face in his shoulder, both hands clasped around his neck. Even then she was in control, holding back the body wracking sobs he'd expected. It bothered him. He didn't expect her to be an out of control, blubbering mess—but he wanted some kind of relief for her.

He understood though and held his tongue. She'd had to be strong for her children. She'd had to find a way to grieve for a husband who'd committed the ultimate sin, the ultimate betrayal—was still committing it at his time of death. Jesus. What a soul-crushing dilemma.

He made an honest attempt not to hate the man who'd done this to her. She said he'd always treated her well. He'd been a good man with one flaw, one mark against him. But damn, it was one hellacious black, ugly mark. Try as he might, he couldn't understand how a man who loved his wife could deceive her in such a way. There wasn't a doubt in his mind Gene had loved his wife. No way could he have been married to this woman and not loved her.

Cynthia's too-brief allowance of tears ended and she tried to lift herself away from him. "I'm probably too heavy for you."

He held her there with a firm, but gentle grip. "You're kidding, right? You weigh nothing." He sensed the moment of her surrender, the second she quit trying to run and settled into his embrace. It took a few more seconds of waiting patiently before she finally began to speak, her voice cracking at first, until she found her reserve of strength. The same strength she'd, no doubt, been relying so heavily on since her nightmare had begun.

"Two years ago, around our anniversary, Gene was scheduled for a week of training in Tulsa. The last night, he'd made reservations at this fancy restaurant and asked me to meet him. The plan was to spend one night at the hotel and drive home together the next morning.

I made it there a little early so I was sitting at the bar waiting for him. He walked up behind me as the bartender brought me my second drink and asked if I was alone. I played along, and said I was for the time being. He asked if he could buy me a drink. I said it depended on whether he expected anything in return because I was a married woman."

She used the handkerchief he gave her to wipe her eyes. "He gave me some corny line. I said he was wasting his time. He'd have to be a hell of a man to steal me away from my husband. He said if I gave him one chance, he'd make me forget all about him. We ended up cancelling the dinner reservation and I followed him to his hotel room, where we kept up the pretense of being strangers."

She stopped, drew in a long breath and released it slowly. "It was the hottest night of sex I'd had with my husband in years. I thought it was the simple change in routine. But Gene admitted it had been the temptation of forbidden fruit. He said it excited the hell out of him."

"This was two years ago, and he died—what—about twenty months ago? So . . ."

Her low chuckle was tinged with the slightest hint of hysteria. "You got it. My husband must have been running on sensory overload that night. Not one, but *two* dirty little affairs."

John examined her hand, turned it over to place a soft kiss on the inside of her palm, wanting more than ever to erase every miserable ghost of a memory the son of a bitch had left her.

"After he died it took me a year not to get physically ill every time I thought of that night."

He swallowed the bile rising in his own throat at the level of betrayal and pain it must have caused her. "I can see why. Hell, I'm halfway there myself."

"You know, he asked me never to tell another soul about it, like it would be our little secret—something to keep the heat in our marriage." She shook her head. "I didn't know why, but it made me a little nervous at the time—self-conscious and unsure of myself. I asked him if he thought what we had, our life, our marriage, wasn't *enough* for him. He laughed at me, said it was more than enough, it was perfect and he'd never need anything else."

Cynthia turned to face him, her eyes filled with a sadness he hated seeing there. "Obviously, he lied."

John pulled her close, placed a soft kiss on her forehead. "So what did your shrink have to say when you told her about you and Gene's little sex-capade?"

"You're the only person I've ever told."

Her admission shocked him. "Are you kidding me?"

"It shamed me, John Michael. It still does. I didn't want another human being on earth to know about it."

"But you told me."

"Yes, I did."

"Does that make me special?"

"Yes. I believe it does." She lifted her plump lips to his and kissed him, chastely at first, then deepened it, tugging at his tongue. She nipped at his lower lip then wiggled out of his lap and stood, her hand reaching out for him.

He took it and pulled himself to his feet.

She turned, tugging at his hand. "Follow me, John Michael."

He balked slightly. "Where to?"

"Don't ask questions."

She pulled him down the hall to what was obviously her bedroom. He stopped in the doorway. "So, you want our first time to be in your mom's house?"

Her eyes sparkled with something—something not quite humorous. "Maybe. What's wrong? Don't you want to do it in my mom's house?"

"Not really, no."

She reached up onto her toes and nipped at his lower lip. "Why? Are you afraid she'll come home and catch us?"

He set her at arm's length. "As a matter of fact, I am. I wouldn't want to disrespect your mother, and frankly, I don't want her to lose respect for either of us."

Her lower lip jutted out in a sexy pout. "Don't you want me, John Michael?"

His gut soured at her question, knowing full-well what was behind it. "By now, you *should* know better than to ask, Cyn. Even if you don't, you need to remember one thing. I'm not Gene."

The light in her eyes dimmed. "I didn't imply you were."

"Implied, no. Assumed my preferences would mirror his—maybe." The thought irked the hell out of him. "Do I want you? Hell yeah, but not because you're forbidden fruit. Not here in your mother's house because we'd risk getting caught."

He pointed at his chest to emphasize his next comment. "I already know I don't want anyone else. When you can say the same thing about me then we'll make love. It'll be a night when we know we're committed to each other and only each other, and it will be both sexually and emotionally fulfilling and satisfying. Not just an afternoon romp of forbidden sex to act out a little revenge on a husband who died cheating on you."

She turned away, her arms crossed tightly across her chest. "I don't understand why you're so upset."

"Really, Cyn? You told me something you'd never told another living soul. I don't know why you can't see it, but I have to ask myself why—why wouldn't you share something like that with your shrink during six months of sessions with her? She's the one person who could help you to sort out your feelings."

He shook his head. "Maybe this is all too soon for you. Maybe you're not finished nursing the hurt Gene left you with. It's like an old, flat beer—one you keep taking tiny little sips from, even though it does nothing to quench your thirst."

Cyn swung around to face him again, her eyes bright with anger. She had to see it. She was far too intelligent not to realize his words rang with truthfulness.

"You're being ridiculous now."

"Am I? I don't think so."

"Well, maybe you should go, then."

He stared at the stubborn lift of her chin. "I'm sorry, Cyn, but I'd rather our first time be somewhere we don't have to sneak around, and preferably when you're not using me to hurt a dead man."

Her eyes narrowed. "Well, what if I don't want to do it at *your* house? How is it fair to me—in the house you shared with Beth?"

He stepped forward, leaned in low until they were nose to nose. "I'll tell you what, hon. When you're ready to commit to me, and only me, you let me know. I'll take you someplace neither of us has ever been before and we'll make love all day and all damn night if you can keep up with me. If by some chance you decide I'm worth keeping around, I'll sell my damn house and everything in it if you want me to. I'll buy or build us another house. Would that make you happy?"

"Maybe." She paired her two syllable comeback with a careless shrug.

Her actions irritated the living hell out of him, but he let it go, suspecting her anger and hurt feelings were really targeted at Gene rather than himself. "When you know for sure, you let me know, Cyn. I'm not here to play games."

John grabbed his Stetson and walked calmly out of the house. His feelings contradicted the storm rumbling in his chest, even as the phrase "tough love" bounced around in his head. He buckled himself into his truck and peeled out of the driveway before he could change his mind.

During the entire trip home it took a concentrated effort not to turn his truck around. All he could think about right now was going back there to take what she'd offered so generously.

Chapter Ten

After two days of nursing the hurt from John Michael's rejection, Cynthia found herself reconsidering his words. He'd accused her of wanting to have sex for all the wrong reasons—not only as revenge against Gene, but because the danger of being caught pushed the excitement level to maximum. Suddenly the facts hit her square in the face. A painful, secret, hidden ache—the reason she couldn't seem to let the past go.

She was far too comfortable being angry with Gene to admit knowing why he'd done what he did. Although she didn't agree with it, she understood it. So, why *hadn't* she told her therapist what she'd shared John?

It was one thing to admit it to herself. It took another long miserable week, a week of no contact with John Michael, of moping around at work and at home, before she could do what she should have done a year earlier.

She picked up the phone and called the number she still had memorized. After a brief exchange with the answering service, she got the phone call back from the woman she'd spent hundreds of hours speaking to about her marriage, Gene, and the other woman.

Two hours later, she hit the end button, knowing this time she'd truly crossed a threshold. She'd put the old hurt behind her.

Cynthia glanced at her bedroom alarm clock—six-fifteen on a Tuesday evening. Should she call or just show up at John Michael's place for a long overdue apology? She called his mobile and got no answer, and then his landline with the same result before calling his dad's place.

"Hey, Mr. J.D., it's Cynthia. Would John Michael happen to be there? He didn't answer his cell or home phone."

"He left for home a few minutes ago, Cynthia. I know his cell phone was about to die. Is everything all right? He's seemed kind of down the last several days."

"My fault entirely, sir, but I'm about to make it right."

His deep laughter echoed from her speaker. "Good to hear. Oh, in case you're wondering, I won't bother or call him for the rest of the evening."

"Thanks Mr. J.D." She ended the call and grabbed her purse as she headed into the living room. "Mom, I'm going to John Michael's place. I have my phone with me if you need anything at all."

Bess looked up from her spot on the sofa, reading glasses perched on the tip of her nose as she worked out the daily paper's crossword puzzle. "Okay sweet girl. Take your time."

Cynthia grabbed her keys, paused long enough to hear her mom's mumbled comment.

"About damn time, if you ask me."

Cynthia approached John Michael's door ten minutes later, her stomach a ball of queasy nervous tension. What if he booted her ass to the curb without hearing her out?

When several knocks on the front door produced nothing, Cynthia walked to the kitchen entry. The wooden door was open, but the glass storm door was closed. She knocked, again with no answer, and tried the latch. It opened easily, so she took a tentative step inside and called out to him.

No answer.

Her gaze landed on two large bags on the kitchen counter, one filled with tomatoes and the other with yellow squash. Two huge purple eggplants sat next to the bags—all products of his greenhouse gardening skills, no doubt.

"John, are you here?" She paused as a door opened in the hallway.

"I'm coming!" he called out, the sound of his voice slightly muffled.

She turned toward the doorway, froze in place when he appeared, bare-chested and damp from his shower, a dark blue towel draped around his waist as he dried his hair with a smaller hand towel.

"Take everything I left for you there on the table, Zach. I'm not in the mood to mess with any of it right now and there's no more room in my fridge. I guess I need to plant fewer vegetables from now on."

She swallowed at the sight of his broad, bare chest, feathered with a mixture of silky dark and silvery hair. He may not have the twelve pack abs of a body builder, but the abdominal muscles of his naturally lean torso were still nicely defined with no sign of flab. His bare biceps rippled with strength as he rubbed the towel briskly in his hair.

She cleared her throat, putting a halt to his towel action. "Or I could show you how to freeze and can some of this stuff.

He lowered the hand towel, his eyes wide with the shock of seeing her. "Oh sh-i-i-it! I thought you were Zachary." He backed into the hallway, presumably to put some clothes on.

"Don't go on my account." She lifted one brow as he froze in place. "I'm kind of liking the view."

He crossed his arms before striking a nonchalant pose against the doorframe, one size twelve foot crossed over the other. "Well, all right then. What is it you want, Cyn?"

"I'm here to apologize to you, John Michael. You were right about everything, and I'm so sorry if I insulted you."

He nodded. "Apology accepted, hon. But what I really want to hear is whether or not you've dealt with what Gene did to you. Are you ready to put it behind you? I can't see us moving forward until you do."

Several slow, deliberate steps had her standing before him. Her hands itched to reach out and touch him, to flatten her palms against his glorious bare abs. Her fingers longed to yank out that tucked-in-corner of the towel draped loosely around his hips. "I had a two hour phone session with my therapist. She says you were right by the way."

"Good to know." He lifted one hand to rub his chin. "Maybe I should hang a sign out front and take in patients." He sucked in his breath as she placed her hands on his waist.

"Maybe you won't have time for any patients other than the one standing in front of you."

He leaned forward to place a kiss on the tip of her nose. "Maybe you're right. I'm thinking you may be a hand full all by your lonesome."

Her hands traced twin sensuous paths up his sides and shoulders to link behind his neck as his arms wrapped around her. She lifted up to her toes to accept the kiss he offered freely. Tongues entwined, fingers knotted in his hair, his hands clutching her shoulders then pressing gently at the back of her head— they finally parted, both breathing hard and gasping for air.

Her gaze landed on the obvious below-the-waist "tenting" of his towel and cleared her throat. "Speaking of a hand full—"

"I've got enough."

Her mouth twisted in a sardonic grin. "Looks like more than enough." She cocked her head and reached slowly for the towel. He remained in place, his expression frozen except for the slightest lift of his left brow over "Ferguson blue" eyes sparkling with amusement. Emboldened, the forefinger of her right hand slipped under the towel's edge, slid a path along the front of his hard belly. Her left hand reached for the folded edge, tugged gently at it. The corner slipped free the exact moment the sound of shoes hit the front porch, followed by the sound of two people conversing.

John Michael uttered a mild curse and clutched the towel tightly as he ducked into the hallway and then his room.

"Hello! We're here for the vegetables, Dad."

Momentarily at a loss, Cynthia rushed to the kitchen where both Zach and Cathryn were stepping inside, each carrying a seat holding an infant. "Hey, you two—and you have the babies." She clapped her hands excitedly. "Oh, give!" She found a bottle of hand sanitizer while Cathryn freed the blue-clad infant from the seat.

"Here you go." Cat handed her son over to Cynthia. "This one ate recently so he should be good for a while."

"Oh, hello there, Caleb. You are growing like a weed, aren't you, young man?" Cynthia settled onto the couch, cuddling the baby to her chest. Cat sat beside her, holding Cassandra. Cynthia gasped at the beautiful baby girl. "Look at these two. I'm a pediatrician and it always amazes me to see how quickly these little human beings grow. Your breast milk must be agreeing with them."

Cat nodded. "It must be. They aren't showing signs of colic or anything, thank goodness."

Zach sat across from them on the stuffed ottoman. "They actually slept six hours straight last night. Man, we thought we'd died and gone to heaven."

"It's fabulous when that starts happening, isn't it? All it takes is a few uninterrupted hours of sleep to remind you all's right with the world again." Cynthia ran her fingers through Caleb's soft, dark hair. "It's funny how those memories stick with you."

She heard a sound at the door and looked up to where John Michael stood watching them, his handsome face covered in a satisfied smile. Her heart skipped a beat—strange how she found the sight of him dressed in faded jeans, a T-shirt, and bare feet, almost as alluring as him wearing a dark blue towel, and nothing else. Both visages equally turned her insides to mush. "Hey there, Paw Paw Johnny. You have visitors."

"So I see. It's about time these two make it over to my place. Mom and Dad must have needed a change of scenery."

Cat groaned at his comment. "You have no idea. Sometimes Zach walks in the door and I run out with a grocery list I've been adding to all day long—just so I can get out for a bit. I stay home with them unless I have help. It takes entirely too much baby paraphernalia to haul them around."

John leaned over to take Cassandra from Cat. "Hey, pretty girl, come to Paw Paw." Cat stood to make room for him beside Cynthia. He placed a kiss on his daughter in law's cheek. "Sit, Cathryn."

Cathryn ignored him and sat on Zachary's lap. "You sit there next to Doc Cynthia. I've got a better spot." She looped her arm around her husband's neck and sent Cynthia a secretive smile. "I hope we didn't interrupt anything. We can cut this visit short if the two of you have plans."

"No. I popped in for a short visit myself." Cynthia nudged John gently with her shoulder. "I owed him an apology. And I also wanted to let him know I need a date for a road trip this weekend, if he's interested." She turned to John Michael and made a face. "Something came up on August 1st, so Jeremy's surprise party has been moved up a week to *this* Friday, July 25th. I understand if you can't make it on such short notice."

He stared down at her. "Are you still planning on driving to Little Rock?"

"Absolutely."

"Then I'm going with you. I don't want you making the drive alone."

"If you'd rather not go—"

"And I *want* to go with you to meet your kids."

She leaned in to kiss him on the cheek, lingering there long enough to whisper a quick "Thank you." He surprised her by shifting his head to kiss her on the lips.

"Anytime, Cyn."

Cat clapped her hands together. "Oh my God—you two are the sweetest couple."

"Cat—don't embarrass them."

Zach's grumbled comment had Cynthia laughing. "We're not embarrassed."

"Okay, then. Don't embarrass *me*," Zach said. "I'm not used to seeing my dad make out with a chick. And besides—" He turned to his wife. "I thought *we* were the sweetest couple."

Cat lowered her chin but looked up at her husband with huge brown eyes. "We are, but I'm thinking *that* particular chick is here to stay, so you'd better get accustomed to them acting all touchy-feely, kissy-kissy—and quickly, Zach-Attack."

Zach cleared his throat, threw a glance at his dad for a little support from the only other man in the room.

John Michael shrugged. "Don't look at me. I'm hoping she's right."

John Michael sent one last wave to the little family of four before closing the door and turning to Cynthia. He wrapped his large hands around her hips and pulled her close. "So, what time are we leaving on Friday?"

She tucked her chin into the crook of his neck. "Mm—I'd like to leave around eight a.m. It'll give us a little time to rest up before the party." She curled her hands around the back of his neck and lifted her face. "I want to apologize again for acting the way I did on Sunday."

John leaned in to kiss her, released a low growl as her hands slipped beneath his shirt, her cool fingertips teasing and tantalizing against the rapid heating of his skin. He pivoted, shoved her gently against the wall for another kiss. Cynthia responded with a satisfied groan—her sweet lips, warm, pliant mouth molding to his, returning everything he offered. He pressed against her, his arousal thick, hard, and too damned obvious to ignore. He sucked in his breath, joining in with her perfectly harmonized groan—their shared ache unifying them in their need.

Face flushed, she tried to catch her breath. "I think I may be ready, John Michael."

He kissed her again, ended it by nibbling on her lower lip, eliciting another needy groan from her. He pulled back, smoothed her hair, her blouse, and stepped away after a short period of painful contemplation. "*May* be ready isn't exactly a given, Cyn. When you know for sure, I'll be here." He kissed her neck, satisfaction rolling through him at her involuntary shiver.

He placed his hands on her shoulders and turned her gently toward the door. "Now, get the hell out of here before I change my mind. If I'm going on a long weekend with you, I've got some business to tend to. I've got a distinct feeling if you're around, the only business I'll be taking care of is you."

She grabbed her purse from the wall hook and turned, wearing a smug grin. "Sounds good to me." She reached up and kissed him, her mouth lingering on his long enough to let him know she was on the brink of wanting so much more. She pulled back, peeking up at him through her long lashes. "I have a feeling it's going to be an interesting weekend."

He clenched his jaw against the all-too-familiar tightening in his groin. "Mm . . . I can hardly wait."

Chapter Eleven

They made it to Bryant, a city southwest of Little Rock by two-thirty on Friday afternoon, stopping only once for a quick-lunch, bathroom-break, leg-stretching opportunity. The drive from Louisiana had been rampant with sexual tension—each simple skin-to-skin contact led to something more sensual. Each secretive smile, each common phrase suddenly turned into something loaded with sexual innuendo, each song filled with subliminal messaging. Each passing moment of what should have been an ordinary trip had transformed the interior of her car into their personal torture chamber of sexually charged atmosphere.

They'd begun the trip listening to Cyn's collection of music from her Mp3 player plugged into her sedan's stereo system. Somehow they'd both thought music would be a safe way to pass the time. It had started innocently enough with James Otto's upbeat *Somewhere Tonight*, along with a few choice numbers from Florida Georgia Line, Luke Bryan, and Hunter Hayes. When Chuck Wicks upped the sexy factor with *Hold That Thought* it clearly smashed their theory to bits. John Michael had come close to pulling the car over onto the side of the road for a serious make-out session. They'd switched it to a country radio station, only to have Jake Owen continue the torture tactics by crooning *Alone With You*. As a result, they'd stuck to the Classic Rock radio stations. Singing along to CCR and The Doobie Brothers proved to be a much safer mode of entertainment for their particular afflictions.

Finally, they arrived, thus ending the six and a half hour long foreplay session.

John stood beside her at the hotel's check-in desk. He pulled out his wallet, slipped out his credit card. "We should have two rooms reserved under John Ferguson, and I'll take care of both."

The auburn haired man behind the desk flashed them a bright smile as he took his card. "Yes sir." The man's fingers flew over the computer keyboard and stopped suddenly. "Uh, sir. I seem to have one room reserved in this name."

Cynthia placed a hand on his arm. "John Michael—"

He raised his hand to halt her comment. "That's not acceptable, we'll need another."

"I'm sorry sir, but we have no other availabilities."

"Are you serious?"

"Yes sir. I'm sorry, but we're booked solid for a softball tournament."

"John Mi—"

He turned to her, mortified by the situation. "I'm sorry Cyn. I don't know how this happened. You booked two rooms, didn't you?"

"I booked one room, John Michael—only one."

He froze—his gaze glued to her face as the realization of what she'd done finally hit home. This was her personal message—her way of telling him she was ready to commit. "Are you sure?"

"Absolutely."

He turned back to the desk clerk and cleared his throat. "I'll be taking care of the room with this card."

The clerk's gaze caught his for a split second, long enough to exchange a barely perceptible, silent, man-to-man, high-five, atta-boy moment, before returning quickly to his business at the keyboard. "All right, sir. I've got you set up. It's a corner room on the south side of the hotel with plenty of privacy." He handed over an envelope containing two card keys. "If you pull your car under the awning, I'll have the bellman unload your luggage and bring it to your room."

John Michael met Cyn's gaze as she slipped her right hand inside of his and squeezed. He repressed a shiver as she stood close and ran the fingers of her opposite hand up the inside of his arm, a gentle reminder he supposed, of things to come. He forced himself to turn his attention back to the hotel employee. He rejected the thought of the two of them alone in a room and having to wait for a bellman to deliver their luggage. "That won't be necessary. I have a single duffle and whatever she has, I can handle."

"Yes sir." The clerk's brow rose. "You certainly look like you can. If you'd prefer, you can drive around and park on the south end entrance. Your room is around the corner from the elevator."

Wordlessly, they drove around to the south entrance, found a parking spot under a tree for a little protection from the blazing sun. John Michael made short work of stacking her luggage and carrying it inside. They stood, arms touching as they waited for an elevator to reach the first floor. Once inside, they stood as near as they could to each other, a prelude to what was coming. John's heart thumped loudly in his chest as the doors opened with a gentle swoosh. As the clerk described, their room was around the corner.

After Cyn tried unsuccessfully several times to swipe her card, he took it from her shaky hands. Guided by sheer determination and a need to get her alone in their room, John got the door opened in one try. He pushed it open and followed her inside, practically throwing the luggage inside the room. He turned, saw her hook the DO NOT DISTURB placard on the door knob before closing and locking the door. She faced him then, the rapid rising and falling of her chest a sure sign her itch was every bit as bad as his.

He forced himself to take a deep breath and swallow. "Cyn, are you absolutely sure ab—"

She threw herself at him, her mouth on his, immediately smothering any question, stifling any doubt he may have been harboring toward this weekend.

She pulled at his shirt, jerked it roughly out of his jeans, pushing it off of his arms. Bare-chested, he lifted her shirt over her head in a single motion, and then unsnapped her jean shorts. With a gentle swipe of his fingers they fell to the floor. She stepped out of them without hesitation, her fingers clawing at the button and then the zipper of his jeans. In seconds she'd pushed them down then shoved him back onto the bed.

His breath failed him as she kneeled in front of him, only to help him out of his boots. Once those were off she pulled the jeans from his legs. He managed to hold her off until he stood beside her.

"Slow down, Cyn. I want to see you."

She shook her head, panting now. "I can't slow down, John Michael. I can't. Not yet." She cupped her hand around him through his boxer briefs.

He sucked in his breath in a loud hiss that turned to a low groan as she wrapped her hand around him, her eyes widening in undisguised appreciation at what she found.

He reached out for the front hook closure of her lacy pink bra, unfastened it, freeing her full pale breasts to his touch. She groaned, her head falling back helplessly as he cupped one, then the other, his thumbs rubbing in light circular motions.

"Oh . . . that feels . . . oh Jo—"

His mouth closing over her right nipple cut off any reply she'd been formulating. He tasted her then cupped the back of her head, lifting her head so he could kiss her. With one hand he slipped off her matching lace panties and laid her gently on the bed. Taking her hands when she tried to cover the faint stretch marks on her belly, he shook his head. "Don't cover yourself, Cyn. You bore three children. You have nothing to be ashamed of."

She took a deep breath, released it slowly. "Now you, John Michael."

He stood tall, used both hands to slip out of his boxer briefs, finally freeing himself to her gaze. He tried like hell to relax, to acclimate himself to this kind of exposure to the first woman since his wife. His body had gone through some changes since he'd last bared his all to anyone.

"Cyn . . . I haven't . . . not since . . . her."

She nodded slowly. "I know."

He passed his fingers through his hair and grinned. "I hope I remember how."

Her eyes sparkled with mischief. "I'm not worried." She reached out.

He took her hand, stretched out beside her on the bed, and supported himself on one elbow. He cupped her breast gently, and began the slow circular motion with his thumb, smiled when her eyelids closed—even as her beautiful lips parted with a sigh.

"Do I need to get you ready, babe?"

Her eyelashes fluttered opened. "What?"

He leaned over to kiss her, pulled back to nibble on her lip, then her earlobe. "It's been a while but I'm fairly certain I can find that G-spot for you if you need me to."

She raised herself onto her elbow to face him, tunneled the fingers of her free hand into his hair. "I don't need any extra stimulation at the moment. How about we save it for later?" She curled her fingers around the back of his neck and pulled him on top of her.

She opened for him, sighed as he nudged himself up against her and waited.

"You can show me your tricks next time, John Michael. Right now I want you inside me."

He grinned, found himself wondering if she would have been this impatient had they been a couple three decades or so ago. And then he complied.

Cyn curled her fingers in his chest hair, hitched her knee a little higher on his thigh, willing her heartbeat to return to normal. "Is it me, or was that extraordinarily great?"

"No," he gasped. "It was pretty damn great." He lifted his head and eyed her. "You think there's a chance it was mediocre and we were both too hard up to realize it?"

"Maybe." She rested her chin on his chest and gazed into his eyes. "I suppose we'll have to do it again—you know, for comparison's sake."

His chest rumbled with laughter. "I'll need a little while to build up the old reserves, babe." He dropped his head back on the bed. "What I'd really like right now is a hot shower to work the kinks out from the drive. If memory serves, I caught a glimpse of a pretty nice set-up before you attacked me." He lifted her hand to his lips and kissed the spot above her knuckles. "Would you care to join me?"

"Hm. How about you go and I'll think about it?"

He rolled out of bed. "Sounds like a plan."

She watched him walk away from her, bare-ass naked and not a bit self-conscious. Of course, he had no reason to be, did he? Even at their age, the man was sexy as hell and easy on the eyes. The shower spewed and sputtered before it blasted to full pressure.

She rose from the rumpled bed and stood in front of the mirror at the desk. She passed her hands up her sides, and let them rest on her belly. Her fingers found the stretch marks as though magically drawn to the slight discolorations of skin. If only he could have seen her in her prime. Before she could feel too sorry for herself she remembered his words.

You have nothing to be ashamed of.

Those words had sounded as sweet as any declaration of love.

Love.

Did what she feel for John Michael compare to what she'd felt for her husband? The sound of him humming in the shower had her smiling. She took two steps toward the door to meet him then stopped suddenly, her mind flooded with memories. The morning of Gene's very last day on this earth, he'd joined her in the shower after her morning workout. They'd made love, giggling like a couple of school kids. Her mind made a feeble attempt to cloud with guilt, but then came to a screeching halt.

No guilt. This thing with John Michael wasn't about any need for revenge. This was between two people who were free to love whomever they wanted—and she damn sure knew she wanted him.

She smiled at her reflection in the mirror, however imperfect it may be, finally able to accept the flaws of a body that had passed the half-century mark by nearly four years.

She approached the shower stall, the steam only blocking part of the view from her hungry eyes. She opened the clear glass door and stepped inside. "Is there room in here for one more?"

John Michael turned, a wide smile plastered across his face. "We could fit a couch in this thing and still have room to move around. Come over here." His soapy arm slipped around her waist. He pulled her close and covered her mouth in a toe curling kiss.

She pulled back, already aching with need for him. "It *is* rather roomy, isn't it?"

He stuck his head under the spray of hot water to get the last bit of shampoo out of his hair then wiped his face with his hands. "I'm approving of this built-in shower seat. I may have to invest in one of these." He seated himself and crooked his finger at her until she stood before him. "Just because I need a little rest, doesn't mean you do." He lifted one of her legs, resting her foot beside him on the seat. Using his right hand to keep her balanced, he slid his left upward along the silky thigh to her core.

She sighed, closed her eyes at his gentle manipulation; let her head fall back as the sweet warmth, and the promise of more to come seeped through her. She sucked in her breath as he found it, pressed upward, applying a slight pressure in a steady rhythm. Within a few short minutes, he brought her—gasping, grasping at him, clutching at his shoulders, his neck, and calling out his name—to her second orgasm of the day. He stayed with it, letting her ride out the wave until the quaking and shudders deep within her had finally rolled to a stop.

Too weak to stand, she allowed him to pull her onto his lap. He held her there, speaking softly, soothing her until she regained her strength.

They exited the bathroom several minutes later, clean, dry, and too relaxed to do anything other than collapse onto the bed. All cozy and wrapped in his arms, her last thought before succumbing to sleep was to wonder if anything in her previous life had ever been this good.

Cynthia stood in the doorway of the small club, clutching at John Michael's hand. Within seconds, Tyler called out to her, rushed over to meet them.

"Mom!" He hugged her tightly. "I've been trying to call you. We were starting to worry you got lost or had car trouble or something."

"I'm sorry, Tyler. My ringer must be set to silent. We made it in earlier and took a nap. You know how us old people need our rest." She somehow managed to stifle the giggle threatening to bubble forth at any second.

"God, you look fantastic. You look happy, Mom."

She beamed at her youngest son. "I am, Ty. And this man is the main reason for my happiness. This is John Michael Ferguson, an old friend of mine."

Tyler extended his hand, his smile genuine. "And a little more than a friend if my guess is correct. Welcome, Mr. Ferguson. I'm Tyler Ellender, but everyone calls me Ty."

John Michael's chest seemed to broaden before her eyes as he shook her son's hand. "Thank you. Ty. Please call me John." He straightened, slipped his left hand lightly around Cynthia's waist and gave her a brilliant smile. "And your guess is right on the money."

Tyler's gaze flipped between the two of them. "Well, my mother has never looked more beautiful, and I trust her judgment completely. So, whatever this is, I approve whole-heartedly—not that it's a requirement."

Cynthia gazed up at John, waiting for his reaction to this first sign of acceptance.

"Required or not, it certainly is appreciated. Thank you, Ty."

His reply warmed Cynthia clear down to her freshly pedicured toenails.

Tyler introduced them both to his new girlfriend, Jessie, an exotically beautiful girl with an olive complexion, long, dark hair and warm brown eyes.

Jeremy's girl, Lena, the party planner, approached the foursome, breathless with excitement. "I'm so glad you could all make this. I apologize again for having to change the date."

Cynthia hugged her tightly and introduced Lena to John Michael. *So far, so good.* She looked around for her middle child. "Ty, is your sister here, yet?"

He checked his watch. "They should be here any minute. She sent a text a few minutes ago saying they were right around the corner." He looked up as the door opened. "There they are now." He gave John a sympathetic look. "I should probably apologize now for whatever selfish, thoughtless thing my sister does or says to upset you. Trini has been in a perpetual state of bitchiness for at least a decade."

Jessie slapped at his arm. "Ty, stop!"

"Well, it's true. *She* won't approve of John. She doesn't approve of anyone, not even you and Lena, and you two are perfect."

Jessie faced Lena and returned her grin. "What do you think, Lena? Should I keep him?"

Lena nodded. "Definitely."

Cynthia smiled at the young women who'd obviously already bonded. She prayed they would be her daughters-in-law one day. She turned to Tyler, deciding it wasn't too early to throw in her two cents worth. "You and Jeremy need to hang on to these two ladies."

Tyler gave Jessie a quick kiss. "I can't account for what goes on in my brother's head, but I'm hanging on to this one for as long as she'll have me." He straightened and cleared his throat as he gazed at his approaching sister and her family. "Batten down the hatches everyone. Here comes Hurricane Trini."

Cynthia turned and walked to meet her daughter halfway. "Trin, I'm so glad to see you." She wrapped her in a big hug. Her daughter returned it half-heartedly.

"Hello, Mother. Who's *that?*"

"He's a friend from home and he's with me." She turned to her son-in-law. "Mick. I've missed you, sweetie."

He gave her a big hug. "Hey, Mom. You look great. So, a new man, huh? He must be treating you right to put that glow on your face."

She elbowed him. "Oh stop, Mick. And let me have my granddaughter. Hello, sweetie pie. Grammy's missed you so much."

"Well, you wouldn't have if you hadn't sold our home and moved two states away."

Trini's snarled reply had Cynthia's shoulders stiffening. "I've explained this, Trin. Your father got to spend their entire lifetimes near both his parents. I hadn't seen my dad for six months when he died. I'm spending what's left of my mother's life near her. I'm sorry if you can't understand that."

"Or maybe it's someone else you wanted to be near. It's kind of soon to be replacing Daddy, don't you think?"

Mick stepped in front of his wife, lowered his voice to a dangerously low level. "Okay, Trini. You need to stop this before you say something we'll all regret."

"And you need to mind your own business. This is a *family* matter."

"Excuse me, but I thought I was family."

"*My* family."

Cynthia couldn't take the hurt look on her son-in-law's face one more second. "For God's sake, Trin. This man is your husband."

"Then he needs to act like one and take my side, not yours. Not to mention he needs to stop whatever he's doing when he's not with his daughter and his wife."

Mick's face darkened with anger. "So, you want me to quit my job and be a stay at home bum who doesn't support his family? Work Trini, that's all I *do* when I'm not with you." He threw his hands in the air and headed toward Tyler and the others.

Tyler groaned as Mick approached their group, his face a study in tightly reined fury. "Here come's brother-in-law. Poor guy's obviously incurred the gorgon's wrath early on." He handed him his newly opened beer. "Here Mick, you look like you need this more than I do right now."

Cynthia's son-in-law took the beer and chugged from it. He wiped his mouth and used one finger to single out Ty. "Your sister, man. I don't know what the hell to do about her."

"Jeremy and I tried to warn you. We said you were too nice for her, but you wouldn't listen." Tyler turned to John. "His wife is the biggest brat you ever saw, and it's all Dad's fault. He spoiled her rotten, then died on us, and left poor Mick holding the bag."

John Michael figured he had a good grip on the situation. It was one thing to hear it from Cynthia. The siblings and son-in-law being in full agreement only strengthened her statement. "Hi Mick. I'm John Ferguson."

Tyler nudged Mick's side. "He's Mom's boyfriend. How do you think my big sis is going to take the news?"

Mick shook John's hand and gave him a sympathetic smile. "It's real nice to meet you, John. I feel for you, man. Just remember one thing. You get to leave."

"You could too, if she's not careful," Tyler threw in. "Maybe it's time you remind my sister. I don't know how the hell you put up with her."

"I married Trini before God, for better or worse. I figure this is part of the worst. We'll work through it."

John Michael's admiration of Cynthia's son-in-law grew by leaps and bounds at the man's answer. He nodded. "I've heard wonderful things about you from Cyn—and now I understand why. Speaking of which, your mother-in-law looks like she could use a buffer right about now." He took two steps in Cyn and Trini's direction.

"*And* John's going into the depths of hell for the woman he loves, aka *my mom*. Cue the love theme from *Act of Valor*." Tyler's movie trailer narration had John pausing to wipe a grin from his face as Lena and Jessie dissolved into laughter.

"Dude, you *must* be in love."

Mick's comment had John nodding in agreement.

"Good luck, Mr. John," Jessie offered.

"It was nice knowing you," Lena volunteered.

He turned to give the group another grin and a one-handed farewell wave.

He approached the two women, his poor Cyn looking like she wanted to throttle the daughter doling out a steady diatribe of viciousness. The tail end of Trini's nasty accusation reached his ears as he joined them.

"—dishonor my father's memory by bringing your boyfriend here? I bet you were even in contact with him before Daddy passed away."

"Excuse me, Trini, but I wanted to introduce myself." He bowed slightly at the waist, knowing damn good and well she wouldn't touch his hand, much less shake it. "I'm John Ferguson. Your mom and I have known each other forever, of course, but up until a couple of months ago, I hadn't seen or spoken to her since our high school graduation. It's wonderful to finally meet you, though. You are every bit as beautiful as I've heard." He turned to the toddler in Cynthia's arms. "And who is this lovely young lady? You're as gorgeous as your mom and grandma, aren't you?"

The golden haired child gave him a gap toothed grin, exposing two adorable dimples as she rested her head on Cynthia's chest. "*My* Gwammy."

John sent "Gwammy" a look of encouragement and a wink as lagniappe. "Yes, she is. So, what's your name, gorgeous?"

She put a chubby finger to her chest and grinned. "Zo-ee."

"Zoe, huh? That's a beautiful name for a beautiful girl. I'm John. Can you say John?"

She gave him an enthusiastic nod. "John!"

"Very good, Zoe. I've got two grandbabies at home, you know. Two month old twins named Caleb and Cassandra. And I bet Cassie grows up to be as pretty as you."

Zoe cocked her head to the side. "Two babies?"

He chuckled. "Yes ma'am. Two of them."

Trini snorted from behind him. "I can't even imagine having to care for two babies. Zoe takes up every spare minute I have."

"Well, my daughter-in-law nearly lost her life bringing those two little miracles into the world. But that doesn't stop her from being the best mother she can be to her children. She adores them and my son, and he feels the same way. That's all any of us want, right Cyn? To know our kids are happy and loved?"

"And where's your wife, John? Did you leave her at home to go traipsing off with my mother?"

He turned to face the young woman. As prepared as he was, the hateful accusation still shocked the hell out of him. He swallowed the *"Perhaps you've mistaken me for your father?"* line he longed to throw in her face, for both Cyn and Trini's sakes. "No, I've been alone since my wife died almost fifteen years ago, so it's been a real blessing to have your mother come into my life when she did."

He'd obviously peaked Trini's curiosity. It won the battle over her desire to ignore him. "Was it cancer? Everyone from *Louisiana* dies from either cancer or diabetes."

John's light touch to Cyn's arm stopped her from chastising her daughter for the rude, insensitive comment. "No, she died during an emergency appendectomy surgery. She had an adverse reaction to the anesthesia."

"Oh, I assumed—"

"But my mother did have cancer at one time, if that makes you feel any more superior than you already do. Unlike your grandfather, Mr. Ham, she beat it. But she'll be gone soon enough. As it turns out, Alzheimer's is no picnic in the park, either."

Trini stared at the floor, apparently having the good sense to feel at least some amount of remorse for her tactlessness. She turned and left them without another word.

"Oh, John, I'm so sor—"

He smothered her apology with a kiss. "It's not your responsibility to apologize for her, Cyn. She'll come around."

"You handled her very well." She patted his chest with one hand, probably more for her own comfort than his.

"It comes from owning and operating a business. I deal with customers—some of them ornery and difficult. I can handle her." His second kiss to comfort her had Zoe giggling.

"Kiss Gwammy."

He laughed. "I sure did. You want to see it again?" Zoe gave him an enthusiastic nod, so he pecked Cyn a third time, causing another round of little girl giggles. In an unexpected move, she reached out for him. He took the toddler from Cyn and rested her on one hip. "Oh yeah, I can't wait for the twins to be this age."

Cyn crossed her arms, wearing a satisfied expression. "It's obvious you have a way with women. You've already won Zoe over, as well as my son's girlfriends." She nudged him into lifting his gaze to the two women watching from several feet over. "Look at that. They're practically melting at the sight of you holding this child."

He grinned and waved to them, then leaned over to give Cynthia another kiss. "There you go, three members of the fairer sex down, and one to go. Don't worry, babe. I got this."

They returned to the other group. Cynthia placed her hand on Lena's arm. "So, when will Jeremy be here, and where do we go to surprise him?"

Lena clapped her hands together then waved her phone. "Jeremy just sent me a text and said he'll be here in about ten minutes, but I've got a look-out in the parking lot. He can stall him for a little extra time if we need it. My plan is brilliant in its simplicity. Your son will never suspect a thing. Everybody with us, follow me, please!"

John had to admire her plan, which truly was simple and brilliant. Jeremy entered the club and joined his girlfriend at the bar. He had a casual drink with a couple of friends they'd met up with, one of whom introduced him to John

Michael, an "acquaintance". Relaxed and discussing business with a couple of old co-workers he'd spotted at the end of the bar, Jeremy followed the group into the restaurant section of the club. One by one, his family members quietly seated themselves at his table while he was deep in conversation with his friends, his back turned.

"I'm starving, babe. Are you ready to order?"

Jeremy paused in his conversation to study the menu Lena pushed in his face.

"So, what do you recommend, bro?"

"The redfish is great here—" He stopped, turned to face his brother. "Ty, what the hell?"

"I hear the T-bone is better, but they have a tendency to overcook it, so order it medium rare, Son."

Jeremy whipped around to where his mother had scooted in behind him. "Mom—what the . . ." He scanned the faces of the multitude of friends and co-workers who'd slipped in around the table while he wasn't paying attention. Another shout out had him searching the crowd who'd lined up behind him. His gaze landed on Lena as his mouth spread in a slow grin. "Oh hell, babe. You got me. You really got me."

"I did, didn't I?"

Mick stepped out from behind a wall, holding his daughter. He cleared his throat. "Hey, Uncle Jeremy, I think Zoe has something to tell you."

"She does?" He turned to his niece. "What's up, Zo?"

The little girl threw her hands up in the air. "Su-pwize!"

Jeremy burst into laughter as everyone followed suit. "Oh man, I cannot believe this." He turned to his girlfriend, gave her a big kiss. "You did good, babe. Well done."

Lena stood and performed an overly dramatic curtsy. "What did I tell you all? My plan was brilliant in its simplicity."

"Happy birthday, Son." Cynthia stood so she could hug her oldest child tightly.

"Mom, it's so good to have you here. Did you fly in?"

"John Michael and I drove in this afternoon. We're staying until Sunday."

"John Michael?"

John stood to take his place beside Cyn.

Jeremy's eyes widened as he made the connection. "So you're not a friend of Chad's?"

John laughed and shook his head. "Nope. I've never met anyone here except for your mother before tonight."

"So you two are—together?"

"Yes, we are." Cyn's tone sounded cautiously optimistic.

"I hope you don't mind me crashing your party," John volunteered. "I'd have been worried sick knowing she was driving up here alone." He shrugged. "Things can happen to women alone on the road, you know?"

Jeremy's gaze gravitated from his mother, to John, then back to his mother. He finally nodded, then pulled her close for another hug. "Good for you, Mom. I'm happy for you." He pulled back and shook John Michael's hand again. "Listen, I don't know the story between you two yet, but all I care about is that she looks happy. Be good to her, please?"

John smiled and nodded, thankful Cyn had at least two loyal and loving children. "You can count on it, Jeremy."

After the meal Mick approached, carrying Zoe. "Tell Grammy goodnight, Zoe."

"Night night Gwammy!" Zoe threw herself into Cynthia's arms and hugged her.

Cynthia covered her nearly two year old granddaughter's face with kisses. "Where are you going, sweet girl?"

"She'll be staying with my parents," Mick explained. "They live a few miles up the road. I won't be long."

Cynthia craned her neck to see her daughter. "Is Trini going with you?"

Mick grinned at his mother-in-law. "Oh no, she's much too exhausted to make the drive. It took us a whole two and a half hours to get here from our place in Van Buren."

She spotted her daughter, who'd already moved to the bar and was sipping on a large mixed drink. "I see." She gave Zoe one last kiss. "Nighty-night, Pumpkin. I'll see all of you again tomorrow, right Mick?"

"Yes ma'am. Trini and I got a hotel room here in town for the night, but we'll pick up Zoe before the cook-out at Jeremy's place tomorrow."

She patted his arm, satisfied for the moment. "You be careful on the road, Mick."

"Yes ma'am, I'll be back in twenty minutes or so." He took his daughter back and headed toward the doorway.

She turned to John Michael. "I'm worried about those two."

He draped his arm loosely around her neck as he turned them toward the club area. "I wouldn't worry about it too much. Mick doesn't take his marriage lightly and he's extremely committed to his wife. I think they'll work it out."

"God, I hope you're right." Her eyes widened as the DJ kicked up *Every Storm* by Gary Allan. "I love this song . . . dance with me?"

"I was thinking I had an *envie* to dance with a pretty lady."

She frowned. "I'm not familiar with the phrase. I'm not sure if it's a compliment or not."

He laughed. "I guess an *envie* would be the Cajun equivalent to an Okie saying . . . a hankering, maybe? So, yeah, it's a compliment."

He finished off the last swig of his beer and led her out to the floor. Within seconds they'd reacquainted themselves with a slow Texas two-step to an old George Strait favorite. They stayed on the dancefloor for the second one to master their dance moves. Several songs later, they headed back out to the floor for Blake Shelton's version of *Home*, a request from the birthday boy himself.

They caught up to Jeremy and Lena in the crowd of dancers. She reached out to tap her oldest child's shoulder. "Nice choice, Son."

He nodded. "It's my girl's favorite song. She gets plumb steamy for old BS."

Lena gave her an enthusiastic nod. "Blake is the only man I'd ever consider leaving your son for."

Cynthia nodded. "Understandable."

John Michael cleared his throat. "I don't much like the sound of that."

"I know, right?" Jeremy added.

Cynthia patted his shoulder. "Relax, sweetie. I like my men more mature."

He grunted. "Good thing."

Jeremy laughed and waved them on. "Carry on, you two."

John Michael threw a "Likewise," over his shoulder.

Cynthia closed the gap between her partner and herself. The belly rubbing song had her wishing she was alone with him—preferably back in their hotel room. "Lord, I love the way you dance."

He squeezed her hand. "I love so many things about you I've lost count."

She waited until they were positioned in the far corner of the room before looping her arms around his neck. She kissed him long enough and thoroughly enough to prompt a guttural groan from John Michael.

He pulled back slightly, kissed her nose and touched his forehead to hers. "Mm . . . what did I do to deserve that?"

She smiled at the tenderness in his voice. "Oh, it's just a little show of appreciation for you being here with me—and a promise of more to come."

His low chuckle vibrated between them, making her shiver. "I can't wait to get you alone, Cyn."

"*Seriously,* Mother?"

The shrillness of her daughter's grating voice jarred Cynthia instantly, like an ice bucket bath with no warning. "Excuse me?"

Trini's face contorted with anger. "Oh my God! You don't even have the good sense to be embarrassed by what you're doing. You two are making a spectacle of yourselves."

Cynthia gazed around the room. People were starting to stare. "I'm sure we weren't. But thanks to you, we're all beginning to be."

"I have never been so ashamed to call you my mother."

"Shut up, Trini." Tyler stepped forward, grabbed his sister's arm. "Have you lost your flipping mind?"

She shook her brother's arm off. "Didn't you even love Daddy? He must have known. That's why he turned to another woman."

"Trini!" This time it was Jeremy's booming voice, sounding so much like his father's that it got Trini's attention.

She swung around to face him. "She's humiliating all of us by carrying on the way she is."

Lena spoke up in Cynthia's defense. "What's she doing besides dancing, like the rest of us?"

Trini lifted one hand. "Family busi—"

Jeremy shoved her hand aside before she could finish. "Don't even *think* about being rude to my girl." He poked a finger in her face. "You know, Sis. You should work a little harder at hiding your crazy. You really should."

"*I'm* not crazy!" Trini waved her finger at her two brothers. "You two are if you think I'm going to accept any of mother's appalling behavior. Aren't either of you ashamed? You should be, for Dad's sake."

Mick stepped forward, apparently having just returned to the club. "What the hell's going on here, Trin?"

She turned on her husband, armed with plenty of self-righteous fury as fodder. "I already told you, this is a family matter, so it's none of your concern. But, as a cautionary warning, don't even think of humiliating me by dancing with your slut of a girlfriend in a public place. It's bad enough I have to witness my mother acting like a tramp."

"That's enough." John stepped in front of her, obviously determined to defend his lady.

"You don't have the right to speak to me that way," she snarled. "*You're* not my father."

"That's obvious. If I had been, you'd be as respectful toward your mother as your brothers are."

She turned to Mick. "Are you going to let him speak to me that way?"

Mick raised his hands in the air. "None of my business, remember? Besides, it sounds like John here knows what he's talking about."

"You're a lousy husband!"

Cynthia snapped. "Okay, Trini. I've had enough of your temper tantrums. It's time to grow up." She grabbed her daughter by the arm, totally fed up with the attention-grabbing-drama-queen-antics.

"Let go of me!" Trini tried to twist out of the iron grip on her arm, but she was no match for an irate mother.

Cynthia pushed her into the women's restroom, checked the stalls to make sure they were empty before turning on her daughter.

"What the hell is wrong with you, Trini? I can overlook your reaction to me finding love with another man. Your reaction is way out of the normal range but considering how badly your dad spoiled you, I'm willing to give you more time. But, I cannot stand by and watch you ruin your own marriage because of your father's stupidity."

Trini's eyes narrowed to angry slits. "My father was not stupid."

"Your father made a stupid choice, and then compounded it with a series of even more stupid choices over a two year period. He wasn't perfect, Trin. Get over it!" She took a step forward to get in her daughter's face. "Trust me, if I can, it can't be nearly as difficult for you."

"You don't understand anything."

"Don't I? I was his wife. I loved him. I honored him. I doted on him. I was faithful to him—*always*. He. Betrayed. *Me*. He betrayed *my* marriage—not yours."

"You couldn't have loved him if you've moved on so quickly."

Cynthia couldn't stop the hysterical laughter from bubbling up at her daughter's ludicrous accusation. "Quickly? A year and a half of wondering what the hell I could have possibly done wrong to make him turn to a woman the same age as our daughter? Trust me, Trin. There was nothing quick about those eighteen months."

Trini shook her head but somehow managed to keep her silence.

Cynthia paced the length of the room to gather her thoughts. "Was Gene remorseful? Probably. He died of a massive heart attack in the prime of his life, probably due to the stress from living a huge lie—from living the separate life he'd kept hidden from us, his family. It had to be eating at him."

She turned on her daughter again. "But I can tell you this. Your father didn't turn to another woman because he wasn't getting what he needed at home. I gave that man everything he wanted; everything he needed from me. He got greedy. That's on him. He's to blame, not me, and sure as hell not Mick.

I'm not going to let what Gene did ruin the rest of my life. And you damn well shouldn't either."

Trini covered her face, began to sob into her hands.

Cynthia's heart constricted at the sight of her daughter in so much pain. "Listen up, Trin. It's time to grow up. Stop being a selfish, self-centered little brat. If you don't, you'll lose a good man, one who loves you."

She approached her daughter. "The one thing Gene and I agreed on when it came to you was that you had somehow managed to marry one of the very few men in the world who was willing and able to put up with your prima donna attitude." She placed her hands lightly on Trini's shoulders. "Please don't push your husband away over a mistake your father made. His lack of morals, or good judgment had nothing whatsoever to do with you—or me either, to tell you the truth."

"Mom . . ."

Cynthia pulled her sobbing daughter close. "I know, Trin, I know." She let her daughter cry until she got it out of her system then gave her a handful of tissue. "Now, as Grammy Bess would say, dry your eyes, *ma petite femme*. There's a party waiting for us out there."

Trini splashed cold water around her eyes and dabbed at them with tissues. "How do I make this right? Jeremy's going to be so pissed because I ruined his party . . . all Lena's hard work and effort. And Mick—God, Mick is probably on the phone right now with a good divorce lawyer."

Cynthia had to hold back her threatening grin. "Nonsense. Lawyers don't work this late on Friday nights." Trini's laughter had her smiling. "Nothing's ruined. Your brothers are used to your dramatics, and no doubt Mick is too, by now."

"You'd think he would be, wouldn't you? But, I may have pushed him past his limit this time, Mom."

"You're not giving the man nearly enough credit. But first, you're going to go out there and apologize to your brother and Lena, and then make it up to Mick. Take advantage of this time away from your child. Appreciate the chance to be a couple rather than a mommy and daddy. Dance with your husband. And at the end of the night, take him back to your hotel room and make love the rest of the night. And most importantly, learn to trust again, Trin. It makes all the difference in the world."

Trini nodded, walked toward the door. She stopped, turned back to look at her mother. "I'm so sorry Dad was such a fool, Mom. I love you."

She met her at the door and wrapped her in a hug. "Good to know, because I had my doubts for a while there, baby girl. We've both got good men out there, and in case you're wondering, I plan on taking my own advice when I get mine back to our hotel room. You'd better get accustomed to the idea—and fast."

Trini made her classic TMI face. "Ew. Still my mom. Don't want to think about it." She took a step toward the door and turned back. "But, I have to admit Mr. John's kinda hot for an old guy."

Deciding not to remind her daughter they were the same age, she nodded. "Yes. He certainly is." They left the room together, each making a bee line for their own men.

Three hours later, the party was still going strong. Out on the dance floor again, Cynthia tucked her face into John's neck and took a deep breath, savoring the masculine smell of his cologne tinged with the aroma of dance hall and beer.

Tyler spoke up from beside them. "Get a room you two, would you?"

Cynthia lifted her head. "It doesn't sound like a bad idea. I'm exhausted."

Jessie added her laughter to Tyler's. "I don't think he was talking to you."

"Nope," Tyler confirmed. "I'm talking to Trini and Mick. They're about to do the nasty on the dance floor." He raised his voice to insure the other couple heard. "Hey, the rest of us think it's kind of disgusting what you two are doing over there. Just go, would you?"

Trini stuck her tongue out at Tyler then grabbed Mick's hand, shooting her brother a grin. "Actually, that's the best suggestion I've heard all night." Trini winked at Cynthia. "Well, almost the best," she added, before giving her a quick hug. "Thanks Mom, and I'm sorry."

Chapter Twelve

Cynthia lifted her knee, slid it higher along the muscular thigh belonging to the man in her bed. She released a deep sigh and snuggled closer to him. His arm tightened around her shoulders to aid her endeavor. She smiled. The only thing better than falling asleep wrapped in this man's arms, was waking up the same way.

"Mm . . . morning Cyn."

Keeping her head flat on his broad chest to spare him from morning breath, she answered. "Good morning, John Michael. Are you stiff?" His silence had her rephrasing the question. "I mean your shoulders . . . you know . . . from holding me all night?"

"Oh. A little there, actually." His hand lowered to a spot under the covers. "But here—significantly more." He lifted his head. "Seems like a waste not to make good use of it."

She grinned at his comment. "A shameful waste. No sense throwing away a perfect opportunity."

"Mm . . . absolutely."

"If I go brush my teeth will it wait?"

He sucked in his breath. "Absolutely."

Cynthia rolled out of bed, thankful for the hotel's room-darkening drapes. Facing the bathroom mirror, she cringed at her bed head and used her fingers to fluff out her hair. Closer examination had her using a dampened tissue to wipe the mascara from under her eyes.

John Michael appeared suddenly in the mirror—gloriously, unabashedly naked, and owning his erection like a badge of honor. He approached her from behind, resting himself against her back to send a chill through her. She swallowed the lump in her throat. "Hey there."

John nodded and grabbed the small bottle of mouthwash provided by the hotel. He cracked the seal, poured half into his mouth and handed her the bottle.

"Great idea." She chugged the rest of it, joined him in swishing the stuff in her mouth for several seconds before spitting into separate sinks.

Immediately, he pulled her close and kissed her, all the while backing her up slowly to the bed. "I'm sorry. I can't wait," he whispered, cupping her breasts gently.

She gasped at how his touch awakened her need for him. "What took you so long?" His sexy grin lit her up. She turned him, pushed him down on the bed and crawled on top of him, grinning. "Let's change things up a bit, shall we?"

His eyes widened, revealing the mild shock at her forcefulness. A slow grin spread across his handsome face. "Well, all right, then."

The cook-out at Jeremy and Lena's place was in full swing by the time John Michael found himself alone in the kitchen. He and Cynthia had started the clean-up process when Grammy duty had called. She'd abandoned him, with his blessing of course, to put Zoe down for her afternoon nap.

He opened several cabinets before finding the one containing baking pans, slid the clean one in with the others.

"Need some help in here?"

He turned to find Trini standing sheepishly in the doorway. "I've about got it, but I certainly don't mind the company." He pointed down the hallway. "Your mom went to put Zoe down for her nap if you're looking for her."

"I—I was looking for you, actually."

He stopped what he was doing to give her his full attention.

"I wanted to apologize again for what I said, what I did last night." She shook her head brusquely. "I was so rude to you, Mr. John."

He raised one hand to stop her. "Look, all's well between you and your mom. The rest isn't necessary."

She stepped forward. "It is. Mom was right when she said I acted like a spoiled brat. My dad did spoil me. I always got away with so much more than the boys. I knew it even then." She shrugged. "I liked it, what can I say?"

John had to smile at her honesty. "Well, sure. Who wouldn't?"

"But that doesn't make it right. When Dad died—the younger woman situation—God, it was so humiliating to all of us the way she came barging into the funeral home. I guess I couldn't face facts. My hero, my daddy, had done something despicable to us—to Mom. Jesus, she handled it with such grace . . ." She shook her head. "I would have lost my mind in the same situation—at the very least scratched little Miss *Tamara's* eyes right out of her head."

"Well, your mom's one tough lady, but she did have to deal with some issues before we could be a couple."

Trini's brow furrowed. "She did? I'm surprised. I really thought she had it all together."

John leaned his hips against the granite counter top and crossed his arms. "Maybe you ought to ask her about it. I've probably already said too much."

"Maybe you're right." She nodded thoughtfully, as if making a mental list of questions to ask her mother. "Thanks, Mr. John."

"I will tell you this, though. It's just between you and me." He wagged his finger between the two of them.

Trini perked up, giving him her undivided attention.

"She wasn't quite as 'gracious' as you all seem to think she was. She told me when the door was closed she slapped Tamara."

Trini's mouth dropped in undisguised awe. "Did she really?"

He nodded. "Then she threatened to slap a restraining order against her."

She nodded thoughtfully, as though she were playing out the scene in her mind. "Way to go Mom. Do you know what brought it on?"

He shrugged. "If you really want to know, why don't you ask her? It might help you to work through some things if you know the entire truth. The same goes for your brothers."

"But, what if she doesn't want to talk about it?"

"What'll it hurt to ask? The worst she could do is to say no."

Trini bit her bottom lip as she considered his words. She met his gaze and gave him a half smile. "You're pretty cool, Mr. John. So . . . do you plan on sticking around for a while?"

He tried not to laugh at the obvious. "Are you asking if my intentions toward your mother are honorable?"

She sobered suddenly. "Are they? I don't want to see her hurt . . ." Her gaze dropped to her shoes.

"Again?"

She nodded. "Yeah. My dad hurt her so badly. Even though she tried to cover it up with anger, I could see through that. Mom acted so calm and collected throughout the rest of the wake. She didn't even cry for the burial at the cemetery. She must have been devastated."

He pushed himself away from the counter and stood straight. "I believe she's worked through it. As for me, I will never do anything like that to hurt your mother." He placed his hand over his heart. "She filled a void when she came back into my life."

Her eyes narrowed. "Are you going to be my step-dad one day?"

He crossed his arms. "I can't answer for her, but I sure would like to think so."

Cynthia stepped into the kitchen, slightly out of breath. "Zoe must have been exhausted. She's out like a light." She paused, her gaze jumping from him to her daughter. "What are you two talking about in here?"

He reached for her, pulled her into his arms, her back to his front and facing Trini. "You, and how you look more beautiful every day." He winked conspiratorially at her daughter.

"That's right, Mom. I was about to go all Billy Currington on Mr. John here—telling him he must be doing something right, judging from the smile on your face." She stepped toward her mother. "Seriously, you look radiant, and if this man has anything to do with it—I can't help but approve of . . . well, whatever this is between you."

John Michael smiled. "Thanks, Trini. I appreciate it."

"As do I, sweetie." Cynthia held her arms out to embrace her daughter. She looked over her shoulder. "John Michael, you're welcome to get in on this group hug if you want to."

He reached out to hug Trini, sandwiching Cyn between them. "I thought you'd never ask."

Lena entered the kitchen holding Cyn's ringing phone. "Ms. Cyndi, your phone. It's a Mr. J.D."

Cynthia grabbed the phone. "Yes sir, it's Cynthia. Do you need to speak to John Michael? Yes, he's right here." She handed him the phone.

"Sorry Pop, my phone must have died. What's going on?" He straightened suddenly, his stomach lurching at his father's dreaded news. Without thinking, he reached for Cynthia. She clutched at his hand and met his gaze, her eyes wide with concern. "When, Pop? How'd it happen?"

The moment he reached for her, she knew. Her hand flew to her mouth at his words. "Oh, no. Oh, John. No." Her words were only a whisper but he must have heard them anyway. He blinked once, very slowly, and gave her a slight nod, a silent message to confirm her worst fears. Teary-eyed, she slipped her arms around him and held tight, waiting until he finished up the conversation with his dad.

"Okay, Pop. Yeah. I'll be there as soon as I can. I guess—uh—I don't know. I'll call you when I know more. Is someone there with you? Call Zachary or Ms. Bess. Okay, Pop. I'll get Cyn to call her for you. I love you, too. And Pop?" He paused here, his voice cracking. "I'm sorry. And I'm sorry I wasn't there for you." He nodded at whatever his dad said to him, answered with a final "Okay," before disconnecting. He gave Cynthia one final hug before setting her away from him.

"Pop went to see Mom this morning. He said they had her sitting up in her bed. She was still awake when he got there, but totally unresponsive. The nurse came in to get her situated for her nap as he was leaving. He did some shopping and got home about an hour ago. The facility just called him, said it looked like she went peacefully in her sleep."

"I'm so sorry, John Michael."

"I know, but it's better it happened this way, Cyn. You know it, I know it, and Pop probably does too. I just—I need to get home. What do you think my chances are of getting a flight out of here anytime soon?"

Cynthia gave her head an adamant shake. "No sir. We're driving home today. Immediately. Come on."

"I don't want to mess up your visit with your kids, Cyn. Not when you've all just straightened things out."

Trini stepped forward. "That's right, we have. Now you two can go on home to help your dad take care of things. We'll do this again." She reached up to give him a hug. "I'm so sorry, Mr. John. I wish I could have met her."

He smiled at her heartfelt words of sympathy. "Well, she hasn't been herself for a while now. But thank you, Trini."

Lena hugged him also, as did Jessie once word made the round. The three men gave him handshakes and the requisite "man-hug/pat on back".

Within ten minutes, they were on their way to the hotel. Thirty minutes later, they'd checked out and had started the first leg of the journey home.

Cyn ended the call from her mother. "Mom's with your dad already. She said Zachary and Cat just made it there with the twins. They have to wait for the coroner to . . ." She let her voice trail off, knowing he wouldn't want to hear the cold technicalities.

He nodded. "I'm glad he's not alone." He swallowed loudly in the silence of her car. "I should have been there with him."

Her heart constricted at the hurt in his voice. "You can't blame yourself for this. You couldn't have known. No one suspected it would happen so quickly."

"I know. And dammit, I never go anywhere, Cyn. Don't you know, the one time I do, *this* happens." He hit the steering wheel for emphasis. "I should have been there for him."

Guilt washed over her like acid rain, eating away at any trace of joy she'd experienced over the last twenty-four hours, and leaving sour regret in its wake. It transported her back to the day of Jenna Ferguson's death. That day John Michael came barreling out of the high school office and ran as fast as he could, away from *her*. He'd said he couldn't face her afterwards, how every time he saw her, it reminded him that his sister was gone. Would this affect him the same way? What if it did? What if he turned away from her again because of this?

Oh. God. No.

The next five hours of driving were excruciatingly quiet and tense. She pushed her bladder to its limits, refusing to ask him to stop to relieve herself. Finally, he noticed her squirming and pulled in at a fast food restaurant.

He threw it into park and looked pointedly at her. "Come on, we need a bathroom break and a coffee."

"I can hold it for another hour," she argued.

He reached over to squeeze her hand. "But I can't, and I'm not one for pissing in a coke bottle while I'm driving."

Praying to the toilet gods for working facilities, she preceded him inside and headed straight for the ladies room. A few minutes later, she walked out feeling much relieved, to find John Michael at the counter. She approached him, slid her hand down his arm, hoping to send him some small measure of comfort.

He laced the fingers of his free hand through hers. "You want a coffee, or a bite to eat?"

"Just coffee please, no sugar but plenty of cream."

He nodded and gave their order to the young man behind the register. Within a few minutes they were back in her car."

She let him get back on the highway before shifting herself to face him. "Please don't shut me out, John Michael."

He stared at her, his face drawn in a frown. "Why would you think I'd shut you out?"

"It feels like it did when you heard about Jenna. You ran from me then. I don't want you to run from me again."

He reached out to cup her face with one hand. "If I run this time, I'll be running *to* you, Cyn. Not away from you."

"You don't blame me?"

"For my mother's death? That's ludicrous."

"Because you weren't there when she passed away."

"Pop wasn't even there when she passed away, hon. Hell, neither was Mom, for that matter."

"Okay, then, for not being there for your father."

His brow furrowed before he shook his head. "Are you that determined to be the blame for something?"

She shrugged, not knowing how to answer.

"Jesus, Cyn. What kind of marriage did you have? Did you tiptoe around? Did you walk on eggshells, always taking the blame for things, just to pacify your husband?"

"No. Not really."

His right brow lifted drastically. "No? Or not really? Those are two entirely different answers."

She took a deep breath, released it slowly to relieve the tension in her chest. She considered his question seriously. "Thinking back on it now, I may have done a little tip-toeing, but I never really thought about it that way at the time. Gene wasn't a brute or anything, but he could be moody as hell. It's kind of funny, now that I think about it. I always thought he was the perfect husband—until I discovered he wasn't."

John Michael released a combination of a snort with an abrupt burst of laughter. "Oh God. I can't wait."

She frowned, ready to hear some joke at her expense, something else Gene had done on occasion. How the hell had she managed to forget these things, until now? "You can't wait—for *what?*"

"I can't wait until we're married. Then you'll have something better to compare your thirty-something years with Gene to."

"Who says I'm marrying you?"

"Are you saying you'd turn me down if I asked?"

"Not necessarily."

"Are you saying you wouldn't turn me down?"

She picked at a speck of fuzz on her capris. "Not necessarily."

"Well, what *are* you saying, Cyn?"

Her eyes narrowed. "Are you asking me to marry you?"

"Not necessarily."

"Are you asking me not to marry you?"

He squinted, his face a study of masculine confusion. "Not necessarily."

She relaxed against her seat. "Well, when you ask me to marry you, you'll get your answer."

"When I do, will you say yes?"

"Isn't this where we started?"

"Answer the question, Cyn."

"Possibly." She shrugged. "Probably."

His laughter filtered through the car's interior. "Again, those are two entirely different answers."

She brushed at her shirt. "Looks like I was mistaken before. *Now* we're back to where we started."

Laughter rolled deep in his chest again as he shook his head. "Honestly, Cyn. I can't flipping wait to marry you."

She turned to face the window, the now familiar landmarks flying past as they neared their destination. Biting her lip in an effort to suppress a smile, Cynthia took her first cleansing breath since the awful beginning of this trip back to Lake Erin.

He couldn't wait to marry her.

"Mom?"

Cynthia turned, shocked to see not one, but all three of her children standing before her. "Oh my gosh. You're all here for the funeral?"

Jeremy pulled her close for a hug. "We felt like we had to. John's such a nice guy, and if he means as much to you as we think he does . . ." He didn't bother to state the obvious.

She hugged Trini and Tyler. "No Zoe? Grandma Bess will be so disappointed."

Lena appeared suddenly, holding the toddler. "We're here. I took her to go potty so they could find you."

"Oh, thank you for coming, Lena. And come here, sweetie pie. Oh give Grammy a hug."

"Love you, Gwammy!"

"I love you too, Zoe. I've got a great idea. Let's go find Mr. John."

She found him in the kitchen drinking coffee with Zach and Mr. J.D. "Someone wants to tell you hello, Mr. John."

His face lit up instantly. "Hey there, Zoe! I didn't know you'd be here."

"John!" She launched herself into his arms and hugged him, generating a round of lighthearted laughter from the circle of people.

"Aw. Thanks so much sweet girl. How'd you know I needed a hug?" He turned, his face glowing with gratitude as his gaze landed on the group of four standing behind Cynthia. "I can't *believe* you all made the trip for this." Four hugs later, he cleared his throat, still shaking his head as he placed his free hand over his heart. "Honestly, this means a lot to me."

"You made a good impression on us. The way we see it, you'll probably be family one day," Trini explained.

"Yep," Tyler added. "And family's got to stick together." He leaned forward to add. "Jessie sends her love. We couldn't both take two days off. She sacrificed so I could make it here."

"Another reason to hang on to her," John added, as Tyler nodded in agreement.

"May as well get to know everyone now," Jeremy added. "Besides, it's time I introduced Lena to Grandma Bess."

Cynthia dabbed at the corner of her eye with a tissue. "It is, and she should be here any minute."

"But for now," John added, "I want you all to meet my dad and my son."

Several introductions later, Cynthia stood by, amazed at the interaction between her children and John's. Zachary had collected Cathryn and the twins to join them in the kitchen for a meet and greet before the final service began. Cynthia turned as Mr. J.D. appeared beside her, holding a small cup of coffee.

"So these are Ham and Bessie's grandkids."

She nodded. "They're my contribution to the fold, anyway. There are six more between my other two siblings."

"You and Johnny . . ." He paused, lifted one hand to indicate the chattering group, all smiles and laughter. "This is a wonderful thing to happen to our family. He's been alone too long. It started last year when Cathryn came back into Zachary's life after being gone for a dozen years."

Cynthia gazed over at the beautiful girl, her dark eyes sparkling with laughter as she conversed easily with Trini and Lena. "She's a beautiful addition to the family."

J.D. grunted in agreement. "They don't come any sweeter. She was like a little ray of sunshine. Then they had the twins, and boy, am I ever looking forward to having those little pooters running around wreaking havoc in our lives."

Cynthia observed the twins, one in Trini's arms, the other in Lena's, both showing off the smiles they'd so recently learned to control. "God, they're adorable. Look at them. They've already got those two wrapped."

J.D.'s chuckle rumbled like an old outboard motor. "Yep, they know how to take command of an audience, that's for sure. It looks like your little one has mastered it, as well. She's taken a shining to Johnny, over there."

Cynthia frowned at the sight of Zoe patting John Michael's face and plastering him with kisses. "Should I be jealous?"

He grinned and patted her hand. "I think you're solid. You and Johnny are wonderful together. I believe Marilee knew it, too, from something your mother said after one visit."

She cocked her head to get a better look at the man she suspected would be her father-in-law one day. "What did she say?"

"I can't quite remember. Bess was a little mysterious about it. Kind of like Marilee always was when she wrote in her journal."

Cynthia nodded. "Yes, the journal—pink with flowers. She had it with her when I visited that first day. She said, 'You're in it now, too,' or something similar. What's in it?"

He shook his head. "I have no idea. It's in a box with the rest of her things. I haven't had the heart to dig into anything yet."

His mouth drawn and tight, he looked ready to tear-up. She turned to him, laid her face on his big barrel chest. "I love you, Mr. J.D."

He wrapped one arm around her and squeezed. "Same here, sweet girl." He shook with laughter as her mother entered the kitchen and got her first glimpse of Cynthia's brood. "Oh, look out, now. The old hen has seen all her grand-chicks. Look at the smile on her face."

Cynthia straightened, started to go to her mother. Bess looked in their direction, her face beaming with joy—only her gaze wasn't directed at her daughter, but rather at the man beside her. Cynthia glanced up at Mr. J.D., recognized the same look of joy on his face as her mother's.

A sudden thought warmed her heart, even though she said nothing. She'd keep this to herself for the moment. Like a wish made at a magical fountain or a shooting star. The kind you don't speak aloud because then it wouldn't come true.

Over and done.

J.D. sat in his chair, staring at the Visitation Sign-in book the funeral home had given him—unable or unwilling at the moment, to open the thing.

The funeral had gone off without a hitch yesterday. After the burial, dozens of people had come here, to his and Marilee's home. They'd spoken in low whispers at first, had eventually grown louder. Eaten food the bereavement committee had delivered. All delicious, all made by the caring women of Our Lady of the Lake's Catholic Daughters. They'd shared delicious red velvet cake and fig tarts, all freshly baked by Bess.

Friends left first, their social obligations fulfilled for the time being. Immediate family remained, including Cynthia's bunch. He'd insisted they sit as a family in church. Why not? No doubt, Johnny and his "Cyn" would be married at some point in the near future.

Prior to losing Marilee, he'd looked forward to their wedding. Until recently, he'd hoped she would attend. But those hopes had vanished in the last several visits, when his wife turned into a shell of the woman she'd once been.

The thought of attending any joyous occasion made him want to crawl in a hole. How could he justify being happy in any sense of the word, without her by his side?

How could he *do* anything without going to her room at the home two or three times a week to tell her all about it? It didn't matter if she knew him, heard him, understood him, or not—it was his duty, his role in life, his routine.

He pulled out his handkerchief, wiped at his eyes, thanking God one more time she'd at least seen her great grandchildren. He looked over at the picture Cathryn had printed and framed for him—Marilee, dressed and smiling, with him beside her, each of them holding one of Cat and Zach's twins. She'd had such a good afternoon.

He picked up the small photo album Cathryn had made for Marilee to keep in her room, filled with pictures. She'd taken dozens of shots, all to commemorate the wonderful day, to insert those moments permanently into the timeline of their lives. He flipped through the album all the way to the end, had to use the handkerchief again to wipe the moisture from his eyes—chided himself for his weakness.

He closed the album, set it back on his lamp table by his recliner. "Buck up, old man."

His thoughts returned to Johnny and Cynthia—the inevitable wedding. Marilee had been so proud, so thrilled when Johnny and Beth had been married at the Cathedral in Lafayette. Said she'd never seen such a beautiful wedding before, even though it had been simple.

Sadness ripped through his soul, sapping him of energy, of any trace of happiness at the prospect of any future joyous occasion. Marilee would never see any of it.

He lifted the Visitation book from his lap, flipped from one page to another, amazed at how clearly he could see since his surgery two weeks earlier. There were dozens of names of people who'd come to pay their respects.

He recalled several of the old acquaintances who'd been in his home yesterday after the burial. How many times had he heard them say it was "for the best"? How many of them had insisted Marilee would have wanted to go in her sleep if she'd had a choice?

Maybe so, but it wasn't what he wanted for her. It never had been. He'd wanted to be beside her, in their own bed, in their own home when she left this world.

And if he was being perfectly honest with himself, he'd hoped to leave this earthly prison at the exact moment she did.

Chapter Thirteen

John Michael glanced at his ringing phone. The single name, *Cyn*, flashed across the screen. The sight gave him both a thrill and a feeling of dread at the prospect of having to cancel yet, another date night with the lady.

Damn, he missed her. He ached at the thought of being able to hold her in his arms, of making love to her as he had at the hotel in Arkansas. The last time had been the morning of his mother's death, on July 26th. Here it was, August 29th, and they'd barely had any time alone together since then. It was agony, knowing how good it had been, and would be again, once his Pop was back to his old self.

He tapped the onscreen answer button. "Hey, babe. How's your day going?"

"Hey sweetie. I've been busy, thank God."

The sound of her voice washed over him like warm sunshine, filling him with the need to see her. "Why is it a good thing?"

"It keeps me from missing you every second of the day. How's Mr. J.D. today? Any better?"

John's gaze shifted over to where his pop sat in the recliner, reading today's weekly edition of the Lake Erin Sun Times. He'd brought the paper to him ten minutes ago at 2:00 p.m. sharp, and he was already half-way through the darn thing. He figured when you had nothing else to look forward to, the local news made for highly anticipated reading material. "About the same, I'm guessing."

"Are we still on for tonight? Or should I cancel the reservation at D.I.'s and bring over a rotisserie chicken for supper?"

"I think maybe that'd be best, babe. Do you mind?" Her sigh told him she *did* mind having to share him with his old man, every bit as much as he minded not having a second alone with her. The thought of another predictably mind-numbing evening of Wheel of Fortune, followed by Gunsmoke and Maverick reruns, made him want to tear his hair out. But her words gave him hope.

"As long as I get to sit next to you on his lumpy old sofa, I'll be happy."

He smiled. "It won't be like this forever, babe. Don't give up on me."

"Never. I love you, John Michael."

As always, hearing those three words from her mouth put a smile on his face. "It never gets old, hearing that. I love you, Cyn. See you tonight." He turned, had to take a step back at the sudden invasion of his dad inside his personal space. "Shit, Pop. Give a guy some warning, would you?"

His dad's brow wrinkled in a frown. "Did I hear you break another date with Cynthia to stay home with me?"

"N-no. Pop, it's fine. She likes spending time with us here."

"Bullshit!"

"Pop—"

"Look son, it's like Bess told me the other day. Between our family and Cynthia's, we've had a lot of gray skies and hard rains. It's high time somebody in this group gets a little clear weather. I'm kinda looking forward to running out of rain, aren't you?" J.D. pointed at the phone in John's hand. "Call her back. Whatever plans you two made for tonight, you go through with 'em. I'm seventy-seven years old, and of sound mind and body. I don't need a damn baby-sitter."

"Really Pop, we don't mi—"

"Boy! Did I raise you to disobey me? To treat me like an old fool?"

"No, sir."

"Then hit a button on that smarter-than-*you* phone, put it to your ear, and call her back. I'm not an invalid, you know."

"I never said you were."

J.D. turned to walk away, a steady diatribe of grumbles pouring from his mouth. "So, I've felt a bit down. It doesn't mean I want to drag you down with me."

"Pop—" One particularly hard glare from his old man cut off any further comeback. "Okay. I'm calling. Right now." He left the room, wanting to keep his old man from seeing the bounce in his step.

She answered immediately when he hit the call button. "Hey, Babe. There's no need to cancel those reservations. I got an unexpected reaming from Pop. We're on for tonight."

"Really?"

"Yep, I'll pick you up at five sharp. And babe?"

"Yes?"

"Wear your dancing shoes." Her squeal of delight put a smile back on his face, one he couldn't erase for the rest of the day.

J.D. stood at the door, sent his son one last wave as he headed off in his truck. Thank goodness he'd over heard him when he did, or he'd have been responsible for another night of boredom for those two. He'd tried to tell them he was okay, to go off and do whatever young folks did these days for fun.

He was glad they were going for a meal and dancing at D.I.'s. He and Marilee loved that place. They'd had some mighty fine times dancing to good old Cajun music at quite a few clubs and dancehalls in this area over the first fifty years of their marriage. Here in Lake Erin, The Lakeshore Club had topped the list. They'd danced many a night there to live bands, eaten many a meal in its Anchor Room restaurant. He couldn't remember a time he hadn't purchased a bingo card or two so Marilee could play bingo while she ate her meal. Many a time he'd heard his sweet wife mutter mild expletives as someone else had "Bingo-ed" in the Anchor Room when all she lacked was one lousy square.

Later, they'd eaten many a meal at the old Wave Café at the south end of Lake Erin Avenue, passed many good times with friends at The Red Rose, attended wedding dances and receptions at the Knights of Columbus and VFW Halls. They'd spent the occasional evening with friends at Lu-Lu Broussard's Lounge and the Circle Top in Gardiner when decent bands appeared. Neither of them had ever been drinkers, but they'd both loved to dance.

They'd showed off some fine dance moves at the Town and Country Club over in Riceville, a dot on a map just north of Gardiner. Some of the best Cajun bands they'd ever heard played right there at the place the locals had dubbed "Chicky Town" for whatever reason. Some claimed it was because of the women that always seemed to gather there in the "old days", others insisted its nickname was derived from the distinctive "chanky-chank" sound of the music, produced from the Cajun accordion and drums to keep the beat going. Still others said it was because of the Cajun dance moves.

Why, hell, they'd seen musical royalty there; the *queen* of country music, Ms. Loretta Lynn, as well as the *king* of Zydeco, Clifton Chenier.

It pleased him to know his son and grandson were both avid dancers of Cajun, Zydeco, and country music. He and Marilee had been thrilled to see them waltzing and jitter-bugging during Cat and Zach's wedding reception last year. It had done their hearts good to see the young couple keep the old Cajun way of starting off their reception with the traditional Cajun Wedding March.

A new wave of sadness washed over him at the memory. He made his way to the bedroom he'd shared with his wife of nearly sixty years, and stopped in the doorway. His gaze settled on the cardboard box containing personal items from her room at the home. He sighed, resigned to not having a damn thing better to do tonight.

Bess had called earlier, inviting him to supper, but he'd turned her down, of course. He couldn't have people thinking he'd forgotten about his wife, even though he knew Bess was as much a friend of his as she had been Marilee's. The old gal probably missed his wife as much as he did.

He dragged the box closer to Marilee's overstuffed reading chair, the one she insisted on bringing with her once she'd made the decision to leave here— the same one Johnny had picked up and delivered back home because J.D. couldn't bear to set foot in that room of hers again.

"This ain't gonna get any easier, old man. Let's get it over with." He got comfortable in Marilee's 'spot', flipped open the box top. His breath hitched as his gaze fell on the top item in the box. Her treasured crocheted afghan— treasured because it had been her last gift from her beloved daughter-in-law. Bethie had taught herself to crochet and had thought enough of her in-laws to gift them both with the beautiful, hand-made blankets for Christmas. From that day on, Marilee's blanket, in pretty blue and rose colors, had a place of honor on the back of her reading chair. He stood, unfolded the afghan and placed it on the back of the chair, where it belonged.

He sat again, peered into the box and his heart plummeted to his toes at the sight of his wife's journal. Guilt ate at him. How the hell had he managed to forget about the one item that had been his wife's constant companion throughout her stay at the home.

He picked it up, sat back in the chair and examined the cloth covered book, worn from her constant handling over the past year. She wrote in it when she remembered. Read from it when she didn't. He'd only asked once to see the contents. She'd turned him down flat—said it was for another time—after she was gone.

He pictured her gazing up at him from her chair, her eyes brimming with sadness and a trace of tears. "Read this when you're ready, John. Not a moment before. Do you understand?"

He'd nodded. "Yes ma'am."

"You must promise me, John. There are some important . . ." She'd flailed her hands then, frustrated at not being able to come up with the right words, finally settled. "It's important you read this."

She'd mentioned the same thing on many occasions since then, always forgetting she'd already told him.

He took a deep breath and opened the book. "Let's see what words of wisdom you've left for me, sweet Marilee."

Aided by his cataract free eyes, and new spectacles, he began to read. It was all there in blue ink upon bright white lined pages, sometimes a different shade of blue, but always blue ink, as was her way.

Her first entry hit him hard:

I almost killed my husband yesterday. I dropped a dishcloth next to a lit burner and walked right out of the house. Wandered around for God knows how long until the nice deputy I've known all my life (but whose name I can't seem to recall) picked me up and brought me home. Thank God the smoke alarm had gone off and woke J.D. from his nap. He'd almost put out the fire by the time I got home. I shudder to think what could have happened had he not awakened when he did. I hate being away from him, but I'm where I need to be. I didn't want to see it before, but I know this now. I love my husband too much to put him at risk again.

The next several entries were about the multitude of visits from him and Johnny, and Zachary and Cathryn. How overjoyed she was to see the earlier ultrasounds of the twins. How thrilled she was her grandson had found the love of his life. How sad she was her son had lost his so many years ago.

After the first twenty pages or so, she began to make notes of people who'd visited during the periods when she wasn't "herself". She'd asked her nurse to have them sign a separate spiral bound notebook so she'd know later on who'd visited with her. She'd check the list when she returned, and sometimes called her visitors to thank them.

J.D. knew all of this. They'd discussed it. He figured she needed to write it all down for her own peace of mind. By the time he got to the middle of the journal, things began to change. She began making references to a section she'd added to the back called *John's Guide to Life.*

I've decided J.D. needs to remarry after I'm gone. He's only 77 after all. The last four generations of Ferguson men have lived until their mid-90's. I need to consider that he may also. I can't stand the thought of him being alone. I need to find him someone. Not just anyone. It has to be someone I admire, someone I respect. This is my priority. I've started a section at the back of this journal called John's Guide to Life (from here on out referenced as the Guide)

Several more references to her "priority" had him saddened. He hadn't realized how much she'd fretted over leaving him alone. How much she fought to keep returning. She spoke of how sometimes when she was herself it seemed like she was gone for seconds. She claimed to remember seeing a particular look on his face before she left him. It tortured her because she knew she'd return to him and he'd have to suffer losing her one more time.

Her notes became erratic, as though a panic had set in, anxiety over when God would answer her prayers. But one visit from an old friend changed everything, and she turned hopeful.

The first thing I did when I woke up as 'myself' this morning was to look at my list of visitors. Bess Robicheaux's name is on there several times, sometimes alone, sometimes with her daughter, Cynthia., who happens to be Johnny's new girlfriend. I found snapshots in an album Zachary and Cat left here for me of Johnny with Cynthia. I'm thrilled! Our Johnny has found someone, and such a lovely young lady. Cynthia was always such a kind girl. Thank you God for small blessings.

Shortly after her entry, there was an addition to the journal.

New development! I've found my replacement. It is duly noted as #11 in the Guide at the back of this journal. Thank God for huge blessings. I have a plan for J.D. This has come just in time. I'm tired, so very tired of fighting my way back only to leave him again.

That would be her last legible entry toward the front of the book. There were some minor scribbles on the following page, as though she'd made an attempt, but failed. Heartsick, he turned to the back of the book. And there it was, in her neat penmanship:

John's Guide to Life

1. Wake up every morning thanking the good Lord that you are still breathing.
2. Get up, Get dressed, and Get OUT of the house.
3. Try new things, meet new people, do not stay stuck in a rut.

He nearly laughed aloud reading the words, practically able to hear her preaching to him.

4. Get those cataracts removed (I know you've been putting off the surgery because I'm in this place but it's time to do it if you haven't already)
5. Get that prostate exam. Medicine will probably help with that problem if you have the guts and good sense to admit you have one.

He snorted. "Ha! I got you beat, ol' girl. I've already had the cataract surgery and got my new specs." He shivered at a particular memory—the dreaded prostate exam—with good reason, too. The jury was still out on the meds his doc had prescribed. He adjusted his glasses and continued to read.

6. Spend as much time with our great grandchildren as you can. Youth has a way of rubbing off on people.

7. Do NOT spend the rest of your life mourning me John David Ferguson. If you only knew how difficult it is for me to come back to this place, you'd stop being so hard headed about this. I don't want you to be alone.

He probably would have gotten a little weepy over number seven if number eight hadn't made him laugh out loud.

8. Get out in the evenings, visit people, or take a drive. No Wheel of Fortune or endless reruns of old westerns all night long. The least you could do is watch Sex And the City every now and then. You can always balance it out with an episode or two of Gunsmoke. The point is, don't plan your night by what's on television.

His smile faded as he began to read the next item on her agenda.

9. Find someone new. I can't stress this enough. I can't bear the thought of leaving you all alone in that big old house without companionship.

10. I saw where Lavyrle Fruge came by while I was "away". I know what that old tramp wants. Do NOT let that woman step one foot inside my house. If she comes sniffing around after I'm gone, you send her on her way and keep looking for something better.

"Now Marilee, how could you ever think I'd look twice at Lavyrle Fruge? If that old chienne ever came sniffin', around I'd throw her a dog biscuit and tell her to be on her way." He shivered again.

11. Bessie Robicheaux! She's the one, John David. I want her for you. It's nothing short of divine intervention. She's always been such a good friend. She helped me so much when sweet Jenna was taken from us. She's a good, kind person and she's alone too. She's the one. She's. I want. She's for _____

He shook his head. "No, Marilee, No. Bess is a good friend, but she can't replace you. No one can ever replace you."

He started to shut the book, and stopped. Near the bottom of the page, in a barely legible scrawl, she'd somehow managed to add one last item. After some concentration, he finally managed to decipher number twelve.

12. Let me go

A sudden realization hit J.D. like a wrecking ball blasting into a condemned building. He sat forward in her chair, hugging the book to his chest, suddenly feeling much older.

"Oh, God. No."

He couldn't bear it.

He raked one hand in his hair, pulled his handkerchief from his pocket, fisting it in his right hand again.

J.D. pictured Marilee scribbling in that book during visits when she was herself. She'd done that when Zachary, Cathryn, and the twins were there last, along with Johnny and Cynthia.

He *remembered* that visit with Bess, and how she'd stepped out of the room to give him and Marilee alone time. His wife had been writing in this journal like a mad woman, as though she had to get it all down before—before she left again.

He remembered the moment she *had* begun to leave him—her pen's movement had slowed, stuttered, the scribbling eventually turning into a somewhat straight line, almost as though her brainwaves had shut down for a moment before lifting her gaze to his, without a hint of recognition.

He shook his head, used his handkerchief to wipe the moisture from his eyes. "So why the hell don't I remember number twelve, Marilee?"

Where had he been when she'd written that last directive—the one much messier, much less legible than the others?

It could only mean one thing.

She'd been alone—totally alone—and had apparently been herself just long enough to get one last item on paper. It was her last message to him, her goodbye, the very last time she'd been herself.

"And I wasn't there for you."

He flipped to the front of the book again, passed his fingers over the scribbles, examining the failed attempt to put down the words locked away in her mind. J.D. slammed the journal shut, collapsed back in the chair, suddenly too weak to stand, overcome by a flood of regret—angry and bitter over the years that had been stolen from his wife. Eyes closed and head back on the chair, he wallowed in his own self-pity until he drifted off to sleep, the feel of the book's worn fabric under his fingers.

He dreamed of Marilee, the sweet sound of her voice near his ear—chiding him, insisting he stop feeling sorry for himself. In his dream he turned to her voice, opened his eyes, saw her holding an abbreviated version of that stupid "Guide". "Look John David. *Look!*" she insisted. He did, because she was so unusually demanding, how could he not? The list was similar to the other, with the identical heading, but cut down to two items, the first, *Bessie Robicheaux*, the second, *Let. Me. Go.*

"*I can't, Marilee.*"

"*You can. You must. I want this for you.*"

"*But, I love you.*"

"*I know. I've always known.*"

"*I didn't get to say goodbye.*"

"*It doesn't matter. I said goodbye. Now wake up, J.D.*"

"*I can't.*"

"*Wake up.*"

"*I don't want to.*"

"*Wake up!*" *She shook him.*

"*No.*"

"Wake up, Pop!"

She shook him again, rougher this time.

"Pop!"

A loud clap sounded at his ear and he jumped. "Son of a—what!"

Johnny stood there, hands in the air, a horrified expression on his face. "Good grief! I thought you were dead."

"Well, almost! You about gave me a heart attack."

"Are you all right?"

J.D. sat up. "Of course I am." He waved his hand in front of his face. "I'm a little dizzy, though."

Concern etched Johnny's face. "From what? Should I call an ambulance? Bring you to the emergency room?"

"I'm dizzy from whatever smell-good you drenched yourself in. Back the hell away from me, boy. You're making my eyes burn."

Johnny sniffed at his shirt. "Cyn likes it. She picked it out with me."

"Well, it doesn't mean you had to take a bath in it. You could use a lesson in subtlety."

"Well—I'm nervous, dammit."

J.D. eyed his son suspiciously. "Oh, yeah? What for?"

"I'm taking Cyn dancing for the first time in a month."

"So what the hell are you doing here?"

"I came by to see if you needed anything before I left town."

"No. I'm okay."

"All right, then. I'm gonna go ahead and go."

"Okay. Do yourself and Cyn, a favor. Drive with your windows down on your way to pick her up."

"It's still ninety degrees outside. I'll be all sweaty by the time I get there."

J.D. shook his head on the way to the bathroom. "It's bound to be an improvement. Now get the hell out of here. You're making me woozy."

He entered the bathroom, came out a little later, freshly showered and shaved. He briefly considered putting on his pajamas to make an early night of it, but decided instead to put on a fresh set of clothes.

J.D. took a deep breath and lifted his phone. He hit the speed dial Cynthia had programmed for him and waited. It rang once, twice, and a third time before Bess picked it up.

"Bess, is that invitation still on for supper at your place?" He smiled at her answer. "I'll be over in about fifteen minutes. Thanks."

J.D. placed the phone in its cradle and stood slowly. He leaned over to pick up the journal, considered placing it back inside the box. After a moment of contemplation, he tucked it under his arm instead.

The way he figured it, poor Bess had every right to know what she was getting herself into.

Chapter Fourteen

God, she loved this man. She loved the way he held her as they danced, how he made her feel cherished and protected. She loved the feel of his skin under her hands. She loved the feel of his hair as she ran her fingers through it. She loved the way he—

"Excuse me! I'd like to cut in."

Cynthia turned, her eyes narrowed at the irritating intrusion into her sexual ramblings. "Go away, Robin. You need to accept the fact that John Michael is taken."

"I'm only asking for a friendly dance, not to marry him."

Cynthia spun her date so that his back was to the bimbo and stared pointedly at her. "Go. Away."

"Sheesh! Somebody needs lessons in sharing."

"Somebody needs lessons in how to apply make-up."

"Oh, I'm sure!" Robin gave an indignant huff.

"I am too. You look like Tim Curry dressed as the Sweet Transvestite in *The Rocky Horror Picture Show*. Now *go*!" She shook her head as Robin finally got the message and flounced off. "If that tramp keeps crashing our party like this, we may have to find another place to dance. I'll miss the food, but it'd be worth it not to have to hear her voice."

John waited several seconds before facing her. "Is it safe to turn around now?"

"Yes, sweet baby, the scary lady is gone," she crooned.

"Are you sure? Because she seems to have brought out a side of you I haven't seen before tonight."

"What you're seeing tonight, is the woman who hasn't been alone with the man I love in a month. Be thankful you don't have to work with *this me* all day long. I threatened to castrate Kevin today if he ever asked me out on a date again. And I meant it."

"Ooh . . . Mama's a little testy. Maybe I should get you outta here and back to my place." The look she aimed in his direction had him rushing to explain. "I'm past all that, I promise. But if you have doubts, I can always rent us a hotel room."

She pursed her lips. "Are we talking by the hour, here, or for a full night?"

He chuckled. "Considering the shape you're in, an hourly rate would clean out my bank account."

"The shape *I'm* in?" She scraped her nails over his upper thigh.

He hissed. "You got me. The shape *we're* in. This could be an all-nighter."

She nodded thoughtfully. "It's a possibility. But let's go on to your place, if you don't mind. It's in the country and I can make all the noise I want. Can we go now, please?"

"Mm, thought you'd never ask. I'm going to get a to-go box for our leftovers and an extra order of hush puppies. I have a feeling I'll need sustenance at some point during the night."

"Do what you've got to do." She gave him a kiss and headed for the restroom. By the time she made it out, he was waiting for her at the exit, holding the bag of to-go boxes.

The trip back to Lake Erin was agonizingly slow, until the Louisiana State Trooper's car in front of them turned off onto another highway. By then they were only two minutes from John's place.

He unlocked the door and followed her inside. Cynthia headed straight for the master bathroom to brush her teeth and touch up her makeup and hair. By the time she exited, John Michael was shirtless, barefooted, and sprawled out on his king size bed, waiting for her.

She smiled when she spied the small square foam container of leftovers sitting on the dresser. "Are you expecting to get hungry that soon?"

He lifted one shoulder. "One never knows. I'm expecting quite a work-out from you tonight. Besides, it's not my hushpuppies. It's your dessert."

"D.I.'s serves dessert?"

He nodded. "They did tonight."

She could go for a little dessert. She took a step toward the dresser. "What is it?"

"You'll have to open it to find out."

She reached for the box. His voice stopped her.

"But, you'll have to decide what you want first—the main course, meaning me, or your dessert?" He flexed his arms then linked his fingers behind his head.

The man was dangerous, for sure. All thoughts of dessert pushed aside for the time being, she slipped the straps of her dress off her shoulders. The silky fabric landed on the floor without making a sound. She stepped out of her pumps and approached the bed.

"*Why* are you still in those jeans, John Michael?"

Her question had him stripping them off in double time. He dropped back on the bed, wearing only his black boxer briefs. She crawled over to straddle him, and then ever so sneakily, reached for the dessert container.

He burst into laughter. "I knew it!" he crowed. "I knew you wouldn't be able to resist."

She sat back, landing solidly on his pelvis to put a quick end to his gleeful claim at being right. "It's your own fault. I could always pass up dessert until I started hanging around you. What is this, some yummy bread pudding with rum sauce?" She started to open the box. "Or coconut cream pie . . ." Her voice trailed off as she stared at the contents.

John Michael couldn't contain his laughter. "God, this was so not supposed to happen like this. I figured we'd either be partially clothed or under the covers, basking in the afterglow of our lovemaking. I wasn't expecting your dessert stealing fake-out."

She pursed her lips. "Well, you should have been expecting it, considering I can't seem to pass up sweets anymore. You're gonna regret it, the bigger my butt gets, you know."

"Uh uh . . . the more butt on you, the better, babe." He flipped her off of him and took the to-go carton from her hands before kneeling on the bed. He pulled out the small black box from the container and flipped it open.

"I love you, Cyn, and I'd absolutely love it if you'd marry me."

She stared at the beautiful vintage style engagement ring with a matching band. "Oh. Gorgeous! Where did you find these?"

"It was my mom's set. I brought it in to a jewelry designer, and told her what I wanted. I added a bigger center diamond, smaller ones around the perimeter, and added the opals on each side because it's your favorite gem as well as your birthstone. If you'd rather choose your own, wear this as a dinner ring and I'll take you shopping for rings tomorrow."

"Oh my goodness, I *love* it! Yes. Yes, of course I'll marry you." She waited until he'd slid the ring on her finger before throwing herself on top of him and covering his face with kisses.

He returned her kisses and laughed again. "You realize, of course, when our family and friends ask how this all went down, and you *know* they will, we can never tell them the truth."

She joined in his laughter. "Never, *ever*! My reputation would be permanently sullied."

He fell back on the bed, pulling her with him. "Babe, do you really like it? I called Trini and asked her opinion and she thought you'd prefer this over a new set."

Cynthia's mouth gaped opened. "Trini already knows?"

"Of course. You didn't think I'd ask you to marry me without getting your children's permission first, did you? It's a matter of respect."

"All my children know?"

"Sure. I had a talk with the three of them the day after the funeral. They were all for it."

She shook her head. "Honestly, I had no idea you were such a sneak."

"Well, I have to be, with you being so damn curious. I mean, you couldn't even wait for dessert, when you had *me* here, with not a stitch on, other than my underwear."

She pushed out her lower lip. "Did I hurt your feelings?"

"You might have, if I wasn't so confident about how much you love me. Besides, it's not your fault you've deprived yourself of desserts all these years. I'm happy as hell that you're not so worried about putting on a pound or two. And do you know why?"

Her eyelids closed as his hands found her breasts. "Mm. You seem to have all the answers, so go ahead and tell me."

"It's because you're so confident about my love for you."

She smiled, and gave him a nod. "You're right again."

John Michael's deep rumble of laughter vibrated in his chest. "You're trying to flatter me, now, aren't you?"

She cracked one eye open. "Believe me, if you weren't right, I'd tell you."

He stopped what he was doing, tilted her chin gently to face him. "You wouldn't tip-toe around in order to make me happy, would you?"

"Uh uh. I don't do that anymore."

His beautiful smile returned, in full. "Exactly the answer I wanted to hear from you." He rolled her over on her back, began kissing and nipping his way down her body.

She gasped as his mouth dipped below her belly button. "What are you doing?"

He paused, resting his cheek on her upper thigh. "I'm considering new ways to sully your reputation."

She closed her eyes and relaxed, a slow smile spreading across her face as she visualized all the possibilities. "Well, all right, then."

Recommended Read: (Companion Book)

FULL CIRCLE LOVE - Recommended reading for this book. Four of Lori Leger's short stories from the Seasons of Love Anthology series, combined into one book, giving you the complete background on John Michael's son, Zachary Ferguson, and the love of his life, Cathryn "Cat" McDaniel. Don't miss out on the chance to put faces to their names, and get the full story behind their relationship.

Other books by LORI LEGER

La Fleur de Love Series
Book 1: *Some Day Somebody*
Book 2: *Last First Kiss*
Book 2.5: *Hart's Desire* (Novella)
Book 3: *Brown Eyed Girl*
Book 4: *Heaven in Your Eyes*

Halos & Horns Series
Book 1: *Green Eyed Temptation*
Book 2: *Sarah Smile*
Book 3: *Meagan's Marine*
Book 4: *One Year to Forever*

Seasons of Love Series
Book 1: *Hearts, Hearths & Holidays*
Book 2: *Spring Promise*
Book 3: *Sweet Summertime Love*
Book 4: *Christmas by Candlelight*
Book 5: *It's a Summer Thing*

Full Circle Love - Combined short stories from Seasons of Love series (Books 2-5)
Companion read for *Running Out of Rain*

Prime of Love Series
Book 1: *Running Out of Rain*

ABOUT THE AUTHOR

Lori Leger is a wife, mother, doting grandmother, and Mistress of Procrastination. She lives in Louisiana with the love of her life, her very own Studley-do-Right. He's earned his spot in the Keeper Husband's Hall of Fame by allowing her to walk away from an eighteen year career as an Engineering Technician in Road Design to stay home and write.

She adores writing stories set in her beloved south Louisiana, where good Cajun cooking, helping your neighbors, and saying y'all is as normal as hurricanes, heat, and humidity. She figures as long as she's not tunneling through ten feet of snow to get to her car, it's a perfectly acceptable trade-off.

Lori has nine novels published in two series: La Fleur de Love and its spin-off, Halos & Horns series. She has also contributed to, as well as published, short stories in each of the five Seasons of Love anthologies, an author collaboration series. She's contributed to the Sweet & Savory Cookbook of Amazon Authors, published by Top Ten Press. Lori also has an article published in the non-fiction book Writing After Retirement: Tips From Retired Writers, published by Rowman and Littlefield Publishers, and edited and compiled by Carol Smallwood and Christine Redman-Waldeyer.

Running Out of Rain is the first book in her Prime of Love Series, novels dedicated to mature characters finding love and laughter through the everyday twists and turns of growing older. She has a second planned for a fall 2015 release date, and a third set for the summer of 2016.

www.ingramcontent.com/pod-product-compliance
Lightning Source LLC
Chambersburg PA
CBHW051957220626
47052CB00004B/983